ICE PLANET
BARBARIANS

ICE PLANET BARBARIANS

RUBY DIXON

JOVE
New York

A JOVE BOOK
Published by Berkley
An imprint of Penguin Random House LLC
penguinrandomhouse.com

Library of Congress Cataloging-in-Publication Data

Names: Dixon, Ruby, 1976– author.
Title: Ice planet barbarians / Ruby Dixon.
Description: First Jove edition. | New York: Jove, 2021. |
Series: Ice planet barbarians
Identifiers: LCCN 2021039594 | ISBN 9780593546024 (trade paperback)
Subjects: LCGFT: Science fiction. | Romance fiction. | Novels.
Classification: LCC PS3604.I965 I24 2021 | DDC 813/.6—dc23
LC record available at https://lccn.loc.gov/2021039594

Ice Planet Barbarians was originally self-published, in different form, in 2015.

"Ice Planet Honeymoon: Vektal & Georgie" was originally
self-published in 2019.

First Jove Edition: November 2021

Printed in the United States of America
1st Printing

Book design by Kristin del Rosario

For the readers who are picking up
these books for the first time,
and for the readers who have been telling their friends
about the blue-alien books for over five years now.
Thank you. ❤

ICE PLANET BARBARIANS

PART ONE

Georgie

Up until yesterday, I, Georgie Carruthers, never believed in aliens. Oh, sure, there were all kinds of possibilities out there in the universe, but if someone would have told me that little green men were hanging around Earth in flying saucers, just waiting to abduct people? I would have told them they were crazy.

But that was yesterday.

Today? Today's a very different sort of story.

I suppose it all started last night. It was pretty ordinary, overall. I came home after a long day of working the drive-thru teller window at the bank, nuked a Lean Cuisine, ate it while watching TV, and dozed off on the couch before stumbling to bed. Not exactly the life of the party, but hey. It was a Tuesday, and Tuesdays were all work, no play. I went to sleep, and from there, shit got weird.

My dreams were messed up. Not the usual losing teeth or naked in front of the class dreams. These were far more sinister. Dreams of loss and abandonment. Dreams of pain and cold white rooms. Dreams of walking in a tunnel and seeing an oncoming train. In that dream, I tried to lift my hand to shield me from the light.

Except when I went to raise my hand, I couldn't.

That had woken me up from my slumber. I squinted into the tiny light someone was shining in my eyes. Someone was . . . shining something in my eyes? I blinked, trying to focus, and realized that I wasn't dreaming at all. I wasn't home, either. I was . . . somewhere new.

Then the light clicked off and a bird chirped. I squinted, my eyes adjusting to the darkness, and I found myself surrounded by . . . things. Things with long black eyes and big heads and skinny pale arms. Little green men.

I'd screamed. I'd screamed bloody murder, actually.

One of the aliens tilted its head at me, and the bird chirping sound happened again, even though his mouth didn't move. Something hot and dry wrapped over my mouth, choking me, and a noxious scent filled my nostrils. Oh shit. Was I going to die? Frantically, I worked my jaw, trying to breathe even as the world got dark around me.

Then, I went back to sleep, dreaming of work. I always dreamed of work when I was stressed. For hours on end, angry banking clients yelled at me as I kept trying to tear open packs of twenties that wouldn't seem to come open. I'd try to count out change only to get distracted. Work dreams are the worst, usually, but this one was a relief. No trains. No aliens. Just banking. I could deal with banking.

And that brings me to . . . here.

I'm awake. Awake and not entirely sure where I am. My eyes slide open, and I gaze around me. It smells like I'm in a sewer, I can feel a wall behind me, and my body hurts all freaking over. My head feels blurry and slow, like all of me hasn't quite woken up yet. My limbs feel heavy. Drugged, I realize. Someone's drugged me.

Not someone. Some*thing*.

My breath quickens as a mental image of the dark-eyed aliens returns, and I look for them. Wherever I'm at, I'm alone.

Thank God.

I squint in the low light, trying to make out my surroundings. It seems to be a large, dark room. Faint orange light is emitted from small running tubes in the ceiling about twenty feet above. The walls themselves are black, and if I didn't know better, I'd say this looks like a cargo bay from some weird science fiction movie. On the wall opposite me, I count six large six-foot metal tubes lined up against the wall like lockers. Orange and green lights run up and down the sides of the tubes in a variety of squiggles and dots that might be some sort of alien writing. On the far wall, there's an oblong oval door. I can't get to the door, though, because I'm behind a metal grid of some kind.

And there's a god-awful smell. Actually, it's not just one smell, it's several of them. It's like a piss-shit-vomit-sweat cocktail, and it makes me gag. I try to cover my mouth with my hand, but my arm is slow to respond and all I manage to do is flail a little. Ugh.

I swing my drugged, heavy head, looking around the room. Actually, I'm not alone, now that I look around. There are others piled onto this side of the grid, bodies curled up and asleep. In the low light, I count seven, maybe eight forms about my size, huddled together like puppies. Seeing as how we're all on this side of the metal grid, I'm starting to suspect I'm in a jail cell of some kind.

Or a cage.

I guess if I have to be in a cage, it could be worse. There's room enough to stand, though not much more than that. At least there are no aliens in here with me. I want to panic, but I'm too out of it. This is like going to the dentist's office and getting a dose of laughing gas. I'm having a hard time focusing on anything.

My bare upper arm aches, and I sluggishly rub my fingers on it. There are several raised bumps on my arm that weren't there before, and I rub it harder, feeling something hard under the skin. What the fuck? I try to peer at it in the dark, but I can't see anything. Images of the aliens and the light shining in my eyes, the nightmares, the terror—it all rises, and I panic. A whimper escapes in my throat.

A hand touches my other arm. "Don't scream," a girl whispers.

I roll my too heavy head until I can look over at her. She's about my age, but blonde and thinner than me. Her hair's long and dirty, her eyes big in her lean face. She glances around the room, and then puts a finger to her lips in case I didn't understand her earlier warning.

Silence. Okay. Okay. I choke the cry rising in my throat and try to remain calm. I nod. Don't scream. Don't scream. I can keep my shit together. I *can*.

"You all right?"

"Yeaaah . . ." I slur, my mouth unable to form words. And . . . I drool all over myself. Lovely. I lift one of my heavy hands to swipe at my mouth. "Thorry—"

"You're okay," she says before I can panic again. Her voice is pitched low so as to not wake up the others. "We're all a bit hung over when we wake up. They drug everyone when they arrive. It'll wear off in a bit. I'm Liz."

"Georgie," I tell her, taking time to sound out my name properly. I rub my arm and point at it, at the strange bumps. "Whattth going on?"

"Well," Liz says, "you were abducted by aliens. But I guess that one was obvious, right?"

I smile wryly. Or I try to. I probably just end up drooling on myself again.

Liz shifts next to me. "Okay, let me see if I can hit the big highlights. Everyone else here?" She thumbs a gesture at the others piled into the cage, still sleeping. "They've been abducted, too. All Earth, most American. I think there's a Canadian in there. You twenty-two?"

"Yeth?"

"Yeah, I thought so. We all are. Let me also guess: live alone, not pregnant, no major health issues, no nearby family?"

"How—"

"Because we're all in the same boat," Liz says, her tone bleak. "Every girl they pick up has the same story. Except for Megan. She was pregnant. Two months along, she said, and they vacuumed her out like it was no big deal." Liz shudders. "So I'm guessing that wherever they're taking us, they don't want pregnant girls. Just young and healthy."

Oh God. I swallow hard, fighting the urge to puke. There's really no place to do it, though I'm starting to suspect I know why the place smells like sewage. Liz's scent isn't exactly pleasant. "How . . . long you been heeere?"

"Me?" she asks. "Two weeks. Kira's been here the longest that we know of. She's the one with the earpiece."

I look around, but I don't see an earpiece on anyone in particular.

"It's a translator," Liz explains. "You'll see soon enough. I'm throwing too much at you at once, aren't I? Okay, let's try this again. See those tubes?" She points at the far wall, at the things that reminded me of oversized lockers. "Kira saw what was in them. She said they're more girls, just like us."

I gasp, the sound watery and overloud. More people?

Liz waves a hand at me, indicating we should be quiet, and I nod, rubbing those itchy bumps on my arm. She peers around to see if anyone's coming, and when no one appears, scoots even closer to me. I smell her body next to mine, her scent sweaty but human. "Yeah. So . . . they picked up Kira and she said they kept talking to her and she couldn't understand them, so they took her by the ear and more or less stapled in some sort of earpiece that translates things. But I guess they only had one of the suckers, so she has to translate for the rest of us."

"S-stapled?" I repeat, horrified at the thought.

"Yep. Tagged her like a cow." Liz grimaces. "Sorry, I'm from Oklahoma. I guess that visual doesn't bother me as much as you. Where you from?"

"Orlando." I'm not sure if my mouth will work around "Florida" without a spray of spit.

She nods. "We're kind of scattered all over the place. Anyhow, from what Kira's been able to pick up, our new friends are smugglers of some kind. Guess what they trade in?"

"Girls?"

"Ayup." She points at the lockers again. "My guess is that they came here to pick up six, then had such a good run that they decided to squeeze a few more into the hold and make out like bandits or something. Kira says someone new pops up every other day or so. We figure they're going to pack us up like sardines and then sell us off to . . . I don't know. Wherever." She shudders. "I'm trying not to think that far ahead because I'll just start screaming, and you don't want to know what happens when you start screaming."

Oh no. "What—"

"You'll see soon enough," Liz says in a sick voice. "Just trust me. The skinny ones don't like noise. Remember that, okay?"

I remember her warning from before. "Okay. My . . . arm—"

"Little bumps on it? Yeah. They have a doctor of some kind—or a veterinarian, who knows. He shows up when we first get here, jabs a bunch of needles into us, sticks the silver thing in your skin, and leaves. I'm thinking it's kind of like when the vet shows up at the farm, inoculates the cows, and sticks a tracker in the ear. Except ours is in the arm. But there I go comparing us to cows again. I probably shouldn't, right?"

"Cuz . . . we . . . eat . . . cows," I mumble between drooling on myself.

Liz snorts. "Yeah, pretty much. But I think they're taking too much trouble with us to eat us. Unless we're a delicacy of some kind, which I wouldn't rule out. But . . . yeah."

"Yeah," I echo.

"Try and get some sleep if you can," Liz murmurs, patting my sore arm. "Sleeping's pretty much the only escape we have. Enjoy it."

That Liz, such an optimist. I wrap my arms around my chest and notice I'm still wearing the sleeveless shorty pajama set I'd gone to sleep in. It's not very warm or very concealing, and I absurdly wish that I'd gone to sleep in a big flannel pajama set.

And then I want to weep. To think I haven't dressed properly for alien abduction. My shoulders shake with mirth until mirth turns into tears. So yeah. Yesterday? I didn't believe in aliens. But that was yesterday.

I quietly weep myself back to sleep.

I figure out a few things over the next day on the spaceship.

I figure out that there's no toilet. It seems our captors hadn't thought through the whole stuff-the-hold-full-of-stolen-girls thing. We have to make do with a bucket in a corner, hence the sewage smell. Dignity? Gone. Nothing like waiting your turn on the poop bucket to make you lose what little humanity you have left.

I figure out that food is tiny little bricks that look like dried seaweed and taste like shit. We get two of those a day. Water? It's dispensed from a faucet of some kind that reminds me of a gerbil feeder set in the wall.

The welts on my arm go down over the next several hours, though one rough little bump remains. Through feeling it and peering at the other girls' arms, I'm guessing it's some sort of electronic tracking device they've implanted. Cattle tags, as Liz had called 'em. At the moment, I think it's pretty damn apt.

I figure out that there are two kinds of aliens. There are the fragile green ones that seem to be in charge and the basketball-headed ones that are security. I call them basketball heads not because they've got oversized brains, but because of the pebbly, hairless orangish texture of their skin. It looks bizarre above the collar of the gray bodysuits they wear day in and day out. The basketball heads are pretty horrific, no matter the stupid name. They have weird little bug eyes with an opaque eyelid over them and needle-like teeth. They have two fingers and a thumb instead of five, and they're tall. The little green men, the ones that make the bird noises? They're not more than three feet tall or so, and they rarely show up. The basketball heads, though? They're in the hold constantly.

Everyone's terrified of them, too.

I figure this out when I wake up the next morning—though I suppose it could be the afternoon—and see everyone else is awake. The last of the dopey meds seem to have worn off, and I stifle a yawn, blinking. I want to be silent, because silent is good. It takes me a moment to realize everyone's moving to the far side of the cage, huddling away from the bars. The hairs on the back of my neck rise, and I follow the others, heading to the back. I want to ask what's going on, but the moment I open my mouth, Liz shakes her head silently, her gaze fixed on something over my shoulder.

I turn and flinch at the sight of a basketball-headed alien peering through the bars at me. I flinch again when he gives me a leering grin, and I scoot closer to the others.

"No screaming," someone murmurs as a warning.

God, this is freaking me out. I nod. No way am I making a sound.

The ball heads remain in our room all day. It's like they're waiting for something. I'm afraid to wonder what it is. We huddle in the corner of the cage, on edge, and another unconscious girl is brought into the room after a few hours. No one even tries to escape when they open the door. We just sit and watch as they shove the newest girl inside and close the door again.

I can guess why no one wants to attempt a breakout. Where would we go? And the consequences of disobedience must be bad, because everyone in the cage is utterly frightened by the basketball heads.

Someone grabs the new girl by the arm and tries to pull her into our huddled pile. She's about my age and has pretty red hair. I notice the ball heads keep coming back to the cage and commenting on her in their weird garbled language, making hand gestures from time to time. Then they laugh, a high-pitched, eerie sound that grates on my frayed nerves.

It's almost like they're taking bets on the new girl.

A few hours later, she wakes up. I'm hunkered down next to Liz, and I startle out of my stupor when she inhales sharply.

The girl sobs aloud, her eyes going wide.

"Don't scream," I hear a low voice hiss. I can't make out who's said it, but I know we're all thinking it.

The redhead isn't listening, though. She takes one look around her, panics, and begins to scream. Her shrill cry echoes in the hold. She won't stop, even though others are waving their hands and touching her, trying to calm her down. She's hysterical, her cries getting louder and more panicked the more awake she gets. She flails and thrashes against our warning touches.

Something beeps overhead.

The others in the cage go utterly still.

Weird birdlike chirps fill the air from the intercom.

One of the ball heads touches a panel that lights up, and he gargles a response. The crowd of girls seems to shrink back as the other ball head approaches the cage and opens the door.

It's freedom, but no one's reaching.

The redhead is snagged. She's a fighter, I'll give her that. She thrashes and flails as they touch her, screaming obscenities in French and shrieking for help. Everyone else sits quietly, watching.

I can't stand this. I try to get up, to go help her. Liz grabs my leg. "Don't," she hisses. "Don't call attention to yourself, Georgie. Trust me."

Even though it goes against everything inside me to do nothing, I'm terrified, too. It's too easy to sit down and huddle with the mass of girls again. To sit and wait and see what happens when someone disobeys the unspoken gag order. And I hate myself for it.

"Don't look," Liz whispers to me.

I look, though. Someone has to look. Someone has to see. When it's over and she's no longer fighting anything, I feel sick. What I just saw . . .

Liz squeezes my hand. "Kira says they have standing orders that they're allowed to 'discipline' any misbehaving captives."

I nod and finally look away as the aliens talk in their weird language and switch places once more. I'm guessing she's good and "disciplined" by now. I want to scream, but loud noises aren't allowed. I dig my nails into my palms and gaze down the row of pale faces in the pen with me, trying to figure out which one is Kira. A girl at the end with silky, flat brown hair is weeping with her hands pressed to her ears. It's as if she can't stand to hear what's going on, but the redhead is silent. There's only alien chatter.

That must be Kira. She's the only one who can understand them, thanks to the device implanted in her ear. I scan the others. They're in shock, eyes averted. One girl wears a look of horrified grief, and I wonder if she was a screamer, too. I decide I don't want to know. I squeeze my eyes shut, trying to drown out the world. Trying to exist in a quiet bubble where none of this is real. Where if I pinch my arm hard enough, everything will go away and I'll wake up.

But when I close my eyes, I see the redhead's face as she's attacked, and the alien responsible for it talks to his friend the entire time. As if it's no big deal, just another day at the office, typical water-cooler shit.

Liz is right. We're nothing but cattle to these things. They're going to sell us to someone else to rape, to eat, or both. Or something else more horrible that I can't even imagine.

I'm not going to take my fate sitting down, though. I cross my arms tightly over my pajamas, draw my legs up, and study my surroundings. I look at each nook and cranny of the strange walls, trying to determine if there's anything I can grab that can be used as a weapon.

Because I'm going to kill those pebbly, gross bastards if they ever try to touch me.

No one else comes on board the ship for the next week, so I'm starting to suspect we're "full." Which is good, considering that our tiny hold gets more and more crowded-feeling with every hour. Now with Dominique—the brutalized redhead—squeezed in with us, we feel like sardines.

Not that anyone is jumping up to complain.

Liz and I talk quietly during the night, when the guards leave us alone. We must be heading out to space now. Our ears have been popping repeatedly during the last few days, and we suspect we've begun traveling at a high speed.

And we don't know what to do about it.

"We start with killing the guards," I tell Liz and Kira for the second time tonight. "The little green men seem to have the basketball heads doing all the grunt work. I think if we get rid of the orange ones, maybe we can bully our way into demanding a return to Earth."

"Tiny flaw in this plan, Georgie," says Liz, ever the practical one. She gestures at the bars of the cage. "We're on this side, and they're on the other side. With guns."

"We need to do something to prompt them to open the door." Kira's quiet voice cuts through the darkness. "I would say we could wait for another captive to show up, but . . ."

"Yeah," I say thoughtfully, my gaze sliding over to where Dominique huddles in a corner, alone. She's been a straight-up mess ever since they'd returned her to the cage. She's quiet now, of course. She spends her waking hours with her fist stuffed against her mouth and biting down on it, tears streaming down her face. And she resists all attempts to befriend her or calm her down. It's going to take time and patience, and because we're all crammed into something the size of a closet, patience is running short at the moment.

I look back over at Kira and Liz's grim faces, thinking hard. "What if we all pretend to be sick the next time they come to feed us?"

"That won't be too hard," Liz says. "Those seaweed bars are fucking nasty."

But Kira shakes her head. "And what if they decide that since we're all sick, they'll just dump everyone into space? We're extras, remember? As long as they have their quota in those pods, we're expendable." She gestures at the lockers on the opposite side of the room.

I can't forget them. I don't know if I'm jealous that they're completely unaware of our situation or even more horrified at what they're going to go through when they wake up. But she's right. The pod people being safe and secure makes us superfluous, and I'm not willing to add "sabotage the pods" to the escape plan. Nor am I willing to leave them behind. We'll simply have to factor them in. "Well then," I say. "What if we scream?"

Kira swallows audibly. "That terrifies me." She peers over my shoulder at Dominique and shudders.

"I don't like it, either," I tell her. "But what are our options? One misbehaving person ensures that everyone else stays safe, right? So we get their attention, get them to open the doors . . ."

"And?" Liz prompts. "What? Get raped?"

"No." I don't even want to think about that. "We need a distraction of some kind. We can rush them when they open the doors. There are more of us than them."

"But they have guns," Kira points out.

"But if we all rush them—"

"Then the ones in front get shot," Liz says. "I don't want to be here, but I don't want to die. And I don't know that the others do, either. They're not really fighters. None of us are."

"But what choice do we have?" I protest. "We can be good little slaves and still get raped and still get sold off for God knows what. At least if we fight back, we have a chance."

"No, you're right." Liz draws her knees up close to her chest, thinking. "So we make a distraction, have them open the doors, rush them, take the guns, and take control. We just need to make sure Kira's protected through all of this."

"Me?" Kira looks surprised. "Why?"

"Because you're the one with the translator," Liz says grimly. "We're not going to be able to convince them to turn around and go back to Earth if you get shot and we can't talk to them."

She has a point. "I'll be the distraction. It's my plan."

"You sure?"

God, no, I'm not sure. Every part of my body vibrates with terror at the thought of those pebbly-skinned creatures touching me. But what choice do I have? Sit back and do nothing? Roll over and let these creatures decide my fate? Screw that. "I'll do it."

As if agreeing with me, the ship lurches and dips, sending us all sprawling.

Not a single person screams, of course. We know better.

For the second time that day, the ship lurches. Turbulence is a little ridiculous, considering that we're in space. Isn't it supposed to be a smooth ride? My stomach lurches along with it, but I ignore it.

It's almost time for our plan.

I stare at the guard pacing outside of our cell. It's what we consider "bedtime," in which we've received the last seaweed bar of the day and the guards are getting bored with harassing us. Normally after the last feeding, they change our waste bucket and then head out.

But tonight, things are off. Even though our waste bucket is nearly full, the ball head isn't coming to get it. Chirping sounds keep coming over the intercom, and the guard in the room is more and more agitated as the minutes tick past.

And the whole time, the ship keeps lurching.

"What's going on?" I whisper to Kira as we watch the single guard pace back and forth, distracted. "Where's the other basketball head?"

"I don't know," she admits, her hand pressing to her ear and the silvery device curled there. "Some of the words don't translate over. Or they do, but I don't know what they mean." She shakes her head. "I think there's something going on with the engine, though. They keep talking about detaching the cargo and offloading to a safe location."

The pit of my stomach curdles. "Um, we're the cargo."

She grimaces. "I know. Apparently they're going to miss a ship date if they do, though, so they're trying to work around it."

"Lucky us," I murmur, glancing at the one guard. Only one. Normally there are two. My body tenses with realization. If we take down the one guard . . . there will only be one to deal with later. Our odds are much better if we divide and conquer.

And if we have his gun.

"I think we should move ahead with our plan," I say in a low voice as the guard begins to pace again.

"I don't know," Kira says, chewing on her lip. But Liz nods at me.

"We're going for it," I whisper to the others in the cage. The girls look uncomfortable, but they move aside to give me room. If I'm willing to be the sacrificial lamb, they're willing to let me sacrifice myself.

So I steel my courage, head to the cage bars, and stick my face between the slats of the prison. "Hey."

The guard doesn't turn. He keeps pacing, his gaze flicking at the ceiling as if expecting more of those weird chirping orders to come down.

I try again. "Hey. Over here." When he doesn't pay attention to me, I admit I'm surprised. Normally they take any excuse to punish us. I've seen another girl raped over the last week because she'd cried out in a nightmare. So I try a new tactic to get his attention.

I hock a big wad of spit at him.

It lands on the back of his big bald head, and he stops in his pacing. His weird little fish eyes get round as he turns to glare at me, then stalks across the storage bay toward our cage.

"Good job, Georgie," Liz breathes.

I suck in a deep breath and nod. I don't feel so good about it, but hey. I retreat to the back of the cage like we've planned—so he'll have to come in after me—and when the other girls close ranks around me, I haul the shit bucket up into my arms.

The idea we've come up with is that I'll throw the crap on him to further distract him, and then the others will use that time to jump him. We'll overwhelm him and take him down, then strip him of his gun. Not that we know how to shoot an alien weapon, but one step at a time. As long as he doesn't have it, that's half the battle.

Of course, hefting the shit bucket into my arms shows just how heavy it is and just how weak and lethargic I am from the shitty rations they're giving us. I stagger under the weight of it, wincing when some slops over the edge and onto my arm. Fuck it.

He growls out something that sounds like a cussword in alien-ese and unlocks the cage.

Unlike how we've planned, the other girls fall back, cringing, leaving me there with the waste bucket and a stupid expression on my face as he slams toward me.

I throw it at him just as he grabs for me, but it's too heavy and ends up slopping on both of us. He grabs my arm, and I shriek in surprise as his fingers dig into the meat of my bicep. Not only is his pebbly skin ugly, it's rough and tears at my skin like it's sandpaper.

He spits an epithet at me and drags me forward.

"No," Liz says, grabbing my other arm even as I twist in his grasp. Where was our big fucking attack plan? Why are the others all huddling like scared rabbits? I look to Kira, my other co-conspirator, but she has her head tilted, a funny expression on her face as she stares at the ceiling. Faint birdlike chirping comes from above.

"Detachment commencing?" Kira asks, a confused look on her face.

The entire floor shifts to the side, and we go flying.

I slam across the room, my body soaring through the air. I land hard against the stasis lockers, and all the air leaves my lungs.

The entire world tilts, topsy-turvy, and the hold is filled with screaming women. Splashes of something wet hit my arms, and the waste bucket flies past overhead. Then everything hangs in the air. The lights go out, leaving us in the darkness.

A red light flickers on. Oh, that's not good. Red lights are always emergency lights, aren't they?

I stare into the now-red room, watching as globules of waste soar past. In the background, someone tumbles in the air. We've lost gravity.

What the hell?

I try to focus my eyes as something dances past my head. Black, oblong, with a thick barrel.

The gun.

Holy cow. I push off of one of the lockers and swim through the air for it, just as gravity kicks in again. I slam to the ground on top of the gun.

A few feet away, the guard slams down as well. All the while, that weird, birdlike chirping keeps going over the intercoms.

I grab the gun and look for a trigger as the guard groans and shakes his head, trying to gather his thoughts. There's no trigger. Well, fuck it. It'll work just as well as a bludgeon. Grabbing it by the thick, heavy base, I raise it over my head and bring it down on the guard's head.

CRACK.

The guard flails.

I don't stop. I hit him again and again. *Crack. Crack.* Over and over, I slam the butt of the rifle into his head. He doesn't move, but I don't stop. I'm terrified he'll somehow have a granite skull and will roll over and overpower me. So I just keep hitting him.

Hands grab mine. "Georgie. Hey, Georgie, stop. I think he's dead." Liz's voice cuts through the haze in my brain. "You can stop now."

I slow, staring blankly at her then down at the guard. Or what's left of the guard. His face is nothing but a pile of meat atop his neck.

I stare. Then I throw up.

"You did it," Liz says, rubbing my back. "Holy shit. You did it, Georgie! You're a fucking Billy Badass!"

I don't feel so badass. I feel sick. I've just killed a man. Kinda a man. Sorta. Definitely a rapist.

Still a living creature.

Was. *Was* a living creature.

My stomach roils uncomfortably again, and I go to wipe my mouth with the back of my hand, then stop. It smells like sewage. Ugh. I'm covered, too, and the cabin is splattered. "What the heck happened?"

"I don't know," Liz says, helping me to my feet.

I ache all over, my ribs feeling bruised from where I landed on the gun. I hold on to it, though. I don't care if it's covered in poop and brains and everything else, it's mine now.

A metallic-sounding chirp blares over the loudspeaker, just as my ears pop hard. Liz clutches her ears at the same time as I do, and we look at each other in surprise.

Kira comes running out of the cage. "Ladies! We've got bigger problems. The message overhead is now saying, 'Prepare for reentry.' I think that means we're crashing!"

Fuck.

We pitch again, and I tumble through the air, banging into the lockers. Something smacks my head, and everything goes black.

"Hey." A familiar voice sounds in my ear. "Hey, wake up. Are you okay, Georgie?"

I slowly come to and groan at the fierce stab of pain shooting through my forehead. Then, a moment later, the pain isn't just in my head. Every part of my body aches, my wrist most of all.

It throbs with an uncomfortable fire that seems to radiate all the way up to my elbow. I squint up at Liz as she hovers over me. "Ow."

She grins back, displaying a fat lip and a growing bruise on one cheek. "You're alive. That's always a plus." She sits back on her haunches and offers me a hand. "Can you sit up?"

With her help, I get to a seated position, wincing. Sitting up just makes everything hurt even more. "What happened?"

"We crashed," she says. "Most of us got knocked out from being bounced around. There are a few broken bones, a few bloody noses, and two who didn't make it."

I stare at her in shock then scan the cabin. "Two people . . . died? Who?"

"In addition to the guard you took down, Krissy and Peg. Looks like broken necks." She nods over at the far side of the room. "Poor kids."

I swallow the knot of grief in my throat. I didn't know them well, but I knew their terror and fear. I'm just glad I'm alive. I hug Liz, and she hugs me back, and for a moment, we're just relieved to be breathing and mostly whole. Over her shoulder, I squint, noticing that the entire cargo bay seems to be slanted at an angle. The metallic floor is covered with debris, tilted, and icy cold. I get to my feet with her help, wobbling, and gaze around in shock.

Several of the girls cling together in a corner—Megan is hugging Dominique and trying to calm her, the latter choking back braying sobs. Other girls are still sprawled on the ground, unconscious, and I see two bodies piled in the corner next to the dead guard. Krissy's dark hair tumbles over her face, obscuring her features. It's for the best. I look away. Over off to the side, Kira's trying to help another girl straighten an obviously broken leg. Kira's own face is bruised and blood's running down from her ear implant.

Everyone looks beaten up, bruised, and damaged. I gaze down at my own legs, but they seem to be okay. My wrist, however, is swollen and getting a little purplish, and my ribs feel like they're on fire. "I think I broke this," I say, holding my bad arm out. I gingerly rotate my wrist and nearly pass out at the shock wave of pain it sends through my body.

"Guess you won't be clubbing any more aliens then," Liz says cheerfully. "If it's not broke, it's sprained pretty bad. You should see my toes on my left foot. They look pretty awful, too. Like they tried to make a strategic retreat into my foot and failed."

I glance over at her skeptically. "Then why are you in such a good mood?"

"Because we're free," she says enthusiastically. "We are fucking free, and we've landed somewhere. I already count those as better odds than what we had before."

"How do you know we landed?"

Liz hobbles to my side, favoring her leg. "Because the floor's tilted and cold, and because of that." She points at something behind me.

I turn and look. Overhead, it seems as if one of the compartments has peeled partially away, leaving a long, narrow scrape in the hull of our storage bay. Through the scrape, weak light filters in and what looks like snowflakes drizzle down. I gasp and push forward, trying to see. "Is that snow?"

"It is," Liz says happily. "And since we're all not asphyxiating from breathing methane or something, there's also oxygen coming in."

Hope thuds in my heart, and I stare up at the ceiling. I turn back to Liz, full of excitement. "Do you think we landed back on Earth somehow?"

"I don't think so," Kira says, her soft voice interrupting my thoughts. I glance over at her and wince. She looks pretty rough, the entire left side of her thin face purple and bloody. One of her eyes has a broken blood vessel, the red stark against her pale skin. And she is limping, too, her knee swollen.

"How do you know we're not on Earth?" I ask. I refuse to give up hope just yet. "How many places can have snow and oxygen? We just might be, I don't know, in Canada or something."

"Except I heard through this thing," she says, pointing at the bloodied earpiece still attached to her head, "that they were dumping us at a 'safe location' for a return pickup at a later date."

Liz crosses her arms, frowning. "Return pickup? So they dropped us so we can sit tight, and they're going to pick us up again in a day or two? Fuck that."

"I don't know when," Kira says, her face solemn. "But when they mentioned this place, it definitely wasn't Earth they were referring to. They kept talking about a particle cloud, but the only particle cloud I remember from science class was on the edge of our solar system: the Oort Cloud. And if we're getting that much light," she says, pointing at the scrape in the hull, "we're not anywhere close to Pluto. I don't think we're on Earth at all. I don't think we're in our solar system, either."

"Gotcha," Liz agrees. She sounds glum.

I'm still skeptical. Glancing up at the snow falling into the crack, it's hard not to get excited. We had to be home, didn't we? It's winter out there. They could have dropped us in Antarctica. Right now I'd take Antarctica over a random planet. "I don't want to stick around until they come back."

"Me either." Kira sighs and winces, rubbing her shoulder. "But everyone's hurt. I don't know how fast we can move, or if it's even safe to move. For all we know, we could be floating on a sea of ice filled with man-eating ice-sharks."

"Good God, you're Suzy Fucking Sunshine, aren't you?" Liz says, staring at Kira.

"Sorry." Kira grimaces, pressing a palm to her forehead. "It's been a hell of a day, and I feel like it's just going to get worse."

She looks so morose that I want to hug her. I refuse to be down about this. One guard is dead, we have his gun, and for now we're away from our captors. "It'll be fine," I tell them brightly. "We'll figure something out."

"Can we figure out food?" Megan calls from the corner of the slanted storage bay. "We're pretty hungry."

"Food is a good start," I agree, nodding at Liz. "Let's see what we have if we're supposed to ride this out and wait for the little green men to return."

An hour later, though, things are looking grim. We've found enough bars for a week, and we have enough water for approximately as long. Beyond that, though, there is nothing.

In addition, other than what belonged to the guard we'd killed—well, *I'd* killed—there were no weapons and no additional clothes. We went through everything, pounding on walls and trying to find hidden compartments in the shuttle bay, but we didn't find much. The only discovery was some sort of thick plastic-like sheet material, but it wasn't warm or flexible enough to be used for much of anything.

"Pretty sure Robinson Crusoe wasn't nearly as fucked as we are," Liz jokes.

I haven't read *Robinson Crusoe*, but I agree. It's clear we're not equipped for survival. We're not equipped for anything, and it's getting colder in the hold by the minute, thanks to the snow and cold air that steadily trickles in from the gap in the hull.

"I mean, I don't understand," Liz says, handing out a few seaweed bars. "If they want us to sit and wait, don't you think they should have left us with more supplies?"

"You forget that we're the extras," I point out, waving away my bar. Someone else can eat it. My stomach is upset enough as it is. "As long as they're intact, that's all that matters, right? And they're not eating." I thumb a gesture at the lockers still lining the wall. "They're still in perfect condition."

Naturally.

"Should we wake them up now?" The thought of a handful of women floating in stasis a few feet away with no comprehension of what was going on is rather unnerving to me. If I'd crash-landed, wouldn't I want to know?

"God no," Liz says. "How do we even know that they're aware of where we are? For all they know, they're still tucked into bed and little green men don't exist. How would you like to wake up to find all this and oh, by the way, we're stranded and don't have much to eat?"

"Good point." I gaze around the empty room, tapping my bare foot and thinking.

"So what do we do?" Kira asks, sliding in next to the other girls huddling together for body warmth. She looks exhausted.

Liz glances at me, waiting.

Am I the leader now? Crap. But . . . someone's got to do it, and I'm tired of no one having ideas. I consider our options for a long moment. "Well, if we're on a planet with oxygen, I'm guessing there are other things living here. I don't know a lot about science, but if Earth can support all kinds of life, doesn't it stand to reason that this planet could, too? We could be really close to a city for all we know."

"A city full of aliens," someone mutters.

"True," I agree. "But we can't stay here and starve to death. Or freeze. The sun's shining right now, but we don't know how long we have until night—"

"Or how long night will last," Kira adds.

"Maybe you quit helping out," Liz tells her. "I'm just saying."

"I think we need to scout around at least," I suggest. "Find out our bearings, look for food and water, and report back."

"But most of us are injured," sniffs one girl. Tiffany. She looks like she is fresh off the farm and utterly terrified. Some of us have taken our captivity with grim determination, and some have completely fallen apart. Tiffany's in the latter category.

"You should go, Georgie," Liz chimes in.

"Me?" I sputter.

"You're kind of our leader."

God, I hate that I'm not the only one who thought that. I glance up at the snow pouring through the crack overhead. It looks cold, and I'm in shorty pajamas. "How am I the leader? I'm practically the last one to arrive." Only Dominique was captured after me.

"Yeah, but you're the one with all the plans. You're the one who killed the guard, and Kira needs to stay here in case the others return, because she's got the ear thing. And my knee's all jacked up. I wouldn't get very far. Besides, you're the one who's good with the gun." Liz flutters her lashes at me.

I snort. "Good at bashing things, you mean."

"Hey, you did better than the rest of us, Georgie. Seriously." She mock-punches at the air, pretending to box. "You want me to hum you some 'Eye of the Tiger' to get you pumped up?"

"Gee, thanks," I tell her, trying to be upset that I just got volunteered. But it kinda has to be me, I think. Other than Kira and Liz, the others aren't much of leaders. Everyone is hurt, and I want to point out that my wrist is fucked and my ribs ache, but . . . *everyone* is hurt. Liz is limping, Kira's got a busted leg, and the others are a mess. Do I want to leave my fate in the hands of another and hope she could scout decently? "Anyone in here have any survival experience?"

Someone sniffs back tears. Other than that, silence.

Yeah. No one is equipped for this.

At my side, Liz hums "Eye of the Tiger."

I shoot her the bird. "Okay, fine. If I'm going out in the snow, I need a couple of bars, the gun, and some water."

"We don't have canteens," Liz points out. "Just eat the snow."

"Not the yellow snow," someone else quips.

"Oh sure, everyone's a comedian now that I'm the one going out to scout," I grumble, but I stretch my legs and test my wrist and ribs, wincing. It sucks, but we're low on options. "Okay, I'm somehow going to climb out of that hole in the roof, I guess. I need some clothes." I gaze down at my dirty shorty pajamas. "I'm guessing these won't cut it."

"I know where you can get some nice warm clothing," Liz says, and points at the dead guard.

"Ugh," I say, though I was thinking the same thing. "I was kinda hoping someone would miraculously spring out a parka or something."

"No such luck," says Tiffany, getting to her feet. "I'll help you undress him."

A short time later, Tiffany and I have stripped the body of his clothing and try to figure out how to put it back on me. There are weird invisible buckles and fastenings instead of the usual zippers and buttons, and it smells like sewage and blood and some other spicily nauseating scent, but it's surprisingly warm and lined. The jacket's a little tight across my breasts and makes me look like I have a uniboob, but I'm not wearing this for fashion. The biggest problems are that there are no gloves for my hands and the shoes are designed to fit something with only two big toes instead of five little ones. I squeeze my feet into each shoe, but it hurts.

Still better than nothing, I suppose, which is what I had before.

"Keep your hands tucked in your jacket," Tiffany suggests. "Your body warmth should help."

I nod and shove the gun down the front of the jacket, too, letting the long barrel rest between my boobs. I braid my dirty hair to get it out of my face, take the bars Liz offers me, and suck in a deep breath. "I'm going to go as far as I can," I tell the others. "I'm going to look for help. Or people. Or food. Something. But I'll be back. If I don't come back by tomorrow, um, well . . . don't come looking for me."

"God, I wish I had some wood to knock on right about now," Liz says. "Don't say shit like that."

"I'll be fine," I tell her, bluffing. "Now, help me get up to the ceiling so I can climb out."

We maneuver the table over, and two girls hold it in place while I climb and Liz and Megan push me higher. My wrist screams a protest, but I keep climbing, wiggling my way to the top of the breached hull. The scrape is big enough for me to squeeze through, and by the time I make it up to fresh air, my wrist is screaming in pain and it's getting colder by the minute. I've wrapped my sleep shorts around my neck as a scarf and hood, the extra fabric bunched around my exposed throat. My face sticks out of a thigh hole. I'm sure it's not a sexy look, and the shorts are filthy, but I'm glad for them. The wind is bitter, and I haven't even stuck my head up through the hole yet.

I put my hands on the icy metal, hissing when my fingers stick to it. I pull them away carefully, wincing at the needle-like feelings pricking at my skin. It's not only cold out there, it's *damn* cold. I use my good arm—now sleeved in the thick, jacket-like uniform of the alien—to propel myself up a bit higher. As I hoist my torso through the crack in the hull, I have a momentary vision of sticking my head out and having an alien chomp it.

Not helpful, Georgie, I tell myself. I shove the image out of my mind as I push through the gap and stare around me.

The good news is that the wind isn't as bad up here as I thought. Instead, the snow falls in quiet, thick flakes, the two suns shining high overhead.

Two suns.

Two freaking suns.

I squint up at them, making sure I haven't hit my head in the crash and am now seeing double. Sure enough, two of them. They look almost like a figure eight, with one tinier, much duller sun practically overlapping a larger one. Off in the distance, there is an enormous white moon.

"Not Earth," I call below. *Fuck.* I fight back the insane urge to weep in disappointment. I'd so wanted to climb out and see a building in the distance that would tell me *oh, it's just Canada or Finland.*

Two suns have pretty much destroyed that hope.

"What do you see?" someone calls up to me.

I stare around the crashed ship at the endless drifts of snow.

I look up. In the far distance, there are other mountains—or at least I'm pretty sure they're mountains—that look like big icy purple crystals the size of skyscrapers. They're different from this mountain. This one is nothing but barren rock. There are no trees. Nothing but snow and jagged granite. Our tiny ship looks like it bounced off of one of the nearby jaggy cliffs; that was probably how it had torn open.

I look for living creatures or water. Something. Anything. There's nothing but white.

"What's it look like?" someone else calls up.

I lick my lips, hating that they already feel numb with cold. I'm a Southern girl. We do not do well with cold. "You ever see Star Wars? The original ones?"

"Don't tell me—"

"Yep. It looks like we landed on fucking Hoth. Except I see two itty-bitty suns and a huge-ass moon."

"Not Hoth," Liz yells. "It was the sixth planet from its sun, and I don't recall it having a moon."

"Okay, nerd," I call back to her. "We'll call this place Not-Hoth then. You guys cover this hole with the plastic while I'm gone. It'll help keep things warm."

"Stay safe," Liz tells me.

"Your lips to God's ears," I yell. Then I haul my ass out of the protection of the ship.

Walking out into that snowy landscape with nothing but borrowed alien clothing and a gun I don't know how to fire? Pretty much takes every ounce of courage I have in my body. I tremble as I trudge through the snow. I don't know squat about winter conditions. I'm from Florida, for chrissakes. Palmetto bugs, I can handle. Gators, I can handle. My pinching boots sinking up to my knees in the snow with every step? I cannot handle that.

But there are half a dozen girls waiting for me back at the spaceship, depending on me to find something. Anything. And we don't have much in the way of options. I can always turn around. I don't think anyone would blame me for being afraid.

And then I'll just sit in the cracked hull and slowly starve to death with the others. Or we'll get picked up by the aliens again.

Or I can risk freezing and try to do something out here.

So I walk on.

I'll say one thing for the ball-headed alien I killed: His clothes are decently warm. Despite the fact that every step is a struggle and I sink into the powder with each one, my feet are doing all right.

My face feels like a block of ice, though. My hands, too. The sleeves are too tight for me to pull them down over my hands, so I walk with one hand tucked inside my shirt and the other under an armpit. When it gets too cold, I switch them out. My bad wrist hurts like hell, and my ribs still burn. Actually they burn worse, now, because I have to take deep breaths, and that makes a stabbing pain shoot through my chest each time.

Most of all? I just want to curl up and cry.

But there are others depending on me. So I can't.

After walking for what feels like forever, the ground starts to slope a bit more, and I follow it down. In the distance, I see stalk-like tall, skinny things that I think are trees. At least, I hope they're trees. There's no other foliage to be found, so I head toward them. The wind is picking up, and my suit—no matter how well it endures the weather—is starting to feel cold. Actually, I'm cold all over. It sucks.

I wish I was back at the hull. I turn around and squint up the side of the rocky hill. The hull is like a small black dot against the hillside. It looks fragile from here. Broken. And there's still no food or animals or even water. Just snow.

Well, shit. I guess I'll keep walking.

The stalks are further away than I realize, and it feels like I'm walking forever down the slope of the mountain. As I do, I start to see things. Foliage-looking things. At least, I think they're foliage. There are tufts of pale bluish-green that look more like feathers than actual leaves, but there's a veritable forest of them. These must be the trees of this strange place. As I pass through them, I touch one. The bark—if you can call it that—feels moist and sticky, and I wipe my palm with a wince. That was gross.

Okay, I've found trees. If there are trees, I'm hoping there's a way the trees are getting nutrition. Trees need sunlight and water. I squint up at the double suns. They're moving toward the edge of the sky, and the enormous moon is rising higher.

A sudden thought occurs to me. What if I'm out here alone overnight? "That'll suck," I mutter to myself. I pull out the gun just because it feels good to have a weapon at hand. It means my fingers feel like ice as I hold it, but I don't care. I'd rather have a shitty weapon than no weapon.

As I trudge onward, I'm starting to feel despair. What if they dropped us here on this planet precisely because we won't be able to fend for ourselves? Even as the terrible thought occurs to me, I hear the sound of trickling liquid.

Water?

I stop, my heart hammering. Oh, please let it be water! If it's water, that means it's warm enough to not turn to ice. That means something is warm. And right now? I'd take a hot drink.

I rush forward. The water sound seems to be coming from

the same direction as the weird, tall stalks. The stalks keep growing bigger the nearer I get, and by the time I find the edge of a burbling, steaming stream, the stalks are taller than some buildings. They tower over me, like a forest of bamboo shoots that stick out of the water. Each one is tipped in a pale pink, sluggish-looking thing. It's rather bizarre looking, but maybe it's normal for this place.

There are a few stalks close to the muddy bank that are human-sized. I grab one. It's warm under my hand. That's a good sign that the water's warm, too. Maybe too warm to touch. I lean down to the surface, holding on to the stalk.

As I do so, I realize there's a face on the other side of the water staring back at me. A face with a huge mouth, jagged teeth, and bulging fish eyes. And the stalk I'm holding? Appears to be attached to its nose.

I scream and stumble backward just as the thing lunges forward, snapping at me.

I keep screaming and crab walk back, away from the edge of the water. The thing stirs, moving slightly away from the surface, its nasty mouth working. Then it sinks in and the stalk gives a small shiver before moving back in place.

Holy fuck.

Holy . . . fuck. I just nearly got eaten by an alien fish . . . thing.

I stare, wide-eyed, at the happily burbling stream. At the enormous stalks sticking out of it. At the ones that are taller than a two-story building. Are all of those . . . monsters?

I turn and run. Breath huffing, I sprint as best as I can through the snow, back up the hill. Back through the feathery blue-green trees. Screw all this. I am not equipped to deal with alien life-forms on an alien planet. My lungs rasp and my ribs hurt like the blazes and I landed on my wrist back there and none of that matters because I am not stopping.

As I pass one of the strange trees, something whips around my ankles.

I barely have time to scream before the thing drags me backward and I'm hauled, upside down, into the branches of the tree, my feet caught and bound together.

I scream over and over again, twisting, turning. The ground is at least a foot or two below me, and I can't touch it. Down there? My club-slash-gun. I dropped it when whatever this is hauled me backward.

When nothing happens, I stop flailing and panicking and try to figure things out. I bend over, flopping through the air, and get a good look at my feet. They're tied with something that looks like rope. If I wriggle enough . . . that definitely looks like a knot. The other end of the cord is tied higher in the branches. I whimper and fall quiet, and I just sway back and forth gently in the tree.

I . . . I've walked into a snare of some kind.

On one hand, this is encouraging. There's intelligent life here, right? Which is exciting because it means we're not alone.

But I can't overlook the fact that I'm in a hunting snare and something could decide I'm dinner. I remember a scene in Star Wars where Luke found himself upside down in the snow creature's cave. And I start panicking again, because I know how this sort of thing goes down. Luke's able to free himself before the creature eats him, because he's a Jedi.

Me? I'm just a Floridian in a stolen space suit with no weapon and a busted wrist. I know how this is going to end.

I whimper and wriggle some more, working my feet and trying to free them from the noose that's holding me fast, upside down.

I don't want to be here when the owner of this trap comes back looking for dinner.

Wiggling my feet doesn't work, so for the next minute or two, I concentrate on trying to stretch far enough to reach my gun. Not that I know how to fire it, but I'll feel better if I have it. It's getting harder to think, though, and the longer I hang here, the harder my head pounds.

It's probably not good for me to hang upside down for a long time, I realize. How long can a human hang upside down before all the blood rushes to their head and they die?

I twist even harder, and as I do, I realize there's something new on the edge of my vision. I stop moving and stare as a white, furry figure approaches.

Shit. It's too late. I'm dinner.

"No," I moan and struggle again. But my body can't keep up with the demands I'm putting on it. My head throbs, and then I pass out cold just as the monster starts to move toward me.

At least I won't be awake to feel it eat me.

Vektal

I don't recognize the . . . thing . . . squirming in my trap.

This is new.

I approach it cautiously, my blade drawn. A moment ago it was dancing and writhing, and now it's gone limp. The smell is *sa-khui* and yet . . . not. Curious. I poke it with the tip of my sword to see if it will jump once more, but it does not. The wind is picking up, the cold air preparing for the little moon's arrival, the twin suns heading to their beds.

With the tip of my sword, I slice the cord binding its legs, and it flops to the ground, lying in the snow.

And then I am shocked anew as my *khui* resonates inside me. My inward being, which has lain dormant for so long, which recognizes no mate amongst my people? It vibrates and sings at the sight of this new creature. I stare at it.

My thoughts confused and whirling, I snatch it into my arms and sprint for the nearest hunting cave.

It is the bitter season, when hunters are free to journey out far from the home caves. There are a series of hunting caves that only see use on the coldest of nights, when a hunter is many sprints away from home. They are ingrained into my brain after turn upon countless turn of hunts, and I find the nearest one's location easily. I push aside the leathery flap protecting the entrance and set my burden down on the floor. A quick shake of the furs does not reveal hidden occupants, so I move the she-creature—for it must be a *she*—to them. Her teeth clack together, making the cold sound that young sometimes make before they're sa-khui, so I touch her eyelid and pry it open to see if she is lit from within.

The eye underneath is white, dull. There is no khui inside her, or if there is, it is dead. She will need to be treated as if a child, then. I make a fire quickly and wait for it to warm her. And because my curiosity has the best of me, I examine her. I tell myself it's simply to determine if she is wounded, but my mind sings with curiosity, my khui vibrating within my chest with a song that's growing greater with every possible moment.

She is making me resonate. She is mine.

I run a hand over her limbs. She is wearing some sort of clothing that stinks of old, bitter memories. I want to rip it off her, but if she is as helpless as a kit, she will need it. So I take time to find the fastenings and undo them, revealing the flesh underneath.

She's smooth. Not like a sa-khui. Her flesh is almost completely hairless, save for the long, flowing locks on her crown and a small tuft between her thighs that's revealed as I pull her leathers from her. I snort with amusement at that small tuft.

Adorable. Adorable and nonsensical.

She has no ridges under her skin to define her muscles, and the overwhelming sensation I have as I view her body is one of softness and weakness. Perhaps she has been sick, and that is why her khui is gone. I run my fingers over her strange face. It's smooth, too, her brow flat. She has no ridges anywhere. Just softness.

How did one so weak as her find their way to the outer hunting grounds? It's a mystery, almost as much of one as the fact that she's making my khui resonate hard in my chest. It's thrumming with the call, and the need to mate slams through my body as her soft, rounded thighs part and her scent fills my nostrils.

A groan escapes me as my cock grows hard, the ridges on it swelling.

I bury my face between her legs so I can taste all of her.

Georgie

Pretty sure I'm dreaming.

Maybe that's all this is. One big, bad dream. I've just been stuck in the bad part of my head for a while, and now I'm getting to the wet part of the dream. Because I'm pretty sure I'm naked, and there's a mouth between my legs, licking me like there's no tomorrow.

I moan softly, because this? *This* is a much better dream than that spaceship crap.

Something slick with hard, nubby bumps runs up and down my pussy. A mouth, a tongue. It glides through my folds, and I press a hand to my forehead because it feels *so* good. A flash of pain shoots up my wrist, but it's quickly buried under another round of pleasure. Soft rumbling sounds come from nearby, almost like language, except I can't understand a word of it. This guy is eating my pussy like a champ.

His head lifts, and he nuzzles at my bush, mumbling something again. My hands go to push his head back down to where I want it.

Except I encounter horns.

I jerk awake, realizing it's not a dream. None of this is. I look down at my body in shock. I'm naked. I'm naked, and there's some guy with a pair of massive curled horns rising from his head between my legs. As I watch, his tongue drags over my pussy again.

"Oh my God," I whisper. I push at his head, trying to shove him away. *This is not normal. This is not normal.*

He looks up at me, and as he does, I gasp.

He's not human. I mean, I knew that with the horns and all, but looking at his face, I can tell he's *really* not human. Horns rise from his hairline and curl around his scalp like a spiky, lethal helmet. He's blue, for one thing. Well, bluish-gray with a black mane of hair that reminds me of a lion's mane. His brows are heavy, heavier than any human brow I've seen, his face rugged like it's carved from stone. Going straight down his forehead to the tip of his nose is a striated pattern of ridges of some kind, his bluish-gray skin slightly darker there.

And his eyes are a glowing shade of blue that I've never seen. Blue like Caribbean waters but completely without pupils of any kind. And they're glowing as if from within.

A small whimper escapes my throat as he rises up over me. I see the shaggy white furs covering his shoulders, and I realize I saw them from hanging upside down. It wasn't a monster come to eat me. It was this monster.

Who's come to eat me out.

It strikes me as incredibly ludicrous, and I want to laugh, but I'm too terrified. "What are you going to do with me?" I ask softly, my eyes wide. The refrain of *please don't kill me please don't kill me* echoes through my head.

He says something and runs a hand down my stomach. Then those weird glowing eyes break my gaze and his head dips.

And he begins to lick me again. Long, slow, delicious licks right down the slick folds of my pussy.

I can't help it. I start to giggle. It's ticklish and it makes me squirm and I should be screaming *no, help, rape* and instead, I have the giggles. Because he doesn't want to eat me. He just . . . wants to lick my pussy. I've dated guys that I haven't been able to convince to go down on me, and this one's doing it as a greeting.

Laughter sweeps through me, relieved and absurd all at the same time. I might be a bit hysterical. It somehow doesn't matter. I'm not going to die yet, and a strange guy with horns is determined to give me oral pleasure. It's just that . . . out of all the worst-case scenarios I've come up with since being abducted by aliens, being licked until I come isn't anywhere on the list.

And he's really, *really* good at licking.

Something ridged and slightly knobbed slicks against the entrance of my core, and I realize he's got a texture on his tongue. And it feels incredible. And even though my every instinct is telling me to find my clothes and get the hell outta Dodge, I don't move. I'm barely even breathing.

When one big hand pushes on my thigh, urging me to spread my legs wider, I do so. I'll get up and protest in just a minute.

Just.

A.

Minute.

He licks me again, and his tongue grazes my clit. And I can't help it. An undignified squeal erupts from me. My clit's especially sensitive, and he's been avoiding it until now.

The horned man's head jerks up, and he looks at me in what I can only assume is surprise. I quiver because those weird eyes are staring at me, and I press my good hand to my mouth, determined not to make another noise and startle him. What if he gets mad and, like, gores me with those gigantic horns?

But he only looks confused for a moment. Then, as I watch, big fingers spread my folds, and he studies me intently. Humiliation burns, and I try to snap my legs closed. Fuck all this. His big hands hold my legs down, though, preventing me from doing that, and he goes to spread my folds again. He looks shocked—downright *shocked*—at the sight of my clit. He says something that sounds like *sa sa*, and it's definitely a question.

I try to clamp my legs shut again and rise. "Now is not the time for an anatomy lesson, buddy."

The big alien pushes me back down on the furs with a stern word.

I shove at his hands, but he's much stronger than me and determined. He keeps my thighs pried apart, and I can't help but notice that his hand is enormous, like a baseball glove. How tall is this guy? His hand spreads the folds of my pussy again, and to my utter humiliation, he touches my clit like it's going to bite him.

I remain perfectly still.

That doesn't satisfy him. He mutters something, and then he begins to rub the hood of my clit, as if trying to figure out the right touch to make me react again.

And I respond despite myself. I close my eyes so I don't have to see the look on his face. He continues to touch me, stroking my clit very carefully. I'm doing pretty good at controlling my reaction, even though every touch of his fingers makes me want to moan.

Then I feel his mouth on my clit, and he sucks it gently.

My hips buck against him, and I cry out.

He murmurs something and sounds pleased, and continues to

lick and suck at my clit until my thighs are shaking. I'm going to come. Damn him. Damn him and the fact that he's making me feel incredible. Those bumps and ridges on his tongue move against my clit, and my entire body quakes, and then I'm coming hard. Over and over, my pussy clenches and the orgasm rocks through me, my entire body locked and tense with the strain of it.

I collapse on his furs, exhausted. My hand goes over my eyes, and I rub my face.

Okay, so I just did that. I just had an orgasm from an alien. I have no idea how I'm going to explain this to Liz and the others.

The alien says something else, and I open one eye to peek at him. The look on his face is fierce, and there's no mistaking the masculine look of pride on his inhuman face. He's pleased he made me come. I shoot him the finger. "You're an asshole," I mutter.

In response, he says something else. Then he grabs me by my hips and turns me onto my stomach.

I know what's coming next. And even though I just came, a girl's got to have boundaries. I don't want to have sex. Oral is okay as long as I'm the recipient, but this is too much, too fast. I twist in his grip, then kick and lash out at him. My foot connects with his chest.

It feels like I broke it—my foot, that is. Not his chest.

It feels like I kicked iron. I give a cry of pain and collapse on the blankets again, my leg throbbing and my ankle shooting pain clear up my entire body.

When I look up, the alien's furious.

PART TWO

PART TWO

Vektal

My mate, the resonance of my khui, my new reason for existing, has just planted her tiny, strange foot in my chest and kicked. It's almost as if she does not want to mate.

Her strange, dead eyes are wide with fear, no comforting glow in them. I want to tell her that she'll be fine. That she's mine now and I'll take care of her. That we'll take down one of the monstrous *sa-kohtsk* and pull a new khui from its depths so she will no longer suffer.

But I'm puzzled as to why she would hurt herself. I rub my chest where her tiny foot landed. Without her leathers, her body seems even smaller, and she's soft and ridge-less. She seems to have forgotten this, too, as she gives me an indignant look, then howls with pain and clings to her foot.

I don't understand her. Maybe her lack of khui is affecting her senses. "I will not harm you," I say to her slowly, because she looks terrified. "You are my mate, now."

"Tht hrt dmmt!"

"Let me see your foot," I demand. If she has no khui, she

probably does not heal as she should, either. When she continues to give me a frightened look, I reach forward and place my hand on her ankle.

She bellows something and thrashes at me again. Her hand curls into a fist, and she smacks it into my face, knocking my lip against my teeth. A flash of pain shoots through my mouth, and I snarl.

She immediately goes quiet, flinching backward, her hands raised to shield herself.

I am sickened at her reaction.

This woman, this small creature who has half the stature of a sa-khui, is my mate. How can she possibly think I would harm her? But she is cringing back even now, as if expecting a blow to fall. Rage fills me, because this is not a normal response.

Someone has hurt my mate in the past.

I reach forward and turn her pale face toward me. She fights, but her eyes close again, and she begins to tremble. I gaze at her small, flat features. Her skin tone is regular, except for mottled bruising along one side. There is the evidence I suspected.

"Who did this to you?" I ask.

She trembles, but she doesn't answer me. She's not mute. She makes sounds, and I wonder if she hit her head. Or perhaps her people speak the nonsensical language of hard syllables she's been filling my ears with. It sounds nothing like my language.

But then again, she is nothing like one of the sa-khui. I should not expect similarities.

I'm fascinated by her, though. The men of my tribe say that there is no pleasure like the taste of a resonance mate on your lips, and they're right. Burying my face between her legs was one of the truest pleasures I have ever felt, and I want to feel it again.

It's clear from her reaction and the way she cringes away that I'm the only one feeling this way, though. I'm mystified by her reaction, but it must be her lack of khui. She doesn't feel the resonance like I do.

She doesn't feel the teeth-aching need to claim. She doesn't feel the hollowness of a lonely spirit. How can she? There is no khui inside her to resonate.

Clearly the spirits have sent her to me so I might learn patience. I smile ruefully. It is not my strongest trait. "Very well, little one," I say to her and brush my fingers over her strange, smooth skin. "You and I shall learn patience together."

"*Dnt nnerstnd yew.*"

Her words trip and tumble off of her agile mouth. I notice her fangs are gone, and my heart stills in my breast, my khui ceasing its resonance. Despite her slapping touch, I peel her lips back to examine her teeth. Are they broken?

But no, it appears as if her small teeth are just that: whole and not nearly as large as my own front tusks. Strange creature.

I release her, and she slaps my hands away, her strange eyes narrowing. "*Fckoffwth tht.*"

Her body is different than that of a sa-khui. She's soft and hairless in most places, and I haven't seen a tail. And then there's that strange nipple between her legs. I find it arousing because it makes me think of how she tastes. I want her on my tongue again. Even now, my mouth waters in remembrance, and my khui resonates in my chest.

So I just sit back and watch her, to see what she will do next.

She gathers her strange leathers around her, determined to cover her small, soft body. Is she cold? My protective instinct rises, and I turn to the fire, feeding more of the stored wood to it. I will need to chop wood and refill the stores here for the next hunter, but it's a task I will gladly do for my mate. I want her to be warm and comfortable.

Once I build up the fire, she moves closer to it and puts her hands near the flames. They look . . . strange. "You have five fingers," I tell her and hold my own hand up. I have four. It is yet another difference between us. I'm fascinated and a little revolted by those extra fingers.

Her hand touches her chest. *"Shhheorshie."* She pats her breast again and looks at me. *"Haim sheorshie."*

Is there something wrong with her chest now? Is she trying to tell me her khui is gone? It's as obvious as her dull white eyes. "Yes, I know," I tell her. "Fear not. We will perform the ceremony when we return home to the tribe."

"Shhheorshie," she says, patting her breast again, and then reaches out and pats my chest. She looks at me expectantly.

Is she asking about my resonance? I press her small hand to my chest so she can feel my khui vibrate. She jerks away, startled, and looks up at me with wide eyes. *"Whtws tht? Thtcher naym?"*

"Resonance," I explain to her, and my khui hums at her touch.

She looks at me with such shock that I start to feel a sense of unease. When she puts her hand on my chest again and I resonate, she pulls her hand away so quickly that it's as if she's touched something ice cold.

"Hiee cnt pru nownsce tht," she tells me and presses her hand to my chest again, then back to hers. *"Sheeorshie."*

"Sheeorshie," I echo.

Her face brightens. *"Ys!"* She gives her chest a happy pat. *"Shrsie!"*

It's not her trying to tell me about her khui or her lack of resonance. It's her name.

She touches her chest again and looks at me expectantly.

Baffled, I touch my own chest. "Vektal."

Her jaw juts, and she tries to say my name properly. It comes out more as "Huptal." She's unable to make the swallowed first syllable properly. It's all right. It's a start.

"Huptal," she says happily and pats her shoulders again. "Shorshie."

Her own name is garbled syllables, but I try to pronounce it to make her happy. Shorshie she is.

And Shorshie is a mystery to me. She has no tail, no fur. She wears strange leathers and walks the dangerous hunting lands with no weapons. She's weak and soft and has no khui, and she does not speak a word of proper language.

It makes no sense. How can Shorshie be here? Every creature has a khui. My people, the sa-khui, are the only intelligent people in the world. There are *metlaks*, but they are covered in hair and no smarter than rocks. They have not yet mastered fire.

Shorshie is smart. She doesn't flinch away from the fire like a metlak. She recognizes it. And she is wearing cured leather. Her boots are finer than any I have seen. Shorshie has come from a people from somewhere.

But where? I can't ask her. We can barely communicate.

And then it occurs to me that . . . she is not resonating. She doesn't feel what I do, because she has no khui. Maybe she never has.

I'm hit with a sense of loss so strong it makes me bare my teeth. This . . . this cannot happen. How is it that she cannot resonate to me? That we are not connected? It is as if I have found my other half after so long . . . and she is dead to me. The thought chokes me. To lack a khui is a death sentence. To see Shorshie so vibrant and so doomed makes my soul ache.

But no. She is *my* mate. My other half. I'll do whatever is necessary to keep her.

Georgie

He's got fire. That's a big plus in my book. I rub my hands close to the flames and bask in its warmth. It's driving away the chill from the outside. The wind is whistling through the door flap, and I can see it's getting dark outside, but I'm decently warm in this cave as long as I'm near the fire. Guiltily, I think of Liz and Kira and the others. Surely they can stay warm by huddling together, can't they?

I look up as Vektal begins to pace in the small cave. He looks troubled, and that makes me feel edgy. It's like I've done something wrong, and I've no clue what. He keeps purring at me, so I thought he was happy? But I guess not.

My stomach growls, and I press a hand to it. Time for a seaweed bar. I check the pockets of my stolen jumpsuit, but I don't find anything and begin to panic. Now I've lost my food and my weapon. The only things I've got left are the boots that pinch my feet and the jumpsuit. Man, I am shitty at this exploring thing. Ugh.

He moves and kneels next to me, and I instinctively shrink

back. I give Vektal a wary look. His mouth felt good on me a short time ago, but I know what he wants and I'm leery of him standing too close.

But he only gestures at my stomach. *"Kuuuusk?"* There are a wealth of tones in that word that I won't be able to emulate. It's like he's doing some weird vibrating thing in the back of his throat.

"Hungry," I say to him and pat my stomach. Then I mime eating.

He points at my teeth and asks another question. Right. Something about them bothers him. I bare them to show him they're fine, and he bares his own in response to me.

Fangs. Of course he's got fangs. His canines are three times the size of mine, and they look brutal. No wonder he's mystified by my short, blunt teeth. "Hope those are for chewing vegetables," I tell him brightly.

He pulls off a fur cape and boy, am I glad to see that it's clothing and not part of him. I can handle the horns, I think. But I'm glad that the shaggy fur isn't his. Looking at him again, I see that a lot of his bulk might be clothing. That's good. There's no disguising that he's seven feet tall, though.

I watch as he undresses, wary. "I hope you didn't mistake my stomach growling for nookie-time."

The fur cape goes to the floor of the cave, and my eyes open wide at the sight of his clothing underneath. I think it's leather, and it's all a similar soft bluish-gray shade that makes me think of a cloudy day. It also doesn't look very warm. His arms are bare, and his chest is covered by a vest that seems to be made entirely of pockets and laces. It holds a few wicked-looking bone knives strapped to his chest. He's got a lot of flesh exposed despite the blizzard raging outside, and I wonder just how warm that stupid cape is.

And if I can steal it.

"Probably a bad idea, Georgie," I tell myself. "This guy's your only buddy at the moment."

Even if he does want to just lick my pussy. I clamp my thighs together tightly at the memory and try not to blush. I go back to ogling the alien. His arms are bare and show a crazy amount of corded muscle. They're enormous and intimidating, and I imagine the pectorals under the leather vest are equally as staggering.

He pulls a strap from over one shoulder, and I see that in addition to the myriad buckles and pouches, he's got a bag slung across his chest. My stomach growls again. He might have food.

Real food. Not seaweed bars.

My mouth waters, and I clasp my hands together tightly to keep from reaching for him. I've never been so hungry in my life. He opens his satchel and produces a bladder of some kind that must be a waterskin along with a leather-wrapped package. He hands it to me, and I unwrap it. There in the wrappings are a few thick bars of what looks like meat mixed with an oatmeal of some kind. Travel rations. Has to be. I tremble and look up at him. "Is this for me?"

"*Kuuus-kah*," he says in that weird language of his, and he mimes breaking off a piece and eating it.

I could kiss him right now, fangs and all. "Thank you," I say and break off a large piece. I don't care if I seem greedy or not. I'm starving. I cram the entire piece into my mouth and begin to chew.

Right away, I can tell it's a mistake.

The taste is . . . well, "awful" is the kindest word I can think of. It's like I've bitten into a package of jalapeno peppers mixed with a vile, mealy texture. The spices are so strong that my nose and eyes immediately water. I cough, desperately trying to swallow the mouthful I've got, but it's burning my tongue. I end up choking and spitting out half the food into my hand; all the while the alien looks on curiously.

It's brutal. I gag and cough for a moment more, until he pushes the skin into my hand and barks out a short word. I cautiously take a sip, afraid of what it'll taste like. To my relief, the water is cool and refreshing, and has a masked hint of citrus to the taste. I guzzle it with relief, and my choked coughing slowly abates.

I push the dried food back to him and shake my head. Even if I wanted to eat it—and oh, do I want to—I can't. Just the thought of putting even a small piece into my mouth makes my jaw clench up. My stomach issues a miserable protest.

The alien is mystified by my rejection of the food. He examines my mouth again and tries to touch my tongue. I brush his questioning hand aside. "The problem isn't my mouth, it's your food."

He says something in his gibberish language and gestures at my bruises. Oh. He thinks I'm hurt and that's why I can't eat. I shake my head. "I'm fine. Really."

The alien—Vektal—gazes at me curiously.

"I don't suppose there's a nice city full of friendly aliens a short distance away?" I ask. The small cave's getting colder, and the air whistles, so I hitch my jacket a bit closer to my body.

Vektal picks up his fur cape and drapes it over my shoulders, talking to me in that weird rumbly language.

"Thanks," I say and hug it closer. He's not putting clothes on, so the cold must not be bothering him as much. I eye him as he bends over and feeds another log to the fire.

He's got a tail. Okay. Lots of things have tails. That's not so weird. I'm trying not to get weirded out by him, but he's just so . . . different. His horns, for one. The hand that places another piece of wood on the fire has only four fingers. The boots on his feet look like a soft leather but are shaped extremely wide at the toes, so I can only wonder what's going on in there.

Oh, and he's a smoky gray-blue. Can't forget that part. And he purrs. So yeah, other than being bipedal, maybe he's not much like me after all.

"Sheorshie," he says, mangling my name. He repeats it and then gives me a frown and a shake of his braided black hair. "Sheorshie Vektal," he says again, then points at his eye and then shakes his head.

"I don't know what you're trying to say to me," I tell him. "That I'm not like you? I know I'm not." I point at his food. "I wish to God I could eat this, but I can't." My eyes brim with exhausted tears. Everything feels as if it's crashing down on me. "You have no idea how much my life has sucked in the last two weeks."

He says something in a softer voice and wipes away the tear that spills down my cheek. I notice his skin feels like suede or chamois. It's . . . nice. It feels friendly even if everything else in the world is all fucked up.

Vektal tugs the cloak down tighter on me. He pats the furs by the fire and says something else. My guess is that it's something akin to "rest here" because he pats the furs again and waits. I lie down. I'm warm and snuggled in furs and for the first time in what feels like forever, I don't feel like I'm in imminent danger. All this alien wants is oral sex.

The thought makes me giggle inwardly, and I'm smiling as I fall asleep.

I wake up later, feeling better than I have in a long, long time. I'm warm and under a thick blanket, and I'm cuddled up against a big, hard form that's warmer than any heating pad. My fingers move over the surface. It feels like suede over bone, and I realize after I hear the soft purring begin that I'm pressed up against Vektal's chest.

It's . . . not the worst place in the world to be. I mean, if I have my choice between the old cargo bay, alone in the snow, or snuggled next to the pussy-loving alien, I'm going to go with option number three.

I debate pretending to remain asleep, but there's something big and hard prodding into my stomach that tells me that Vektal's conscious, acutely aware of my presence, and far more generously equipped than any guy I've ever met.

I sit up, tugging the blankets around me. My breath fogs in the air, and I glance around the cave. Weak sunlight is pouring in through the door flap, and the fire has gone out. It's bitterly cold unless I'm pressed next to Vektal, and the urge to crawl back against him and huddle for warmth is real and strong.

But he sits up and begins to adjust his clothing. "*Vy droskh,*" he tells me. I don't know if that's "good morning" or "damn it's cold" or what. He gets up, and as he does, my stomach rumbles again.

Vektal squints at me.

"I know," I say. "Trust me, I know." It's embarrassing for me, too.

He begins to unwrap the food from last night, but I make a face and shake my head. I mime that it burns my tongue. He chuckles and then makes a gesture that looks like a rocking baby, which puzzles me. I'm not following this conversation at all.

"Hungry," I say. I rub my stomach and mime eating something. "Food?" Every inch of me feels like a mooch for finding a guy and then demanding he feed me, but "food" is easier to mime than "If you'd give me a nice weapon I'd catch my own breakfast." For right now, we have to proceed in baby steps.

Vektal nods and begins to put on the gear he discarded overnight. He's bare-chested this morning, and his pectorals are just as grimly fascinating as I suspected they would be. They're like slabs of cold iron over his smoky blue chest. I remember the warm, suede feel of his skin. He sure was nice to rub up against. I watch him dress, intrigued by the differences in our bodies. Over certain spots on his body, he has knobby ridges. They trail along the back of each arm to his elbow. The ridges glide down the center of his chest and smooth out somewhere between his pectorals and his navel. And his thighs have the bumpy, textured ridges, too. I wonder what purpose they're for. They decorate his brow, too, and right down his nose.

He's in a talky mood this morning, too. He holds a one-sided conversation with me as he slings his vest back over his chest and begins to tie his knives and blades back to their proper spots. I want to ask for one, but I don't know his culture. Maybe it's taboo for him to give me one and I'd insult him by asking. Right now I'm wary of pissing him off, because he's the only lifeline I've got. I watch my breath fog in the air again as he continues talking, and I think of the girls at the ship, huddled together.

I hope they're okay. God, I hope they're okay. I need to get back to them today so they don't worry. I can tell them what I've found . . .

Which, really, isn't much. I've found face-eating fish that have stalks that look like bamboo. I've found a warm stream (full of the aforementioned face-eating fish), and I've found an alien that likes to eat pussy as a greeting.

All three things won't help us get home. I haven't found a city. I haven't found another ship. I sure haven't found anyone that speaks English. And to make matters worse, I've lost our only weapon. I'm not doing so hot at this save-the-day thing.

Vektal finishes tying his bags and pouches and then slips on boots. I sneak a peek at his toes just to satisfy my curiosity. Three large, splayed toes and a bony heel that was probably a fourth toe at some point in evolution. I probably wouldn't be able to wear his boots, either, and the thought depresses me as I shove my feet back into my uncomfortable stolen boots.

I stand and spots swim before my eyes. I weave, only to be pulled against a hard chest. He murmurs something in my ear and offers the food again, but I push it away. I'm not being picky. I cannot physically eat the stuff. I accept the water he pushes into my hand, and I drink it, but it's not going to last me. Maybe I can convince Vektal to go back to where he captured me so I can hunt for my seaweed bars. At this point, I'm so hungry I'll eat them even if they've turned to a block of ice overnight.

He leads me out of the cave, watching me as I follow him. A new powder has fallen overnight, and I look at the deeper snow with despair. So much for finding my old supplies.

Vektal gestures at his shoulders, bare of any sort of cloak since I'm wearing it. He kneels and indicates that I should climb onto his back and put my arms around his neck, piggyback style. Well, this is humiliating. But I'm so tired and weak that I don't protest. I put my arms around him and cling to his back, wrapping my legs around his waist. He pats one of the arms around his neck, says something soothing, and then he starts racing down the side of the mountain.

I'm stunned for a moment at how fast he is. He's unaffected by the snow, his boots driving through the powder as if it's nothing. He burns like a furnace inside, too, his skin so warm to the touch that the parts touching him are toasty warm and the parts exposed to the wind are like sticking a hand in a bucket of ice. It makes me burrow down even closer to his body once I realize he doesn't need the cape at all. He's just fine in this wintry land-scape without it. So I push my head against his neck and press my cold face into his warm hair. He smells good, too.

Great, now I've got Stockholm syndrome.

He pushes down the mountainside, moving down the steep slopes as if they're nothing. We pass through another copse of trees, and I realize for the first time that we're heading the wrong way from the crash site. I haven't been paying attention, dazed from hunger and cold. But this is wrong. Everyone up there is waiting for me, shivering and starving. I can't leave them.

"Wait," I say, tapping on his shoulder. "Vektal, wait!"

He pauses, and as he does, I slide off his back. I shiver im-mediately at the bitter cold, but I make him turn so I can point up the hill, back to the direction that I came. "We have to go that way and rescue the others."

He shakes his head and points down the hill. In the direction he's pointing, I can see thick trees and more greenery. He wants to go down the mountain.

But I can't leave everyone behind. I insistently point back up. "Please. I need to go up there. There are more people. More women. They're hungry and cold and don't have anything."

Vektal shakes his shaggy head and mimes eating. Then he points at the forest below us, down the snowy slopes.

I waver. Do I let him take me farther away to eat? Or do we immediately go up to the others and still starve? I hesitate. They probably already think something's happened to me.

My stomach growls again. Vektal gives me an exasperated look. He says the food word again. *"Kuuusk."*

I bite my lip, thinking. I glance back at the mountain. Everything in me says I need to insist. But I'm feeling so weak and starved. I can convince him to go back later, can't I? Once I've gotten something to eat?

And won't it be better to show up not empty-handed?

With a heavy sigh, I look back at him. His glowing blue eyes seem to be burning holes into me. "Kusk then up the hill, okay? Let's get enough kusk for everyone."

Maybe a belly full of food will swallow my guilt.

Vektal

When my mate climbs atop my back again and wraps her small, soft limbs around me, I have to fight my pleasure. She's cold and hungry and upset over something. The need to please her eats at my insides. I'll bring down a meal for her so she can gorge and regain her strength. Right now, her pale skin is even paler, and I worry she'll sicken and be too weak to accept a khui.

I have plans for my sweet mate. Whether she likes it or not, she's going to take a khui. I'm not about to lose her now that I've found her.

The valley blossoms with teeming wildlife. I can tell from my mate's easy grip on my neck that she doesn't see the skulking snow cats in the distance or the form of the scythe-beak hiding behind a nearby tree. My hunter's gaze picks them out, and I search for a safe spot in which I can leave my mate without worry for a short time. She's too weak to hunt for her own food or to defend herself if something should attack.

There's a large boulder I can use for a lookout on the far side of the narrow valley, and I head there, pushing through the ever-deepening snow. Though the weather doesn't bother me, my mate's shivering increases the longer we are out. She won't be able to travel far unless I get her something warmer to wear. So, food first, then skins so I may dress my soft, fragile Shorshie.

I'll protect her with my life if I must.

The need to claim her resonates in my chest, my khui reminding me that I have found my mate and not yet claimed her. I pat my chest as if to tell it *I know. I know she is mine.* Communicating with her is difficult, and she is frightened and weak. Once she is strong and we can share more words, she will see what I have been trying to tell her. Then she will spread those soft, pink thighs for me again, and I will have her on my tongue. I will bury my cock inside her and feel the resonance reverberate between both of us.

My cock grows hard at the thought, and so I force it away.

Once I get to the boulder, I gently set Shorshie down. She climbs up on the rock when I gesture to it. "Stay here," I tell her.

Of course, she tries to follow me.

I gesture that she should stay again, and she gives me a panicky look. "Sheorshie Vektal?"

"I'm not leaving you, sweet resonance," I tell her, brushing a finger over her pale cheek. "It's dangerous." I point at the lurking creatures that are even now watching us. I point out the scythe-beak and then the snow cats. I even point out a lurking quill-bundled rodent that will be her meal. It takes a few moments for her to recognize the creatures hiding in plain view, blending amidst the snow. When she sees them, though, her eyes go wide, and she gives me another frightened look.

"You will stay here," I tell her. "I'll hunt something for you to eat."

She babbles something in her weird language. *"Hly sht thse thngs r hugednt leev me!"*

"It will be fine," I soothe. I bundle the cape tighter around her small shoulders. She responds by reaching for one of my knives, a question in her eyes. I nod and hand her a bone-handled one that I created myself. Now she has protection.

It's clear she feels better with it in her hand. She crouches down on the rock and nods at me, gripping the knife. I brush my fingers over her cold, hairless skin again and then pull my sling from my pack. I keep a few smooth stones at hand and put one in the pouch, then whirl the sling through the air, taking aim. My arms flex as I let the stone fly, and I'm pleased to see that the rodent flops to the ground, staggered.

I approach it before it can recover and slice its throat with a motion of my knife. Then, I cut a slit in the neck to drain the blood and another in the belly to remove the offal. I leave the heart and other tasty bits for my mate, then bring the entire thing back to her. I'm leaving a trail for the snow cats to follow, but they won't attack as long as they scent me. Their memories are long, and they don't like the taste of sa-khui flesh. We are a bitter meal.

I return with my prize and display it to my shivering mate.

She wrinkles her nose and gives me a confused look.

"Not familiar with quilled beasts, are you?" I say, because it feels good to talk to her. I lay the kill down on the cold stone she's crouching upon and notice she flinches backward. "It's dead, sweet resonance. Look, I have saved you the choicest parts." I pull open the belly flap and reveal the heart and liver. They're still warm, though they'll cool fast in this weather and won't taste nearly as good. "Just avoid the quills in the fur. We'll get you something larger for a cloak. There are furred *dvisti* in this area that will make a fine meal."

Shorshie stares at the kill blankly. Then she points at it. *"Yewspectmiteweet thet?"*

Is she not familiar with this food? She ate the meal bar easily enough. I pull the heart out and hold it to her lips. "Here. Taste."

She nearly falls off the rock in her haste to move backward. *"Ohmigodfckno!"* A moment later, she points at the dripping delicacy held between my fingers. *"Fckincookthtshit!"*

I tilt my head at her. "What is it? What are you saying?"

She mimes a gesture, holding her hands out like she did over the fire. Then she points at the food. *"Fiiiiir,"* she tells me. *"Cookhit."*

This time my lip curls. "You want to burn the food? Do you not understand what this is?" I toss the heart into my mouth and chew to show her. Flavorful blood bursts across my tongue, hot and sweet.

Her face crumples, and she gags. Her hand goes up, and she gestures for me to put it away. *"Hmigod. Grss."*

"Eat," I tell her sternly. She's too weak to be picky about her food. "I'll burn it for you later if you like, but you must eat now." I slice another thick portion of the creature's flank off and hand her the meat. I force her small fingers to close around it, ignoring the fact that she makes that gagging noise again. "Eat so you have strength for the rest of the day."

She shakes her head.

I take a bite and show her, then insist she eat as well. Her stomach growls, and she gets a pained look on her face. *"Hopes-likesushi."* Shorshie makes another face and then takes a bite, grimacing the entire time.

I'm pleased. She's not, but at least I'm getting food into her.

She doesn't like the tasty organs, then. I eat them, ignoring her little sounds of distress, because a good hunter does not waste meat. I carve more tasty tidbits and feed them to her, and she protests the entire time, but at least her belly is filling. She drinks all of my water and then motions that she's still thirsty.

I nod. One thing at a time. Caring for Shorshie in such a dangerous territory is something that must be handled carefully. The last thing I want is for her to accidentally run into a snow cat near its den . . . or worse, a pack of hunting metlaks. I must carefully guard her and not let her out of my sight. It will mean slow hunting and an even slower return to the tribal caves, but I am prepared to do whatever it takes.

"Come," I tell Shorshie, hanging my kill from my belt so the meat can freeze in the chill weather. That will keep it until later. I offer her a hand so she can get down off the rock.

She climbs back onto my back, and I realize again just how small and fragile she is. I can carry her as if she weighs nothing. This is not good. Even the daintiest of my tribesmates could crush her like a twig. It rouses my protective instinct, and I fight the urge to snarl at the thought.

Shorshie will be safe, no matter the cost.

We trek through the snow for some time, and I'm pleased to see that she's quiet, observing the world around her. She doesn't call attention to us. She doesn't complain or demand more things in her strange language. She doesn't ask questions when I break a tree limb from a nearby sapling and backtrack, sweeping it over our prints to hide our trail. She's a silent observer.

But I still worry she does not even know the basics of how to fend for herself. Her request for more fire lingers in the back of my mind and worries me. I find an unfrozen stream, heated by the ground itself. It smells of rotten things, but the taste will be pleasant enough and the heat will be nice on weary muscles. It's also a test to see how much my Shorshie knows. There are things that even the smallest of kits know about the wilds that I worry she does not.

Sure enough, she trots trustingly toward the stream, getting far too close. So much for my test. I grab her by the arm before she can step near the bank, and she hisses in pain.

I'm instantly abashed at my own strength. "Shorshie?" If I've hurt my mate, I will be sick with self-loathing. My khui seems to recoil in agreement.

"Sokay," she says, breathing heavy. She winces and flexes her wrist. "Hrtfrmcrash."

I take her small hand in mine, and she trustingly lets me examine her. She is mottled with bruises on her arm, the flesh swollen. She is hurt, and I never even realized. I am furious with myself for missing something so obvious. "I am sorry, my Shorshie. I will not be so careless again."

I lead her away from the stream and look around for something to bind her wrist. I pat my clothing, looking for loose fabric, but she laughs and shakes her head. She jabbers something else at me and points at the water, indicating she'd rather drink than fuss with her wrist.

All right, then. I can show her how to drink. I glance around and find a broken stick at the base of a tree. I pick it up and indicate she should observe me. Then, I get as close as I dare and toss it into the water.

For a long moment, there is nothing. Then, the water boils with activity. I watch Shorshie gasp as the mud-dwelling fang-fish attack. Her surprise is chilling to me. The land is not hospitable many months out of the year, but even the smallest kits know that the foul-smelling warm streams are crowded with dangerous creatures. A fang-fish can strip the flesh from a full-grown dvisti in a matter of moments. Shorshie would have been dead before I'd blinked.

The thought makes me pull her closer to me. She trembles and pushes closer, terrified.

"Watch," I tell her.

"Watch," she agrees, looking up at me with huge, white-rimmed eyes that do not sing with khui-color. It reminds me of her vulnerability. Her fragility. This must be corrected, and soon.

I pull out my traveling pouch. No hunter leaves the tribal caves without one, and in it I have several of the red soap-berries that are so plentiful. I grip two of them, smash them between my fingers, mix the juice with a handful of packed snow at my feet, and then lob the entire thing into the current of the stream. Then I look at Shorshie again. "Watch."

She watches, her face intent. I see her surprise when the water begins to flick and the fang-fish swim upstream, fleeing the waters and the berry-taint they hate so much. "They do not like the juice," I tell her. "They will not return here until the moons go down once more. Now we can drink."

She looks at me curiously, and so I show her by moving toward the water. I dip my waterskin in and fill it, then indicate that she can drink the water directly from the stream.

"*Sokay?*" she asks cautiously. "*Noh mnsters?*"

I nod to whatever nonsense she's saying and drink again, then wash my face in a cupped handful of water.

That gets her attention. "*Wash?*" she asks, plucking at my vest. I see she's now clutching my bone knife in her hand, no doubt frightened of the fang-fish. But her gaze is on my face, and she mimes my gesture from a moment ago. "*Wash?*"

"Yes, you can clean yourself," I say, taking the knife away from her before she can hurt herself. I hand her a few more of the berries instead. In addition to being a taste the stream-dwelling fish dislike, they make a fine soap. I indicate that she can lather with them, and she looks excited.

"Vektal *wash*?" she asks, then speaks another nonsense stream of syllables before repeating the words and miming bathing. "Vektal *wash*?"

"Are you afraid to get into the stream alone, my resonance?" I tease. "Shall I stand upstream so the fang-fish devour my carcass before yours?"

She gives her head a tiny shake indicating she doesn't understand, but there's an excited smile on her face. "*Wash?*" she asks again.

I nod and begin to remove my leathers. I'll wash my mate gladly. I watch her graceful form as she undresses, stripping out of her own strange leathers. For the first time I realize they're covered in stains, and they reek of offal. I've been so enamored of Shorshie that I haven't paid the slightest bit of attention to the fact that she's dirty. No wonder she's so excited at the thought of washing.

My resonance mate is chattering up a storm, shivering and rubbing her arms as she gets naked. Like her hand, her tiny feet have too many toes and are oddly shaped, but I don't point this out. I love every ounce of her strange body, even if she is furless and tailless. My khui starts to resonate with pleasure at the sight of her, and I finish stripping off my leathers and then wade into the water.

"*Hoboy*," she breathes, still standing on the bank. She's staring at my groin. Pleased at her attention, I stretch and rub a hand over my stomach. My cock grows hard at her stare, and my body surges with resonance. Is this Shorshie's way of encouraging mating?

"Come to me, then, my mate." I gesture her forward. "I will fill all your needs."

Georgie

"Hung like a horse" really never had much of a meaning until now.

I try not to stare, and fail.

I can handle fangs. The tail. The suede-like bluish-gray skin. Heck. I'm cool with the horns that curl around his head like a badass crown of some kind.

And I tell myself that I should realize that a dude who's seven feet tall will have an enormous cock. It's size appropriate. I'm *almost* prepared for that, though the sight of it growing erect still makes my thighs clamp together in trepidation.

I'm not prepared for ridges.

He's got freaking ridges on his cock.

Just like the upraised texture along his chest, his brows, and his arms, he's got the bumpy, knotty ridges along the top of his cock. His very big, very thick cock. In addition to those ridges, he has an additional one that almost looks like another horn, except it's blunted at the tip instead of sharp. Small miracle, that. So, okay. He's got a textured, huge cock with a bony, protruding knob an inch or so above it.

I feel like there's an alien bingo card somewhere that just got checked off. Horns? Check. Tail? Check. Crazy-ass cock? Check check check.

And since I'm staring, he's giving me heated looks with those glowing blue eyes of his. It's like he's daring me to touch him.

And . . . okay. I'm a little curious about what all that equipment would feel like on a girl, but I'm more interested in bathing than playing hide the sausage. I eye the water he's now thigh-deep in, and he crosses his big arms over his chest.

Right. My turn. I'm still scared of the fish from earlier, but if he's in the water, I assume it's safe. I move closer to where he's at, though, just in case. And I am shivering with cold, so I need to either get in the damn water with him or re-dress.

I look at my filthy clothing and decide to get in the water. I can still smell blood and the mess from the hold on me, and I desperately want to get clean. So I take a leap of faith and get into the water.

It smells like rotten eggs, which I've heard is what underground hot springs smell like. I don't care. The water's warm like a bath, and considering that it's snowy and bitterly cold, I love it. I moan as it hits my limbs and then I sink deeper, trying to submerge my entire body into the scalding water.

It feels amazing. Right now I could kiss Vektal for bringing me here, scary fish and all. I splash water over my limbs, rubbing at them to get rid of the nasty smells of the last ten days of captivity.

Vektal moves next to me in the water. He says something, then hands me more berries. He motions that I should squeeze them and then rub the juice on me. And maybe I don't move fast enough for him, because he takes the berries from my hand and squeezes the juice onto my shoulders. Then his big hands start rubbing it into my skin.

I stiffen at first, but his touch is very matter-of-fact. It's like he realizes I just want to get clean and won't monkey around, despite the enormous erection he's sporting that says otherwise. And it's kind of . . . sweet, I guess. He's not touching me to be a creep. He's touching me because he wants to show me how to use the soap. I begin rubbing the strange, fruity-smelling lather over my arms and legs, and when he scoops a handful off my shoulder and begins to wash my hair for me, I moan with pleasure.

Being clean has never felt so amazing.

I hear him inhale sharply. Hear the vibrating purr start in his chest again. He murmurs something, voice thick, but all he does is wash my hair. No demanding touches. No insisting of anything. Just pleasure in touching me. In pleasing me.

Actually, other than the fact that he startled the hell out of me with the oral sex thing, he's been kinda sweet. Everything he's done has been designed to please me and give me pleasure. I digest that small bit of information. Maybe it's the Stockholm syndrome talking. Maybe it's the fact that with Vektal, I've felt safe. Safer than I have in the last two weeks. But I don't mind his touch. In fact, I kind of like it, probably a lot more than I should.

I can't look at him while I'm—we're—bathing. My cheeks feel hot, because every so often, he leans in closer and prods me with that enormous cock of his, and it makes me think of dirty things. Of his mouth on me. The suede-like feel of his skin against mine. His warmth. His intriguing scent.

"Shorshie," he murmurs, his hands caressing my scalp.

"Gee-or-gee," I correct him. There must not be any *g* sounds in his language, because he slurs them.

"Shorgee," he tries.

"Gee," I prompt.

"Shhhzhee—" he begins, then stops and tries again. "Corgee."

I giggle. Corgi? Not quite. I turn around and point at my mouth to show him how to move his tongue. "Georgie."

His fingers brush over my lips in a tender caress. "Zheo-rzhe." Then, he tries again. "Geeeeorgie." His *g* is practically purred.

"Very good," I say, my voice soft. I've just now realized that I'm practically pressed up against him and I'm naked.

"Georgie," he repeats, purring my name again. Then he takes my hand and places it over his chest, where he rumbles like a cat. "Georgie *sa-akh* Vektal."

The way he says it, with my hand clasped against his heart, makes me think it has a bigger meaning than I'd like to imagine. His gaze is intense, as if he's waiting for me to respond.

He's an alien. I remind myself of that, even as it occurs to me that I can convince him to help me—help us—escape the other aliens. The captors that want to sell us.

This has to be a multilayered plan, I figure. Vektal's planet is cold as hell and, judging from his gear, probably isn't past the Stone Age. But I refuse to give up hope of a way back home. I just know it's not going to happen with the little green men or the ball-headed aliens. They think we're cattle.

Vektal's my best bet.

Maybe I'm using him a little when I rub my fingers on his chest. They're cold in the frigid, snowy air, and my nipples are hard. I rub up against him deliberately, letting him feel my body.

I lick my lips and then look up into those alien, glowing blue eyes.

And I point at the mountainside in the distance, where I know that so many women (half in pods) are waiting for rescue while I play bubble bath with a native. "Take me up the side of the mountain?"

He caresses my face, a question in his gaze. "Moun . . . tain?"

"Yes," I say and trace my fingers over his skin. "Up there."

His brows draw together, and he gives a shake of his head indicating that no, he's not taking me there.

All right then, time to pull out the big guns. "Vektal," I murmur. "Do you know how to kiss?"

The alien's blank expression tells me he has no clue what I'm saying. Of course he doesn't. So I put a hand to the back of his neck and pull him closer to me. He's warm, and I rather like the feel of him blocking out the chilly wind. "Kiss?" I say again, and then I lean in and brush my lips against his.

The look on his face is stunned. It's like it never occurred to him that people would put their mouths on each other. I stifle the giggle threatening to erupt and drag a finger down the front of his chest. "I can show you more things . . . if you take me up the mountain."

I know I'm playing with fire. Offering him sexual favors in exchange for rescue probably isn't the greatest plan, but I'm working with the weapons I have. As long as he's fascinated by me, I can use that. It's mercenary, but people's lives are at stake. If I have to kiss an alien and flirt with him to get a rescue to my friends, I will.

It's not exactly a hardship, I have to admit. I'm still thinking about his mouth on my skin from last night. The way he licked me until I came. And the way he is staring at me right now makes me think that sex with him wouldn't be something terrible to be endured. It'd be slow and full of discovery and oh-so-wicked. And I'm not hating the idea. Not by a long shot. Maybe I'm not in the right frame of mind to be entertaining sexy thoughts, but I can't help it.

I play with fire a little more when I drape my arms around his neck and press my breasts to his warm—*so warm*—body. His cock pushes against my stomach insistently, and I ignore it, twining my fingers in his thick black hair.

Vektal leans his face close to mine again, his gaze flicking to my mouth and then to my eyes. It's like he's asking for another kiss but unsure how to go about it.

"Do aliens not kiss?" I ask softly, leaning in to brush my lips over his again. "I'll show you how to do all kinds of kissing if you'll go up the mountain with me."

"Moun . . . tain," he repeats, and his eyes narrow. He puts his fingers to my mouth and then his, and then repeats it again. "Georgie mountain?"

"That's right," I say, pleased he's getting it. "Take me to the mountain and Georgie will kiss you again." I press my fingers from my lips to his.

That shrewd gaze watches me. He leans in, and I think he's going to kiss me, but he only nuzzles my nose. "Georgie . . . mountain," he says in a low voice, and then I feel his hand slide down to my bare pussy, where he drags his fingers over my folds. "Mountain."

I gasp. It's as much the startling, arousing touch as it is what he's asking. He wants me to have sex with him if he takes me up the mountain.

I consider for a long moment, gazing up at him. Then I reach down and grip his cock. "Georgie mountain," I agree, and I give him a quick stroke under the water. *You take me up the mountain, this is what you get.*

He groans and tries to push against my hand, but I release him just as quickly. "Mountain," I insist.

"Mountain," he growls and pulls me against him, his bigger body pressed to mine. For a moment I panic, wondering if he's going to just take what I'm bartering. But he only rubs his nose against mine again and then releases me, pointing at my clothing on the bank.

Hot damn, we're going up the mountain. Rescue party of two, coming right up.

We dress quickly, and I make a face at having to put on my filthy jumpsuit again. The chill in the dry winter air is even worse now that I'm wet and cold, and Vektal insists on me covering my wet hair with the cloak. It's a good idea, but it's still icing up in the brutal cold. Maybe a quick dunk in the river wasn't the smartest of ideas, but I'm clean now.

He hauls me back onto his shoulders, and then we set off up the mountain again. He's carrying on a grumbling narrative that I can't make out and occasionally pats my cold hands. He points out landscape, but if I'm supposed to see something other than snow, I can't make it out.

We head up the hill steadily for what feels like forever, and I'm getting colder by the minute. My teeth chatter, and my head feels like a block of ice. I'm cold and hungry, and the raw meat I ate has only made me hungrier. I didn't realize how far down the mountain we'd come until I look up and it seems that the rocky crag that holds the ship is hours away. Which only makes my teeth chatter harder.

The steep ground slopes toward a steep cliff I don't recognize, and I'm surprised when Vektal heads right for it. He sets me down, says something that probably means "stay here," and then moves to the base of the cliff and begins to dig. I watch him for a few confused moments before I realize he's uncovering the mouth of a new cave.

He's not taking me up the mountain at all. He's taking me to another cave.

"You have got to be kidding me," I explode. "No! Vektal, we're going up the mountain!"

The alien turns and gives me an irritated look. He lets forth his own stream of narrative, pointing at my ice-covered hair, the fact that my teeth are clicking madly, and that I'm shivering. He continues talking, gesturing at the cave. I don't have to speak alien to know what he's saying.

You're cold. We'll stay here tonight. Fuck going up the mountain.

And I can't leave the others for another day. I just can't. I'm freezing even with his borrowed cape, and they have nothing. Nothing to eat, nothing to drink, and no shelter. I'm so frustrated I could scream.

Instead, I turn and begin to stomp off, heading to what looks like the path up the mountain. It winds up the valley wall, laden with snow that's trickled down from above. It feels like I'm wading through water, but I'm not going to give up. If I have to march every step back up the mountain to get Vektal to go with me to see the others, I will.

"Georgie," he calls from behind me. Then he bellows out the sharp syllable I now know is "No."

I ignore him and march even faster.

"Georgie, no!"

Too late. I don't see the shadowed snow before I realize that when I step too close to the cliff wall, my foot doesn't connect with anything. The ground beneath my feet disappears, and I scream as I slide down an icy crevasse for forever.

Only it's not forever. It's ten, maybe fifteen seconds. Then I drop and *ploof* into a pile of snow at the bottom, and lie there stunned. Vektal's not so far away that I can't hear him shouting my name from up above.

"Yeah, yeah," I mutter. I can't wait for the alien *I was right, and you were wrong* he's going to deliver to me. I sit up and wince at the throb of my bad wrist. It's getting worse all the time.

Something shuffles nearby, and I freeze. I look at my surroundings for the first time.

I'm in an ice cave of some kind. Icicles hang from the ceiling. Snowdrifts line the walls, and, up above, a trickle of sunlight bleeds in.

It's enough light to let me see the two dozen eyes staring back at me.

I'm not alone. And I'm in deep, deep shit.

PART THREE

Georgie

I stare around me uneasily. Somehow, I've fallen through a hole covered by the falling snow. It's a stupid misstep, and it seems that this planet is absolutely riddled with caverns, because I've landed in one.

And this one's occupied. Really, really occupied.

A dozen pairs of eyes stare at me out of weird, fish-like faces. They're kind of human, kind of not. They're bipedal and have two arms and legs and are tall. Taller than me. Their eyes are enormous in their pointed faces, their mouths small and round. They look almost cartoony, except for the matted pale hair that covers almost every inch of their bodies. And they smell like a wet, dirty dog. Ugh.

One hoots at me, the sound querulous.

"Hi," I say softly. I don't move a muscle as they gaze at me. It's clear they're trying to decide if I'm friend or foe. They remind me a bit of Wookiees from a Star Wars movie—Jesus, I've *really* got to get my mind off of Star Wars—except for the fact that they're white and have enormous eyes. And tails, I realize as one creature moves forward, its tail flicking back and forth like an irritated cat.

It cocks its head and studies me. Then it hoots again.

"Georgie," Vektal snarls from above. "Georgie!" I hear his hands scraping against the ice above, and snow rains down on my head.

"I think I'm okay," I call up to him.

The tail-flicking creature lifts its head and hoots at the air again, sounding a bit like an owl.

More snow flicks onto my face, and I peer up. The rocky cavern has a hole up above, and Vektal's desperately scraping at it, trying to clear enough space for his much larger body to follow me down. He looks frantic and bellows another command at me that I don't understand. Is it "stay put" or "move" or what?

I look at the bug-eyed yeti-things.

One tilts its head at me and wags its tail faster. It's almost like an ugly puppy. Almost. I smile and get to my feet slowly, noticing that the "puppies" are all a foot taller than me. "Hey there," I say, keeping my voice sweet and soft. Maybe if I treat it like a puppy, we'll get along just fine. When its nostrils flare and the tail thumping increases, I extend my good hand out so he can sniff it.

Immediately, the creature snarls. He slaps my hand away and gives me a vicious shove. I give a startled little scream as I fall to the ground. Another creature pounces on me right away, pulling on my hair and my clothing. Another hoots and throws snow at me. I realize they aren't like puppies at all, but more like vicious, angry monkeys.

And I'm in an entire den of them.

The hand twisting in my hair pulls hard, and I scream again, trying to slap it free. Another smacks my injured ribs, and the breath gets knocked out of me. I cough and roll around on the ground, trying to protect myself from their wild swings and hooting calls.

From above, there's a wild, ferocious roar. Then the entire ceiling seems to cave in.

Vektal. Thank God.

Something heavy slams into the ground, and the creatures screech and retreat. I squeeze an eye open just in time to see Vektal roar with fury, the sound vibrating with intensity. The entire cavern shakes, and I watch as he draws his blades.

The creatures back up even more.

I don't blame them—Vektal looks utterly terrifying. The light in his eyes is blazing, and his fangs are bared with fury. I'm even a little frightened when he turns his gaze toward me.

But then he scoops me off of the ground and flings me over his shoulder, caveman-style, before storming his way down an entirely different passageway. The creatures hoot and scream at him, and when one pounces, I feel Vektal's big arm sweep it aside as if it's nothing.

They cluster about, shrieking, and one grabs at my hair again, fisting a handful before I can bat it away. I cry out, and Vektal turns, this time with a knife.

The creature's dead before it hits the ground.

I gasp at the sight, but then Vektal's slamming through the cavern, pushing his way through the grabby creatures, and I'm so relieved at the sight of sunlight a few moments later that I want to weep.

We're out of the cavern, and the creatures aren't following us.

That doesn't mean my alien stops, though. He continues on, trudging through the deep snow with a sense of purpose that makes me a little intimidated. I'm still waiting for the *I told you so.*

But I'm cold and freaked out, and I say nothing to protest my stupid move. If he wants to play caveman, as long as he keeps me safe, I'm fine with that. He's angry. It's pretty obvious to me that he's rather furious, actually. He mutters under his breath in an angry tone, and his body is tense against mine. And the thing that sucks the most is that I can't even apologize for stomping off. We don't have the words. I'm so frustrated and unhappy that I want to kick something.

Except my entire body hurts from my fall, and my ribs feel like they're on fire. So instead of kicking something, maybe I'll just cry instead. If I do, though, the tears will probably just stick to my face.

This whole damn planet is against me.

I'm feeling pretty miserable when Vektal sets me down in the snow and glares fiercely at me. *"Saan tes."* He points at the ground. *"Tes!"*

"Stay here. Got it," I mumble, feeling guilty. I cross my arms over my chest and wait.

He gives me an exasperated look and then heads a few feet away. I notice we're right back at that stupid cliff wall with the buried cave. We're right back where we started a short time ago, except in the meantime I've had half my hair pulled out by rabid yeti, acquired a few more bruises, and now he's pissed at me.

I hate this place. I hate that it's cold and it's snowing all the damn time and everything wants to eat my freaking face. I hate that I'm wearing a smelly, gross jumpsuit and that I ate raw meat and that there are a dozen girls up the hill who would probably kill to be in my place at the moment, and I can't even feel grateful.

I just feel miserable.

I do my best to fight back exhausted, frustrated tears, but they're coming on anyhow. I'm shaking and trembling from cold and misery, and by the time Vektal digs out the mouth of the cave and enters it to make sure it's safe, silent tears are leaking from the corners of my eyes and freezing on my lashes. Because of course they are. Not even his cloak is keeping me warm now, and I stifle a stab of resentment that he's practically in a tank top and leggings and seems to be just fine with the weather.

After a moment, he emerges from the cave and indicates it's safe to come in. I join him, and it's not much to see, the interior a small grotto hacked out of the rocks that opens up near the cliff wall and then snakes further back into the earth. There are supplies near the front, another leather door hanging, a few furs for warmth, and a small stack of what looks like cakes of mud and some wood. It's cozier than anything I've seen recently, and it's out of the wind. As Vektal pushes the leather covering over the entrance to block out the rest of the snow and wind, it's dark inside.

But safe.

I'm safe. I shiver, and then I'm shaking as a sob escapes my throat.

Vektal

Not for the first time, I despair at how helpless my mate is. I'm utterly confused by her—if she knows nothing about the land, how did she get here? Even the metlaks didn't know what to make of her. I'm furious at myself for letting her wander away. I'm furious that the metlaks could have hurt her more grievously than they did. I know of kits that have been torn apart by accidentally encountering a group of metlaks on the prowl.

Georgie, my precious mate, my resonance, fell right into an entire den of them. She could have been killed before I made it down to rescue her.

The thought has my hands shaking and my khui thrumming against my chest with an angry beat. How can I possibly take care of someone who is more helpless than a kit? Someone who demands to go into the dangerous mountains instead of letting me take her home to my people?

Who *is* my Georgie? How did she get here? Other than the metlaks and the sa-khui, there are no other people on this land. She is precious.

And I nearly lost her. I'm twisted in my own anger, stalking about the cave as I prepare a fire for my shivering mate. I stack wood and dung chips, rub the fire-making implements between my palms until I catch a spark, and then create a fire by feeding it tinder. When the flames begin to lick at the wood, I gesture that Georgie, shaking with cold, should move closer.

"*Dankyew,*" she says in a soft voice.

"I don't understand you," I growl at her. It's another obstacle in the way of my mating. I want to tell Georgie that she is mine. That she is my resonance. That she's safe with me and I won't let any harm come to her if she'll just trust me. That she is my light and my reason for being now, and that we shall create a hearth and family together. But I can tell her none of these things.

She sniffs loudly and moves a little closer to the fire, sticking her tiny, five-fingered hands out to warm them. Her bad wrist is an angry color. Maylak, the tribe healer, could cure this with a touch. But she is not here, and my Georgie must suffer. "Give me that," I say gruffly, indicating that she should give me her injured hand. She probably hurt it worse during her fall, and I'm chagrined that my mate is so poorly cared for.

"*Nowyurmadatmeeh,*" she says and sniffs loudly again. Then, she bursts into tears.

"Ah, Georgie," I murmur and pull her against me. Her face presses against my vest, and she sobs. I stroke her hair, now crunchy and hard with ice. She's going to get sick. I've forgotten she has no khui to warm her and dragged her up one side of the mountain and down the next. She's fragile, my small five-fingers. I chide myself for not taking better care of her. "It won't happen again, my resonance," I tell her, stroking her rounded cheek. "I shall take better care of you, starting now."

And even though it's callous of me to use all of the supplies here, I build the fire even higher. I don't care if I'm sweating as long as my Georgie is warm and comfortable. And I hold her against me for what feels like forever. Her hands burrow under my clothing, seeking my warmer skin, and my cock grows hard at her small touches. But she's still crying, and so I hold her and comfort her as best as I can, until the tears die away and she's only sniffling her unhappiness.

Her hands are still under my clothing, though. My cock hasn't forgotten this, and I ache with need, my khui thrumming in my chest. I want to make her happy. I want to make her strange, sweet face smile instead of cry.

So while she warms herself by the fire, I dote on my mate, like I should. I examine her wrist and then cut a strip from one of the furs, binding it tightly and splinting it against one of my bone knives. It will hold until I can take her to the healer. She gives me a grateful smile and points at another one of the bone knives on my vest.

"Kinnihafwon?"

I shake my head to indicate I don't understand, and with gestures, she shows me she wants to hold it. Ah. She wants to defend herself. I give her one of the blades. I wear six, and now I am down to four. Tomorrow, I will show her how to use it and how to stab with it so if she is attacked by metlaks again, she will be able to fight back. They are cowardly creatures at heart and will run if endangered.

At the gifting of the knife, her smile widens and she beams happily at me, as if I have given her the greatest of treasures. *"Iveel betterwit it."*

I nod, though I don't know what she's rambling about. Just that she's smiling. It's enough for me. I will do more, though.

There are furs in this cave, furs left for comfort for hunting warriors who venture out this far. They're stale and stiff with age,
but they're warm. When we leave in the morning, I will break
the rules of hunting politeness and she will wear them as we
travel. I won't have her shivering anymore.

"*Cookh?*" she asks and points at the kill slung at my belt.
"*Cookhnao?*"

"Cookkh?" I repeat, holding the quilled beast up for her to
see. "Is that what you call it? Cookh?"

"*Eeeht,*" she says and smiles up at me, her small teeth gleaming. She points at the beast, then at the fire. "*Cookhden eeht
plis.*"

Ah. Instructions. I point at the fire. "Cookh?"

"*Wellthassfire ifyewont tewget teknikal butyess.*" She nods.
"*Cookh.*"

Even though it goes against every instinct I have, I do as she
asks. I skin the animal and skewer tasty bits on one of my bone
knives, and she holds them up to the fire and then eats one with
happy smacking noises. She exclaims over each bite, and by the
time the food is gone, her eyes are getting drowsy and content.

I'm content, too. We've stopped early, but Georgie is warm
and safe and fed.

I explain to her with hand signals that I must collect more
wood and set traps for more food. She is to stay in the cave and
keep the fire going and rest. She looks uneasy but nods, and I
leave her with my bone knife and waterskin.

I hurry through the gathering, finding dvisti dung instead of
wood. I have no axe with me, and this far up the mountain, the
trees are stunted. I set snares for more quilled beasts and the
scythe-beak birds. Dvisti are the best eating, but Georgie seems
determined to go up the mountain and we cannot carry so much

meat. If she were another sa-khui, it would be easy, but my Georgie is delicate and not nearly as strong as our weakest warrior.

I return to the cave near dark to find Georgie sound asleep, curled up in the blankets, knife in hand. The fire is banked to coals, and her hair has dried into shiny, golden-brown curls that are lovely to see.

They're almost as lovely as the soft smile she gives me when she wakes up. She sits up in the nest of blankets and gives me a sleepy look. "Mountain?"

I shake my head and set down the fire supplies off to one side in the cave. There's a fierce snowstorm outside, and the drifts we must wade through to go up the mountain are getting deeper by the moment. I pull back the hide door to show her the snow, and she looks crestfallen.

"Tomorrow, we will go to the mountain," I tell her. I'm not sure why she is desperate to go, but it must mean something to her. I gesture with my hands, trying to explain that we will go when the sun rises again and the storms stop. Eventually, I just settle for *soon*.

"Soon," she echoes and gives me a smile. She seems satisfied with my answer.

The day is going to be a long one. The suns would still be high in the sky if they were out, and we are snowed in, tucked away against the bitter cold. Georgie cannot withstand it like I can, and having her with me slows me down. I would not trade her presence for the finest hunting, but I must acknowledge that having my mate with me means I must make different choices than I would if I was alone. Caring for her has now taken priority.

The thought of being with her all day feels like a gift.

She gestures at the fire and says my word for fire.

"Yes, fire."

"Fire," she repeats. Then she grabs a handful of the furs she is sitting on and gives me a questioning look.

"Furs."

"Furs," she echoes. The words sound funny in her mouth, as if she has a hard time making the rumbling throat noises that I do. But I'm pleased she wants to learn how to communicate with me. For the next while, we name off things that are easily pointed at, and Georgie tries to pronounce them. Then, she goes back and repeats them in different orders each time, trying to learn the words.

Eventually, we run out of things to name in the cave and proceed to bodies. She pats her curly, disheveled locks.

"Hair," I say automatically, amused that she immediately starts finger-combing her tresses. I will make her a bone comb when we return to my home cave.

"Hair," she grumbles, giving up on the tangles. Then she leans toward me and pats my mane. "Hair?"

"Hair," I agree.

Her fingers move to my horns, and she lightly skims one. "*Whazzis?*"

"Horns," I tell her. I scarcely dare to breathe as she traces along it. Though my horns do not have much feeling, her breasts are close to my face and the scent of her arouses me, as does her fascinated touch. I long to grab her and pull her against me. Instead, I clench my fists and force myself to remain unmoving.

"*Whazzis?*" she asks again, and her fingers brush over my forehead, the bony ridges there, and then my nose.

"Face?" I don't understand what she's asking. I touch her cheek. "Face, like yours."

But she gives a small head shake and rubs one of the ridges with a small fingertip. It makes my cock leap to attention, and now I'm fully erect and aching, my pulse pounding directly in my groin. Her fingers touch the ridges along my nose, and then over my brows, and then brush over my heart. *"Slikeharmr?"*

"It's just skin," I tell her. Hers is smooth all over, while mine has texture in certain places. Her funny, flat brow and tiny nose look odd to me, and her comment makes me think that perhaps I look strange to her.

Her fingers trail down my chest a bit more, and she keeps touching me with soft, ticklish brushes of her fingertips. My khui vibrates with need, and I have to close my eyes to brace myself. I'm going to burst across her hand if she reaches any lower, so I grab her hand before she can keep exploring.

Georgie is in control, but I cannot take much more of this gentle exploration. If she touches me again, I'm going to throw her down on the furs and fuck her until she screams with pleasure.

Georgie

Vektal takes my hand in his as I run my fingers down one big shoulder. It has that ridged, gnarled armor-like plate over one bicep and the back of a hand.

"No," he tells me in his language.

I'm confused. I thought he liked me and wanted me to touch him. His soft leather leggings can't hide the erection straining against them. I'm a little frightened by the sheer size of it, but I know Vektal would never hurt me. He's been fussing over me all afternoon, making sure my wrist was all right, checking my bruises, and shoving small bits of cooked food into my mouth the moment they were ready. All the while, he was touching me with possessive little touches that let me know that he was right there with me, that he was aware of me.

So to be pushed away now? When we're learning about each other? It hurts my feelings. "No?"

He sees the hurt on my face, and I hear his chest thrumming even harder. "Georgie," he says in that soft, unique way of his.

He gestures at himself, then glances heavenward and mutters something I can't make out.

"Are we done playing our game, then?" I ask. I was just getting to the interesting parts. And, okay, I might be flirting a bit. Because touching him and feeling that suede-like skin against mine and watching him react? It's like catnip to a cat. He's just so warm and has such soft skin over those rock-hard muscles, and he looks at me like I hung the moon, and . . . it's intoxicating.

I wonder if he's attractive for his people. He's attractive to me, now that I've gotten past my initial shock of the horns-and-blue-skin-and-glowing-eyes thing. His features are strong and well-defined, his nose straight and regal, even if it is ridged. His cheekbones are high, and he's got a beautifully sculpted mouth.

And he has the most amazing shoulders and biceps. I want to fan myself just thinking about them. Fact is, he's just pure pleasure to touch. I've been enjoying running my hands over him quite a bit, and I can't get our little interlude in the stream a few hours ago out of my mind. About his hand, dragging down to my pussy and claiming it with a touch. Letting me know that he wants me if he's going to take me up the mountain.

I'd touched him back. Gripped that big, delicious cock in my hand and gave it a squeeze to let him know I was willing to play his game.

"Georgie," he says again. He gives me another shake of his proud head and then rubs a hand down his face in a very human-looking gesture of frustration that makes me smile.

"Yes?" I purr, sidling up to him again. Now that the cave is warm, I've stripped off most of the furs I was cocooned in and am down to my jumpsuit. I'm so close I can practically rub my breasts on his arm.

And he won't look at me. Instead, he shakes his head and says something that sounds like, *"Sa nisok ki yemev."*

"Yeah, I don't know what that means," I say, brushing a finger through his mane. His hair is straight, black and coarse, and super thick. It doesn't grow anywhere else on his body, either, which I find interesting.

He pushes my hand away, but I hear the strange purring going wild in his chest. I know he's enjoying my touch. I just don't understand why he won't look at me, or why he pushes me away.

"Vektal?" I ask. "I don't understand."

His eyes flare with light anew, and he takes my wrist and guides my hand to the erection straining his soft breeches. Then he gives me a look as if to say *you see?*

Ah. I get it now. A small smile curves my mouth, and I feel rather powerful at the moment. He won't touch me—won't look at me—because it's arousing him and he doesn't want to push me into anything.

Really, for a big barbarian, he's being the perfect gentleman.

It's ironic because now I'm the one who wants to do more. Maybe it's the need for comfort or the fact that I find him weirdly attractive. Or maybe it's that my belly's full and I feel safe for the first time in what feels like forever, but I'm in the mood. The more he tries to be noble about things? The friskier I get.

"I guess I don't need to ask about birth control, do I?" I say to him and put a hand on his shoulder. God, I love touching him. It feels utterly decadent. "I'm not on the pill, not that it matters now. And I'm pretty sure that since we're different species, you can't get me pregnant."

He watches me with narrowed eyes, as if waiting to see what I'm going to do.

"Allow me to make the first move," I tell him softly, reaching out to undo the top laces on his unusual vest.

Vektal's strange eyes flicker with light, and then he purrs harder than ever, his chest practically vibrating from the strength of it.

"I appreciate the rescue earlier," I say, tugging at the laces. The fabric, a soft hide of unnatural coloration, falls away at my touch. I brush aside the knives and pouches tied to it, revealing Vektal's broad chest and the ridges that cascade down his breast-bone, between two massive, hard pectorals. "Allow me to show you how much."

I lean forward to kiss him—

And he automatically leans away, looking at me with sur-prise.

"Kiss," I say, stifling a giggle. I'd almost be offended at his expression of surprise, but I know Vektal's not familiar with kissing. Maybe he doesn't make love like humans do, either. The thought intrigues me.

"Kiss," he agrees, and when I lean forward again, he doesn't pull away.

I brush my lips over his firm mouth. His lips don't part under mine. If anything, he's stiff and unresponsive while I kiss him. I decide to coax him a bit more, pressing my lips to his over and over again, then nibbling on his lower lip. He doesn't open up no matter how much I coax him, so I gently brush the seam of his mouth with my tongue.

He jerks back in surprise, eyes narrow as he gazes at me.

"Still a kiss," I tell him. I wrap my arms around his neck. "It's called a French kiss. It's where tongues mate. I think you'll like it if you'll give me a chance."

Vektal's gaze remains focused on my mouth as I speak. He

leans in and presses his mouth to me, quickly, and then gives me a suspicious look, as if waiting to see if I'll correct him.

"Kiss," I agree and press my mouth softly to his again.

When I feel his tongue brush my lips, I capture the tip of it and suck lightly.

He groans . . . and so do I. The ridges creasing his brow, his chest, his cock . . . they're also on his tongue. I've forgotten about this, and I moan when I remember how it felt as he licked my pussy.

Vektal thrusts his hands into my tangled hair and holds me against him. "Kiss," he demands again. It's clear he wants more.

So I give him more. I lock my mouth to his and slide my tongue against that textured one, moaning again as he rubs against mine. He's still against me, as if judging my movements. Learning them. So I brush my tongue along one of his long fangs, pleased to feel the purr in his chest escalate. When I'm breathless from kissing, I pull away from him and give him a pleased look. "How was that?"

"Kiss," he says again, and then he takes charge. Pulling my mouth to his, Vektal begins an all-out kissing assault that leaves me utterly dazed. He nibbles and sucks at my own tongue, and then starts a slow, languid thrusting that reminds me of sex and leaves me aching with need.

By the time I pull up for air, we're in the furs together, and I'm pressed against his bare chest. My pulse is throbbing a beat between my thighs, and I'm aching with need.

"You're pretty good at that." Boy, really, really good. He's going to kill me if he gets any better at it.

"Georgie," he murmurs against my mouth. "Kiss." And his hand goes to the collar of my grimy jumpsuit. He presses his mouth along my upper lip. Then my cheek. Then my jaw. "Kiss," he says softly again.

"Yes," I say and pull at the fastenings of my jumper. I tug it open, and my breasts spill free.

He looks at my bare skin with something akin to wonder. His large, three-fingered hand lifts, and he presses his palm not to my breast, as I expect, but the smooth valley between them. He strokes my skin, then runs his knuckles up and down over my breastbone, fascinated.

Then, Vektal's attention turns to my breasts, and he brushes those knuckles over my nipple. I gasp, feeling arousal bolt through my body, and he seems equally surprised at the texture of my skin there. He lightly touches one with a fingertip and the nipple hardens and puckers at his touch.

"*Sem,*" he says in a low, reverent voice. Then he touches my skin between my breasts again. "*Sem.*"

"Soft?" I ask. I touch his chest, the ridges there, and then shake my head. "*Sem?*"

"Georgie *sem,*" he says, voice ragged. The thought looks like it tortures him.

"Yeah, I guess I'm pretty soft," I agree, smiling. "But fun to touch, right?" And I grab his hand and put it back on my breast.

He responds by kissing me again, and I lean into his caresses. There's something about him that's so very delicious. His kisses turn hungrier, and I moan as his hand cups my breast. I press against him, wanting more of his touch.

Vektal's big hand moves over my body, exploring me. He pushes at my open jacket, and I remove it because I want him to touch all of me. Pressing my skin against his is warmer than any piece of clothing. I want to be against him, naked, and the thought of his big body covering mine sends shivers of anticipation through me. I shimmy out of my jacket, the tight sleeves resisting a little thanks to my bad wrist and the wrappings around it, but I'm topless soon enough.

I push at his vest, because turnabout is fair play, and he removes it. Then we're both half-naked and gazing at each other, exploring the differences in our bodies. He has the textured, armor-like patches on his arms and chest; I'm soft all over. He's got suede-like skin that feels like heaven against mine. We both have belly buttons and nipples. I run my hands over his, and they feel hard, textured, like the armor plates. Maybe that's why he's so fascinated at the softness of mine.

I press my breasts against him and tuck my chin against one hard shoulder. This allows me to run my hands down his back, and I sigh with pleasure as I continue touching him. He's purring so hard his entire chest is practically vibrating, and it feels good against my skin. His shoulders are enormous, the strength in them turning me on. His back has more of the textured ripples down his spine, and they lead to his tail. I have to admit that the tail makes me smile. It's a long cord tufted with black hair like on his head, and it's currently lashing back and forth against the blankets.

"Georgie," Vektal murmurs into my ear, and then I feel him nuzzle at my neck.

Oooh. My nipples harden in response, and I cling to him as he licks the tender skin of my neck, then goes to my ears and teases an earlobe with his tongue. By the time he returns to my neck a few moments later, I'm moaning with pleasure and rubbing my breasts against his big chest.

His hands go to my ass, and he pulls me against him. Then he's brushing his lips over my breast, and I cry out when he takes a nipple into his mouth. I cling to his horns, holding on to him as he coaxes and teases my nipple with his lips.

Oh, sweet Jesus, the tongue ridges are a delicious torture. They drag over my sensitive nipples, until I'm practically climbing the big guy. I'm panting and feeding him my breast, and over and over he nuzzles it with his mouth until I want to scream with need.

Vektal's hands tug at my pants, and that seems like a fantastic idea to me. I shuck them with quick movements, eager to be naked against him. "You too," I tell him, pressing my mouth to his again. "Want you naked too."

I get to my feet to pry the tight pants off. I'm pretty wet, and I can feel my juices when I press my thighs together. I have no panties on under the uniform, so by the time I get it off, I'm totally naked—pasty, bruised skin and all.

My big alien pushes my hands aside when I try to go back into his arms. Instead, he insists on checking over all my bruises, I assume looking for new ones. I roll my eyes and endure his ministrations, more interested in getting into his pants than having him peek at my bruises. When he insists I turn around so he can look at my back, I give him an exasperated sigh and put my hands to his breeches, sliding them in to cup his groin.

That gets his attention, fast.

My hands curl around his length, and with touch only, I feel the differences between him and human men. For one, his girth is pretty freaking impressive. He's scalding hot to the touch, and in addition to his huge size, he's got that hard knob, like a knuckle-shaped ridge that protrudes over his cock. I have no idea what it's for and no questions to ask about it. He's also ridged here, though the skin feels less abrasive, more textured like his tongue.

God, I bet it feels amazing inside a girl. I shiver at the thought. Lucky females of his race. "I'm interested in seeing more of this," I tell him. I slide my fingers underneath his cock and feel the base of his sac. I wonder if he's sensitive there.

His hands go to my hair, and he begins to kiss me again, flicking that textured tongue against mine. I moan and grip his cock tighter. I want him naked, but he's still wearing his pants, so I try to fix that for him. Unfortunately, I can't figure out how to unlace them. He's got a breechcloth of some kind over leggings that are rigged with some sort of complex laces that are too much for this needy girl to figure out. I settle for shoving them down his hips.

Vektal chuckles and murmurs something against my mouth. He pulls at the laces, and his pants sag, then fall down. Well, damn it. Maybe I just don't know how alien clothing works. I no longer care, either, because my big, beautiful alien is naked and I get to bask in the glory that is Vektal. When he stands at his full height, he's utterly gorgeous.

He looks down at me, blue eyes glowing brightly, and his chest rumbles with the continuous purr. His hand goes between my breasts again, and I wonder if he's checking for a purr of my own. "Humans don't do that," I tell him. "We get wet instead." And I take his hand and guide it to my pussy, so he can see for himself.

My big alien falls to his knees and groans. He presses kisses to my stomach and then my pussy, and then holds my hips and puts his mouth directly on me.

I gasp and my knees get weak, so I have to cling to one of his horns again. In response, he lifts me off my feet and places me down in the furs, looping my legs over his shoulders and burying his face between my thighs. His tongue sweeps over my labia, and I moan when it circles around my clit.

Oh God. Then he's licking me with that crazy tongue of his, sweeping those ridges over my sensitive flesh and lapping up my juices. I whimper and cling to his horns, spreading my legs wider. It feels utterly incredible. I've had sex before and oral sex several times, but between the purring and the textured tongue? I've never had anything quite like this. Two licks and I'm moaning. Three more and I'm grinding my hips against his face. Two more after that and I'm practically coming off the furs, panting and crying out with need.

And my big, brutal alien just ignores my pleading for an orgasm and keeps on licking me with slow, steady, sensual motions that tell me he's enjoying this as much as I am. He murmurs soft, unintelligible words with every stroke of his tongue, and when it swirls around the entrance to my core, I practically come out of my own skin. "Please," I sob. "Oh God, please!"

But of course he doesn't understand me. So I wail and beg for an orgasm, and he just licks away as I clutch his horns and think this is the most incredible, pleasurable torture I've ever known.

"Stop," I moan. I'm so ready to come I'm aching inside. I want him deep inside me, filling me up. The licking and nibbling is just making me utterly crazy with need. "Oh God, stop, Vektal. I want you in me *now*."

In response, his tongue thrusts into my core.

Deep.

And *rubs*.

I come apart in the hardest orgasm I've ever had, my legs locking around his face. I might be screaming his name and clinging to his horns. I might be thrashing against the furs. I'm not really sure because I'm seeing stars at the moment, and between that and the orgasm, there's no room for any other conscious thought.

He growls, clearly enjoying that I'm coming, and just laps

harder, which makes my orgasm seem to go on for mile after endless mile. I'm utterly spent and exhausted when he finally lifts his head, his eyes practically glowing like headlights, and licks his sinfully wet mouth.

I feel wrung out at the sight of that. I've come so hard and so frequently that I'm pretty sure that wasn't one orgasm but a dozen stacked on top of one another, cascading with every flick of his talented, talented tongue. "God, your women must have some incredible stamina," I tell him weakly as he crawls over my body like a big blue-gray panther and begins to nuzzle at my throat. I need a rest break, but he's raring to go, pressing his mouth along my skin and licking all the parts he finds the softest.

And before long, I'm moaning and dragging my hands over that suede-soft skin, wanting him deep inside me. "Vektal," I breathe and lock a leg around his hips. He's so warm, the purring inside him fierce.

He touches my cheek and murmurs something soft and sweet and then my name. His hips settle between mine, and I realize again just how big his equipment is. Suddenly all of his enthusiastic licking takes on a new meaning because at least I'm wet as hell, which will ease the way.

"Georgie," he murmurs, and I realize he's saying something I've heard before. "Georgie *sa-akh* Vektal." He nuzzles my throat again, and I feel his cock press against my core. It feels enormous, but I'm in this until the end, and I'm ready for him to fill me up. So ready.

Beyond ready, really.

He presses his lips to mine again and then begins to push into me. My body's stretching to accommodate him, and I drag my hands over his skin, stroking and petting as he presses in, inch by thick inch.

When he's seated entirely, I learn something new. That knob? The bony ridge I had no idea what it was for? I've still got no freaking clue, but I do notice that as he sinks into me, it pushes through my labia and brushes against my clit. I'm trying to analyze this unique sensation when he moves his hips and shallowly thrusts again.

And every nerve ending lights up in response to the push of that knob against my clit.

"Oooooh," I moan. It reminds me of the time I had a Rabbit Vibrator and it worked my clit at the same time as my core. Having sex with Vektal? It's like that, but *better*. Even more intense.

This . . . might kill me out of sheer pleasure. I cling to him as he begins to thrust again, sucking in a breath when his ridge pushes against my clit again. Did I think that the pussy-eating was too much to handle because of his sheer enthusiasm? It's nothing compared to the mind-blowing sensation of him fucking the hell out of me, that ridge teasing my clit with every stroke, the ridges inside him humming against my G-spot. I come again. And again. I claw his back and scream my pleasure as he thrusts into me over and over, whispering soft words. I'm coming apart with every stroke of his cock, until I'm boneless and weak and mewing—

—and still coming.

My exhausted legs quiver as his strokes begin to take on a wilder edge. Vektal bares his fangs, his own features tightening as an orgasm rises inside him. I rake my nails down the tough, ridged spots on his chest and arms, and he growls low in his throat and shudders. I can tell he likes that, and I do it again. *Come for me, baby*, I think as he wrings another orgasm out of me and I choke on the overwhelming pleasure.

Then he pulses inside me. Like the rest of his body, his semen feels several degrees hotter than my skin, and I can *feel* it as he comes, his growl of pleasure becoming louder and louder, the purr in his throat a thunderous rumble. He thrusts hard, and his fingers dig into my hips as he comes, and I feel him coming inside me, over and over again. It's a new sensation for me.

Hell, all of this is.

But when he collapses on top of me like a big delicious blanket, and then presses his ridged forehead to my flat one and murmurs my name?

I feel content. Boneless—of course—but utterly, completely content. And I want to ask him if he wants to take me up the mountain tomorrow. But it seems like the wrong time to ask. I don't want him to think I only slept with him because I want him to do something for me.

If I'm totally honest with myself, I slept with him because I'm completely attracted to him. The horns, the blue-gray skin, the tail, the weird cock, all of it. His gruff, protective demeanor. It does it for me.

He shifts over me, clearly trying to pull his weight off of me. I cling to him, because I love the feel of his big warm body over mine, in mine. And I sigh with contentment.

Vektal, on the other hand, begins to kiss me again. I feel him move his hips in a shallow thrust.

A small moan rises from my throat again. "It's a good thing you can't make me pregnant, buddy," I say, even as I lock my feet behind his back.

Vektal

All night long, my khui thrums with contentment in my chest.

I have claimed my mate. Over and over, she's welcomed me into her small, soft body, until we're both exhausted from pleasure. Being with a resonance mate is like no other feeling; I am pleased to my very marrow with my sweet Georgie. I cannot wait to return to the tribal caverns with her. My hand caresses her soft skin even as she snores in my ear, the sunlight streaming in through the gaps in the cave-mouth covering.

I cannot wait for her to swell with my child. Our child. My khui was wise to pick her, even though she is small. She is strong in heart and spirit, and creative and enthusiastic in the furs. She doesn't resonate for me. Not yet. But when she carries a khui, she will thrum with pleasure at my touch, like I do at hers.

From now until my spirit departs this plane, there shall be none for me but her.

I touch her sleeping features reverently, memorizing them. She's a strange, tiny thing and soft all over, but her cunt grips my cock so tightly it's an ecstasy that cannot be described. Her taste is sweet, but the expressions she makes as I fill her with my cock? Even sweeter.

I look forward to tonight, when I will drag my Georgie back to bed until she's mewing with exhaustion but still eager for more as I pump into her.

I press my mouth to hers to wake her. "Georgie?"

Her eyes, still so dull and lifeless without the shine of a khui, flutter open. It will need to be remedied and soon, I decide. She looks tired, the circles under her eyes deep against her pale skin.

"Vektal," she murmurs happily and slides a hand down my chest, which starts my khui to thrumming again.

"Mountain?" I ask her, raising a brow with amusement as she tries to burrow back under the blankets and return to sleep.

That wakes her up. "Mountain?" she asks, eyes wide.

I nod. "Dress yourself. I will check the traps, and then we will go."

"*Dnno wutyew sd butlessgo.*" She looks excited, flinging her pale arms around the cave and searching for her discarded clothing.

It takes some convincing to get her to stay in the cave while I go out to check the traps, but with hand gestures and our few words, I manage to relay that I will go much faster if I am alone. She kisses me frantically before I leave, as if ensuring that I'll return for her.

As if anything would ever keep me from her side again.

Rubbing my pulsing chest, I smile to myself and trudge through the snow. Yet another night of steadily falling powder, and the trails are almost entirely covered. I have walked these grounds many times in the past, though, and know exactly where to set my traps for them to yield prey. Since it is just Georgie and me, my traps are small and their catches, even smaller.

Were I hunting for my people, I would seek dvisti, bring them down, and then bury them in the snow with a marker until a party could be sent back later to retrieve the bounty. This morning, though, I have two quilled beasts and a small hopper to feed my Georgie. There is no nearby stream, so I gather pure, sweet snow in my skin and then hold it against my chest so it can melt.

I check all my traps, and it's not until I'm returning back from the last one that I notice an oddly shaped lump in the newly fallen snow. Curiosity gets the better of me, and I approach it, then nudge it with a boot to uncover what lies underneath.

It's a foot. Small, bare, and five-toed—like my Georgie.

It's frozen solid.

As I stare down at it, I realize my Georgie's not here alone. This is why she's so frantic to get up the mountain. There are others like her.

Or . . . there were.

PART FOUR

Georgie

Vektal's out checking traps and getting me some Not-Hoth breakfast. Since I'm stuck at the cave, I decide that today I'm going to leave with the blankets instead of abandoning them here at the cave like we did last time. Vektal has already indicated that he wants me to be ultra-bundled when we leave, and since we're heading up the mountain, I want blankets for the other girls. The only way that's going to work is if I can wear them.

So I'm busy slicing makeshift ties out of the lining of my jacket and poking holes through the edge of one of the furs with my knife to make it a cloak. I'm not much for sewing, especially with these terrible supplies, but it's something to do while I wait on Vektal to return. I'm testing my second "cloak" when Vektal rushes back to the cave, his glowy eyes frantic.

I get up, alarmed. "What is it?"

He grabs me and pulls me against his chest, stroking my hair. He's breathing hard, and this might be the first time I've heard him winded. Normally nothing fazes him.

But right now? He's rattled. And that makes me scared. "Vektal?"

He cups my cheek and gazes into my face. Then, he peers into my eyes. Puts a hand to my forehead, then to my breast. Asks a question I can't make out.

I frown and shake my head. "I'm fine? What's going on?"

"Georgie," he says and then utters something else that I'm pretty sure is "Come with me."

I put on the heavy furs, and he nods, helping me bundle up. When every inch of me is covered in shaggy hides and I'm practically sweating, he tugs me onto his back and out into the snow we go.

It's a lot warmer this way, and I'm rather enjoying the snowy weather as Vektal does the hard work, tromping through the deep snow. The two sickly-pale suns are out, and the world looks rather beautiful right now. Like a snowy paradise.

I'm so busy admiring my surroundings that I don't notice Vektal has stopped until he nudges my arm and then gestures at the snow.

There's something in the drifts.

Somehow, I don't think this is a hunting kill. My stomach churns sickly, and I slide off his back. Holding my furs against my body, I move forward and brush a bit of the snow aside.

It's a face. Human. Red hair. Her eyes are open and frozen.

I gasp. Dominique. Her clothing is ragged and dirty, and it's clear from the tinge of her skin that she's been out here for a while. She's frozen through and through. A sob escapes me, and I look at Vektal.

He points at the girl, his eyes pale as if with shock. "Georgie?"

"No, I'm Georgie," I say then point at her. "That's Dominique." Then I try to teach him the word "human" by spreading my five fingers. I can't stop sniffling. What is she doing here? Did they send her after me? Another sob catches my throat. "Vektal, we have to go up the mountain. Please."

"Mountain. Human?" he asks, voice low.

"Yes," I say, feeling frantic. While I've been fucking around with an alien and eating and wearing warm furs, the others are starving and cold. I point up the mountain. "Please. Please let's go up the mountain. More humans."

He nods and lets a stream of syllables fly. I don't understand them, but when I gesture that I want on his back again, he hauls me against him and begins a quick pace up the snowy hills and past the cliff we spent the night at.

This time, we're going up the mountain. I want to sob with relief. Instead, I keep thinking of Dominique's frozen face. Poor Dominique. What happened? Why did they send her out with no clothing? It's a death sentence. Were they so desperate they had no choice?

"Hurry, please," I tell him. He doesn't understand the word, but maybe he hears the urgency in my voice. His pace picks up.

It takes at least two hours of Vektal's steady, measured pacing before I get a glimpse of the black hull of the ship. It's almost entirely covered by snow at this point, and I suck in a breath at the sight of it. That can't be warm, no matter the insulation. Up this high, there aren't many trees and there's no wildlife. The air feels thinner, and I wonder if the aliens deliberately stranded us at the most inhospitable site so we wouldn't run away.

Fuck that. We are getting out of here today, and I am taking my girls with me.

I just pray they are still alive.

Vektal points at the black oblong vessel that had broken off from the ship. "*Sa?*"

"Yes," I tell him. *"Sa!"*

It takes a bit longer for us to get up to the discarded portion of the ship. The slope is rocky and steep, and going up proves to be a bit of a challenge that I hadn't had while going down. We get to the edge, and I see a snowy drift is high enough on one side that it can act as a ramp. It must have snowed a lot here. Ugh.

I drop off Vektal's back and nudge ahead, taking the lead. The breeze is picking up, so I swaddle the furs closer about my face and climb up the ramp. The hole is covered by the tarp, so I tug it up.

A snowball immediately hits me in the face.

I sputter, wincing and staggering backward. It's nailed me right on the nose, and my face throbs, my eyes stinging.

"Back the fuck off!" a voice yells. Another snowball lobs in my direction, and I duck it.

Vektal gives a furious cry, pulling me behind him, rage lighting his eyes. As I watch, he pulls two bladed, carved short swords from his vest.

"Wait," I yell. "Guys, it's me! Georgie!"

Silence.

"Georgie?" a voice cries. It sounds like Liz. "You're alive?"

"I am," I yell back. "Fuck off with the snowballs!"

"What's with the lion, Georgie?" someone else yells up. "Call it off!"

"It's not a lion. It's a native, and it's my friend. His name is Vektal." I pat Vektal's arm, trying to soothe him since he still looks as if he wants to crawl inside and murder everyone. "It's okay, big guy. Really." I'm so relieved at finding the others alive that I could blubber big, ugly tears of joy.

I try to move forward, only to have Vektal block me again. I give him an exasperated look. "Really. It's fine. These are my people. Humans."

"Humans," he repeats and points at his fingers.

"That's right."

Grudgingly, he moves aside, and I push the tarp away and duck, just in case another snowball comes flying my way. When nothing does, I peek in.

Five ragged girls stare up at me, faces dirty. Liz, Kira, Megan, Tiffany, and Josie are all still alive, though they look like hell. Their eyes are hollow, their hair is lank, and they shiver as they stare up at me.

I think they're all beautiful. I'm so happy to see them that I burst into tears. "Hi," I sob out.

"Georgie?" Vektal asks. His hands go to my back, his touch possessive.

I turn and pat him, trying not to blubber and failing miserably. "Help me down?"

My wrist is still crap, but Vektal is strong. He helps lower me into the hold just enough that I can grab onto some of the wreckage. I climb down awkwardly, falling forward when I get close to the floor. Then the five girls are grabbing me, hauling me against them in big, smelly hugs.

"You guys smell awful," I say between sobs and hug each one. Liz is grinning wide, but Josie seems listless, her delicate figure practically skeletal. Tiffany's blubbering as much as I am, and both Megan and Kira are quiet. "Here," I say, stripping the furs off my body. "Please. Take these. You guys have to be freezing."

They grab the furs with greedy hands, and I don't even mind. I strip them off, happy to hear their moans of pleasure as they get their first warm clothing in days.

"We thought you were dead," Tiffany says. "You never came back."

"I got held up. Are you guys okay?" I ask as they snuggle in the blankets. Kira's wearing Vektal's traveling cloak, and Liz and Megan are huddling together under one fur, Josie and Tiffany under the other. They're standing and alert, so that's good.

Megan sniffs and then sneezes. The others grimace. Liz rubs her forehead, and she's clearly exhausted. "We're hanging in there," Liz says. "Food's almost gone. Water, too. But—"

Something big and heavy thumps behind me, shaking the entire cargo hold. Everyone's eyes go wide as they scatter, retreating.

I turn and see Vektal shaking a bit of snow off of his leather boots. His nostrils flare with the stench of unwashed bodies and human waste, and then his gaze fixes on me. He frowns at the realization that I've given away all my furs.

"It's okay," I tell him, moving to his side. I pat his big chest, trying to soothe him with small touches. "Vektal, these are my people."

"He understands you?" Liz asks in a small voice.

"Well, only little bits and pieces," I say, watching him. I don't think he's going to greet the others with oral sex, but you never know.

He gazes at the others and then puts a hand on the back of my neck and pulls me against him, possessive.

Yeah, I guess I'm the only one special enough for that greeting. Oddly enough, I'm pleased by the thought. I like being special to him. "Ladies," I say, gesturing at my big blue-gray friend. "This is Vektal. He's from around these parts."

They look at him warily.

"He looks like a demon," Liz says, ever blunt.

"He's nice, I promise," I say and give him another pat on the chest. "He's been keeping me alive for the last few days."

"I don't care if he looks like a demon," Josie says, her small voice trembling. "Is that a dead animal hanging from his belt? Can we eat it?"

I look down. Sure enough, Vektal's got his kills strapped to his waist. They look like gigantic naked rats or rabbits with no hair or ears. That's right. He was checking traps this morning. "I'm sure he'll share," I say and gesture at his belt. "Can I have that, Vektal?"

When I reach to his belt, he grips my hand and gives me an incredulous look, then rattles off a string of syllables.

"He just asked if you want to mate here," Kira says, voice full of disbelief.

"Oh shit," Liz says. "That's what held her up. Alien nookie."

My face feels flaming hot. I jerk my hands back.

They're all staring at me. Megan looks amused while Tiffany looks a little horrified.

"I can explain," I begin.

"I wouldn't," Liz says. "Just let us imagine for a bit. And feed us. I don't care if you fucked an entire stadium of aliens if you give me something hot to eat."

"He's not keen on the 'hot' part," I say, then turn to Vektal and point at the rabbit-things hanging from his belt. "Food? Food for humans?"

"Humans," he agrees, unhooking the meat from his belt. As I take it, he offers me his knife.

"We need fire," I tell him and mime the hand-warming gesture. "Fire."

"Oh shit," Josie says. "I'll even blow him if he can get us a fire."

"Right?" Liz says in agreement.

I feel a flare of annoyance at the girls. They're cold. There's no reason I should be jealous of them. I've been frolicking in the snow with a big sexy alien for the last two days while they've been freezing their butts off and starving. But the thought of them touching him makes me . . . unhappy.

Jealous.

Crap. I cannot be falling for a big blue alien. No matter how good he is in bed.

"Fire?" Vektal asks. He looks around the cargo bay and frowns, then points at the ceiling and spits another stream of syllables.

"He says that there's no wood this high up the mountain. He'll have to go get some from the cave and come back."

I nod at Kira, then at Vektal. "Please do that."

His ridged brows draw down, and then he points at Kira and says something else.

"He wants to know if I understand him," Kira whispers. She edges closer to the others. "What should I say?"

I reach up and brush a hand on Vektal's hard jaw, turning his frowning face toward me. It's impossible to tell what he's thinking right now. "Vektal?" When his attention turns toward me, I gesture at my ear, then move to Kira and pull her forward. "You speak, and she hears it. Understands it." I add a lot of panto-miming of words and lips moving, in the hopes that he'll grasp it.

His face lights up, blue eyes glowing. Another string of words, and he gestures at Kira's ear.

Kira's face wrinkles. "He says I have a shell that is allowing me to understand him. I wonder if the translation isn't all that clear."

"It's something like that," I say, nodding at Vektal.

He turns to Kira and says something else.

"He wants to know if my parasite teaches me his language." She shakes her head. "Just translates." She taps her ear, then her mouth. "Hear, no speak."

Vektal scrutinizes Kira for a long moment and then says something else. Then he turns, grabs me by the waist and tugs me against him, pressing a hard kiss to my mouth in front of everyone.

"He says he's going hunting and to get firewood, and for us to keep an eye on his mate," Kira relays, amusement in her voice. "Mate, huh?"

This time, it's my turn to be shocked. "Mate? *What?* He thinks we're mated?"

But Vektal's already climbing up the side of the hull and back out into the snow.

Vektal

There are five other humans in addition to the dead one in the snow. All female. My mind cannot comprehend this. All female. I think of my own tribe, with over twenty unmated males. There are only five females in our tribe. There have never been many. Maylak was my only age-mate that was not mated, and we were lovers for a time until she resonated for Kashrem. Now they have tiny kit Esha, bringing the count of females in our tribe up to six. Most of our warriors only dream of the resonance of a mate.

And I have found one. And there are five more who could resonate for one of my tribe. Five more who could bring our small, dying people back to life. We are long-lived, thanks to our khui, but it is a long and lonely life, and I have spent much of mine envious of others with their mates.

Now there is Georgie. And Georgie brings hope with her.

I don't know how she and her tribe have come here or why they are so poorly equipped to survive. We cannot communicate well enough. In time, I will have answers. For now, I must hunt and feed my small, fragile humans. I worry they are too weak to make it back to the tribal caves.

None of them have khui.

Before long, they will sicken and die. It's too early to see weakness in my Georgie, but I have been feeding her and keeping her warm. The others lack the spark in her eyes. They look tired. Frail. One has a rattle in her lungs that speaks of sickness.

I think of the dead one in the snow, frozen. That will not become my Georgie.

I travel as quickly as possible through the ever-deepening snow. I clean out first the cave we slept in earlier this morning. Then I will travel further down the mountain and remove the contents of yet another. With luck, I might find something to hunt. I only have one waterskin and many human mouths, though. The humans need everything. They are not equipped to survive, not in the slightest. Thinking about this makes me run through the snow even faster. Raahosh is out on his hunting treks, and his territory is near mine. I could head south, enlist his help, and together we could feed the sickly humans.

But it might take days to find him, and I will not leave my Georgie for that long. Not when she cannot fend for herself. Not when she could already be carrying our kit. Not when there are metlaks in the area and Georgie's tribe has no weapon but snow.

I have no idea why or how they are here, but my protective instincts surge at the thought of my Georgie facing off with more of the rabid, unpredictable metlaks. I must teach her how to defend herself. One small step before the next, I remind myself. First, food and shelter for the humans.

By the time I finish gathering the supplies, both suns are disappearing into the horizon; the larger of the two moons is out, covering the sky. Snow has begun to fall again, and I return to the strange black cave that Georgie's women are huddled in. The cave's contents are strapped to my back, their weight heavy. In addition to the firewood and furs, I've also hunted a small dvisti that will feed all the hungry mouths for at least a few days if they freeze the meat properly. I'm exhausted from spending the day running, and I'm tired as I drop into the cave from above.

Frightened screams ring out as I do.

"*Calmdn,*" I hear Georgie tell the others. "*S'Vektal.*"

I drop my burdens to the hard, cold floor and stretch. My back pops, muscles aching.

"*Fck owtall izzee?*"

"*Ithnk sevnfeet,*" Georgie says, and I hear a hint of pride in her voice. She approaches me, and I see concern on her face as she looks at me. "*Yewrgon lngtime.*"

"I am well, sweet resonance," I tell her. I caress her cheek. "Did you eat something? You are as small and weak as your fellow humans." I look at the other five-fingers. They have taken all her furs and huddle against the walls together. They smell terrible, but they are also trapped inside this cave, so I don't blame them.

"*Eez askinifyewate,*" the one with the shell in her ear says. "*Sezurweak.*"

Georgie makes a funny face, wrinkling her tiny, smooth nose. "*S'frozn.*" She looks at me hopefully and asks in my language, "Fire?"

I nod and pull her close to my body. I'll make fire for her in a moment. For now, I feel the aching need to be next to her. My khui rumbles and begins to resonate in my chest at her presence. The anxiety I felt at leaving her disappears at the sweet press of her cheek to my chest.

One of the others makes smacking noises with her mouth at

the sight, and Georgie's pale cheeks turn pink. *"Fckyew,"* she says but laughs. *"Eyelikhm."*

I breathe in my mate's scent for a moment longer, then release my Georgie and move to the supplies I've brought. I create a small pyramid of wood and dung chips, and add a bit of the fluff that keeps my boots warm to use as tinder. The women all watch quietly as I begin to make a fire. When a spark lights on the tinder, though, and I blow on it to increase the flame, I sit up and see I have six weird, smooth faces peering at me with happiness.

"Fck eyelikhmtew," says one.

They huddle near it for warmth as I put one of my kills on a spit to roast. I don't understand their need to burn the flavor out of their meat, but Georgie has taught me she won't eat it any other way, so burn it I must. At my other side, one with a long mane of pale yellow hair begins to cough again, deep, racking coughs that shake her small body.

Georgie grimaces and looks at me. *"Medsin?"*

I don't know what she's asking, but I shake my head. "Nothing I have can help her. It is the khui-sickness."

Georgie

"What's that word mean?" I ask Kira. "Cwee?"

"I don't know," she says with a shrug of her fur-covered shoulders. The others are bundled up to their necks in the furs, only their heads peeping out from the woolly coverings. I'm a little chilly now that I'm not the one bundled, but I don't complain. How can I? This is the first time they've been warm in days. I'm thrilled I can at least do this much for them.

Or rather, that Vektal can. I mostly just stand around and look proud that I brought him.

The girls have been giving me shit for hours. I don't mind, because I do deserve it. After being taken captive by aliens, I show up with a new one who's calling me his mate? Who kisses me and drags me against his chest every chance he gets?

Who fucked the hell out of me for hours last night until I nearly passed out from orgasms?

Yeah, I totally deserve all the shit I get.

I'm just so freaking happy at the moment. Vektal's getting us fire and food, and all the girls are alive. I've fussed over them for the last few hours, making sure they're warm and retrieving snow to melt in one of the makeshift basins so they can wash a little. They're weak with starvation, and Tiffany's toes and fingers look like they've got frostbite. Josie's listless and weak, and Megan has a deep, racking cough that shakes her entire body. But they're alive. We can fix everything else. Food will go a long way toward making them feel better. In addition to the hairless rat things (which have a thick layer of blubber that Vektal insists we eat, and no one is brave enough to try yet) we have something that looks like a cross between a boar and a pony that he calls a dvisti. The meat's roasting on the fire, and even my mouth is watering, so I can't imagine how hungry they are.

"What's khui-sickness?" Megan asks, a worried look on her face as she crouches nearer to the fire.

"I don't know," I say with a small shake of my head. When I ask Vektal, all he does is press a hand to his chest and then to mine.

"The khui lives here," Kira translates with a shrug. "No clue."

"You just need some food and a warm place to stay," I tell Megan, trying to soothe the worry from her face. "We'll deal with one thing at a time."

She nods. I'm afraid she's going to question more, but Vektal pulls one of the legs off of the hairless rat, and it looks just like a drumstick. He automatically hands it to me.

"Oh gosh," I say, embarrassed. "Don't feed me, Vektal. I'll eat last." I immediately hand it to Megan.

She scarfs it down before someone can take it from her, and Liz gives me a gleeful look and makes more kissy faces. "He's feeding his mate, Georgie. Give the guy a break."

My cheeks heat again. I feel like I've spent all afternoon blushing.

He pulls another leg off and raises a brow at me. I shake my head, and he offers it to Kira instead, who takes it gratefully. One by one, the women are fed. I only take small bites of the dvisti as it cooks, leaving the majority for the others.

This displeases Vektal, who insists on feeding me more. I give the others an unhappy look every time he shoves another cooked piece into my hands.

"Don't piss him off," Tiffany says, licking her dirty fingers to get the last of the grease. "If it makes him happy to feed you, eat."

So I eat. Once everyone is full, Vektal crouches next to me and pulls me against his chest again, and he starts purring. He strokes my hair and touches my face as the others talk quietly. We discuss our kidnappers, who haven't returned, the planet, which seems to be getting snowier every day, and our situation.

Which is grim.

That casts a pall over the conversation, and everyone gets quiet. Liz switches places with Megan, who's helping herself to more food. She sits next to me, cross-legged, her furs draped over her thin form, and she studies me as Vektal runs his fingers through my tangled hair.

"So you and the big guy, huh? Can't leave you alone for two seconds without you getting hitched to the nearest alien."

I shrug uncomfortably. "Seemed like it would help the survival odds." Even as I say it, it feels wrong to make my relationship with Vektal sound like it's just survival. There's attraction, too, but I feel like I'm betraying my fellow captives if I admit to it.

Liz nods and stares at Vektal's horns for a bit. Then she looks at me again. "He's kinda possessive of you."

"Yeah." He is, and I don't hate it. Kinda like it, actually.

"How's he going to act when he finds out we don't want to stay on Not-Hoth?"

I don't respond. It's not something I've thought about yet. I'm still adjusting to the fact that Vektal thinks I'm his mate. I don't want to think about how he's going to act if I get on the first bus ride home. Or the depressing idea that there might not be a ride home.

Liz is still looking at me, waiting for a response.

I shrug and say, "Being with him makes me happier than the other guys. I'll take my chances with him."

"Fair enough." She gazes at the fire. "You haven't asked about Dominique."

I swallow the hard knot in my throat. I've been deliberately avoiding the topic, not sure how the others would respond if pressed. Like Vektal said earlier, they seem fragile. "I . . . saw her dead body. Out in the snow."

Liz nods. She moves in a bit closer. "So the first night we were here, we heard some creatures. They hooted like owls and stuff, but they looked like skinny teddy bears or something."

"I've seen those," I tell her. "They're pretty nasty. Vektal's not a fan."

"Yeah, I'm not either," she says with a grimace. "They weren't smart enough to figure out how to get in, but they still scared the shit out of us. Kept us up all night. Dom cried the entire time."

"I'm sorry."

She bats my arm. "I'm not telling you to make you sorry. Just telling you what happened. Anyhow, we decided we needed a defense of some kind, so me and Tiff and Dominique went up top and made snowballs the next day. Tiff and I turned our backs for one minute, and Dom just ran off into the snow like a crazy girl. We tried to follow her, but we're all kinda broken, and it's too cold to be out there long." She shrugs. "Tiffany went looking for her and had to come back. I think her feet have frostbite."

I nod.

"So we never saw her again. We kinda hoped she found you. Guess not, huh?"

I shake my head. "She was dead when I found her. Long dead."

"I can't even be sad," Liz says with a sigh. She hugs her good leg closer to her body. "She didn't want to be alive. Not after what they did to her." She looks at me, eyes big in her too-thin face. "We have to get out of here, Georgie. We can't be here when they come back to pick us up."

"I know," I tell her quietly. I haven't figured it out yet, but I'm going to get us out of here. I just need a plan.

Vektal

The others watch Georgie and me closely all night. Every time I touch her hair or caress her cheek, their eyes regard us uneasily. Is it because I'm showing her affection in front of them? My people are not shy about such things. Georgie doesn't seem to mind my touches, and her nearness keeps my khui humming pleasantly.

When the human women begin to yawn, they file off to bed with Georgie's blankets, a fact that makes me angry. They are cold, but she is my mate, as small and fragile as the rest of them. When I suggest she take one for herself, she shakes her head.

I make sure my complaints are heard by the solemn-faced one with the shell in her ear who can understand my words. A moment later, she hands her furs to Georgie, and when my sweet mate protests, the girl insists and goes to curl up with another girl. They will be warm enough. The strange cave is closed off from the bitter winds, and despite the smell, it's warm enough inside that they will not freeze. Between the fire and body heat, the temperature inside is pleasant.

There is no watch, though. Either the women are too trusting they will be safe or so sick and exhausted that they cannot stay awake. I suspect it is the latter. I will be their watch, then.

But first, I will spend time with my mate. My khui demands it.

Georgie yawns and wraps the blanket around her, moving to curl up next to the other women. I bank the fire with a large log so it will provide warmth for many hours, and then I move to her side and pick her up, carrying her to the far end of the cave with me, where we will have some privacy.

One of the girls laughs and calls something out. *"Gitsum grlfrend,"* says one.

Another calls, *"Kppdown ovrthr. Weer tryntew sleep!"*

Georgie just buries her face against my chest.

I take her as far from the others as we can get. Here, they will not be able to see much beyond the firelight. I put Georgie on the side closest to the wall, and my body blocks her in. I cover us both with the fur and pull my mate against me.

My khui sings and hums. It wants more of our bodies joining, and I am eager to do so.

She tucks her smaller body against me, her cold hands moving under my clothing to press against my bare skin. *"Sohwarm,"* she murmurs. *"Sohnice."*

My khui rumbles in my chest as she rubs against me. Her eyes are closed, and I'm not sure if she realizes just how much she's tempting me. My cock rises in response to her sleepy touches, but she's not giving me more. I need to make her aware of what I require, then.

So I caress her neck and tilt her head back, and then I press my mouth to hers and claim her tongue with mine.

Georgie gives a soft, moaned sigh and licks me back. I enjoy the human custom of mouth-joining and caressing my mate with my tongue. It's not something I've considered before, but now that

I've done it with Georgie, it seems so obvious. I love tasting all of her. Why not her mouth? My hand pushes between her legs, but she is wearing her strange leathers. I find the waistband of her leggings and push my hand into them, seeking her sweet warmth.

She moans against me, and her hand presses to my arm. "Vektal."

I love it when she says my name. I growl my pleasure, and my khui hums a response. I push my fingers into her soft folds, seeking that strange third nipple. I find it, and she immediately gasps and presses her face against my arm.

"*Eyethnkthyr dewinnit,*" whispers a voice on the other side of the room.

"*Dunlook,*" says another. "*Gohbcktewsleep.*"

"*Eyebeteez gotta monstrdick!*"

This time, Georgie buries her face against my chest, and I feel her push my hand away. "No," she murmurs against my chest.

No? When my khui is throbbing almost painfully in my breast with its need to have us mate? I'm shocked. Is it because the others are awake and possibly listening? Why does that matter? I have seen and heard other sa-khui mate many times. We are not shy people. It seems the humans are not the same, though. Georgie doesn't want me to touch her while the others are paying attention.

I growl again, but I remove my hand.

She makes a downcast little sound and presses her body closer to mine.

And that little disappointed sigh is the only reason I don't get up and toss the other humans out of the cave.

The next morning, I stoke the fire for the humans and we begin to make plans. The humans don't want to stay here. It's clear they're nervous and want to leave. I can't have them stay here, either, but I'm not equipped to take them to safety. The walk to my home caves is at least a day of hard travel, and these fragile humans won't be able to handle that.

After they eat, they look at me with hopeful eyes, as if I will somehow produce clothing and boots for all of the women. I know what they are asking with their sad faces. It grieves me to disappoint my Georgie, but a hunter alone must be practical. "I cannot take you with me," I tell the one with the magic shell in her ear.

"*Sezzee kantakus.*"

One begins to sniffle loudly. The loud one—Leezh—glares at me as if I am the problem.

I point at my shoes. "You have no foot coverings. No clothing. With six of you, I cannot possibly hunt enough game and keep you moving. My home caverns are many hours' walk away. With Georgie, it will take me two days to go there. I will get my people, and we will come and bring you warm clothes and travel rations. Then we will take you home with us. You will be safe there."

Her brows draw down, and then she translates.

"*Eez got ppl?*" Georgie asks, then smacks her forehead. "*Uf kors eeduz.*" She looks at me. "*Yew haf ppl?*" She points at the others, then at herself. "*Human ppl. Vektal ppl?*"

Ah. "Do I have a tribe? Yes. There are four eights of us, plus two kits. I am the chief."

The one translates, and Georgie nods again. "*Shlda known. Eez bosseh.*"

Leezh snickers.

"*Weeve gotwelv,*" Georgie says and counts on her fingers before pointing at the wall behind her. "*Siks indeyr.*" She does counting words at each woman, then points at the wall and does more counting words.

I shake my head. "I do not understand."

Georgie throws her hands up. "*Nvvrmnd. Fun surprz for-laytr.*"

"Ha," says Leezh.

They all start to chatter, and one gestures at the wall. I frown at them. I don't understand their fascination with the back wall with its flashing lights, and our one-sided conversation is not getting us anywhere. "I will return to my people with Georgie, and we will get her a khui. Then I will bring back my hunters, and we will return for all of you. This I promise."

"*Dohn fergetdeez,*" Leezh says and taps a bump on her arm.

"*Eyewohnt,*" Georgie tells her. A determined look comes across my mate's face, and I wonder what they refer to that brings such a grim look to her delicate features.

At Georgie's insistence, we leave all the winter furs and two of my blades with the women. We also leave all the food. This makes me unhappy because my mate will be the one that suffers, but she promises with soft pats and smiling eyes that she is fine. I think it pleases her to be able to provide for her humans, so I don't complain. There are other hunter caves along the paths, and I will raid all of them to clothe my Georgie if I must. They can be replenished in the spring, when the thickest snows melt and the hunters have easier days.

We wave goodbye to the women, and Georgie wipes her eyes frequently. I know she worries about them. Despite the food, they all seem a little more tired this morning, a little more pale.

It is the lack of the khui, which is why it's so important that

I bring Georgie back to my own people, and soon. I cannot bring down a sa-kohtsk by myself. It is a task that requires many hunters with strong spears.

I carry Georgie's smaller form on my back, and I take a different route down the mountain. This time, I do not go to the winding game trails but head straight across the land, as the winged birds fly. This way, instead of many hunter caves along the path home, there is only one: the elders' cave, with its strange smooth walls not unlike Georgie's cave.

My mate seems to understand my sense of urgency. We stop only for brief rests to refill a waterskin or so we can relieve ourselves. When the two suns are high in the sky, I find a quilled beast, and Georgie does not protest when I offer her raw tidbits. It will take too much time to collect wood for a fire. We eat, and then we are on our way once more.

The day is an endless cycle of running and hiking, and even Georgie's slight weight grows heavier over the hours. I do not put her down, though. My strength is far more suited for travel than hers. She's exhausted, too. Her grip on my clothing becomes less strong over the hours, and I worry we're not making good time when a familiar snow-covered hill appears in the distance. I give a sigh of relief and point it out to Georgie.

"*Looksweerd,*" she says with a yawn. "*Wegoinder?*"

"That is our one stop today," I tell her. "We will rest and sleep, and tomorrow we will return to my people." Mentally, I make note of the hunters who can help me shepherd the sick humans back. Maylak will want to come, as tribal healer, but she has a small child. Her mate, Kashrem, then. Raahosh, if he has returned from his own hunts. Rokan. Salukh. Zennek. Haeden. Dagesh.

All of them are unmated hunters, except for Kashrem. It might be smarter to take the mated ones, so there are no fights over the small females, but I do not want to build resentment amongst my tribe. I know the men will be eager to see the female humans, especially after I return with my lovely Georgie.

I rub her arm thoughtfully. I would not deny my men the chance to see if their khui resonate with the humans. Not when I felt the pleasure of my own spring to life.

We make it inside the cave, and Georgie exclaims at the oddness of the walls. I don't blame her for being surprised. They're covered with a thin sheet of ice, but there's no denying there's a uniformity to the walls that is unnerving. It looks as if a gigantic hand has scooped the side of the hill out and smoothed the sides down. But there are furs and wood and a stretched hide to block the door. I set Georgie down and prepare the cave.

To my surprise, she immediately begins to make a firewood pyramid with supplies while I hang the door covering. She gives me a shy smile. *"Wantto lern."*

My heart swells with pride. I move to her side and ignore the fire, cupping her small face instead. She's lovely, flat nose and all, and I am obsessed with touching her.

She smiles up at me, and my khui begins a steady thrumming in my chest. The fire can wait. My khui and my body have been aching with need for her since this morning. Any longer and I feel as if I will be in physical pain. I tug at the collar of her leathers.

Georgie chuckles, the sound sweet. She presses a small, cold hand against my chest, right where my khui vibrates under my skin. *"Luvit wenyew purh,"* she says softly. Then she looks up at me with those strange white eyes and tilts her head back for my kiss.

I grab her and pull her against me, mindful of her wounded wrist. I want to touch her everywhere. Taste her everywhere. The khui inside me demands a mating, and it's a call I want to answer. I kiss her just like she's asking, my lips moving over hers before I slide my tongue into her mouth for a taste. It feels like nothing I have ever experienced, this kiss, and I want it over and over again with Georgie. I love her smooth tongue brushing against mine.

She is just as hungry for my touch. Her fingers tear at her clothing until she exposes her breasts to me. I groan at the sight and drop to my knees to tug one soft nipple into my mouth. I love her breasts, how similar and yet different they are to those of the women of my people. Her pink nipple hardens when I touch it, but it's still like brushing my fingers over soft leather instead of the armored, hard tips of my own women. I wonder how human children are, if their mothers have such soft, tender swells. I picture my child there and crush her against me.

Our child. Part sa-khui, part human.

"Mmm," she says softly, and I don't know if she's humming or saying another one of her strange human words. I lick her breast to distract her, and she moans. Then she reaches down and grips my cock in her hand and strokes me through the leather of my leggings.

I nearly come undone at that touch. With a hiss, I pull apart the knots that keep my clothing at my waist and free my cock. This mating will be quick and not elegant. I don't care. From the sounds Georgie is making and the way she squeezes my cock in her hand, I doubt she cares, either.

"You are my heart," I tell her as I caress her breasts. I tease one, then the other, loving the soft noises she makes. Her skin puckers at my touch, and the scent of her arousal perfumes the air. My mouth waters at the thought of tasting her, and I kiss her flat belly that will be rounded with our child next season.

But children will come later, and I want Georgie now. I tug at her leather leggings until the dark curls between her legs are revealed. She pulls her pants down the rest of the way and kicks them aside, and then she drags her fingers against my pants, doing the same for me. In this way, we undress.

Georgie gives a small shiver and moves to stand closer to me, to share in my warmth. I pull my mate against me, pick her up, and then seek out the furs in the cave. As I do, she presses kisses to my face and runs her fingers along my horns, murmuring soft words.

Then I lay her down in the furs, and she looks utterly beautiful and tempting, my strange human. I cover her small body with my larger one, and her legs go to my waist, her feet brushing against my flicking tail.

Her hands caress my horns as if they are my cock, stroking the length of each one, and I groan at the sensation. I seek the folds between her legs, and she's wet and slick, her body hungry for me as I am for her. I want the taste of her on my mouth, and I push my head between her thighs.

She makes a soft sound and spreads her legs wide for me, welcoming me. I drag my tongue over her sweetness, enjoying her cries. Her flavor is heady, her aroma intoxicating, and I lose myself to her body. I lick and suck each fold, my tongue coaxing more of her nectar from her body. Telltale shivers move through her, and her thighs grip my head and horns tighter with each stroke of my tongue. She is close, my Georgie. And I want to be inside her when she comes.

I shift my body, fitting the head of my cock to her. She feels incredible against me. Wet and willing and oh-so-soft. I push into her, and she gasps, clinging to me. Her body is tight around mine, clasping me like a glove. The sensation is incredible, and I close my eyes, savoring it. My khui responds, thrumming inside me. Soon, I will feel her khui answer mine.

It must be soon, or else Georgie will not survive.

The thought sends a stab of fear through me, and I press my form to hers, holding her close. No. She is mine. I must keep her. With a groan, I stroke into her and feel her body give to mine.

Georgie gasps. "Vektal. *Ohhyes!*"

I pull back and slide into her again, and her legs twitch then grip me tighter. I stroke into her over and over again, need making my motions quicken. Her cries increase as my movements speed up, and when her hot warmth clamps around my cock, I feel her orgasm race through her even before she cries out.

My own khui responds, and I thrust into her again, spilling my seed inside her. I hold her close and stroke her hair as I come, my own body locked in the process of pleasure. Her hands touch me, fluttering over my skin, and she pants small, sweet, unintelligible words.

When the last of my seed is wrung from my body, I press my mouth to hers and then roll to my side, pulling her against me, our bodies still joined. I want to stay like this for hours. All night, even. My exhaustion is gone with my mate in my arms. Already I'm thinking of how to make her cry out with pleasure again.

I stroke a hand over her skin and feel her sex quiver around my cock again. Just a few touches and she would be crying out once more. I'm intrigued by the thought and tug her closer to me, until her small back is pressed against my chest.

As I do, she props up on one elbow. "*Wutwuzzat?*"

I touch her arm. "Hm?" I wish again that I could speak the language of humans.

Georgie pats my hand to get my attention and then points. *"Sawa lyteblink. Wutwuzzat?"*

She indicates the far wall, and sure enough, a star blinks under the ice and then fades. Ah. "This is the cave of elders. The cave of stars. It is full of magic. That is what you are seeing."

But she pulls free of my grip and crawls out of the blankets. I feel a sense of loss as my cock slides from her warm body, but she is preoccupied. So I sit up and watch as she climbs to her feet and runs to the far wall. She presses her face against the thick ice, watching the light as it slowly blinks again. Then she looks back at me again.

"Vektal," she breathes, and there's excitement in her voice. New excitement. *"Izzit a spays ship?"*

PART FIVE

Georgie

Holy crap, it's a spaceship.

I don't know how I didn't see it before.

Well, actually, I do. I was so tired after our journey that my brain was a fog. The need to help save the others constantly burned in the back of my mind. Vektal seemed to have a sense of urgency, too; he crossed over valleys and climbed up sheer walls with me clinging to him, more agile than a mountain goat. I held on for dear life, but it was still exhausting. The cold hadn't let up, and the wind felt as if it had chapped my face into one big cold burn. But I still had it better than the other humans, so I didn't complain.

By the time we finally stopped for the night, I'd barely glanced at my surroundings. Yes, the cave was perfectly made inside. Yes, it was in the side of a hill that also seemed perfectly oval-shaped outside. I'd noted it and stumbled inside, heading for the warm furs that I now knew waited within.

It wasn't until after sex, as I relaxed and cuddled against my alien, that I saw a light flash. I'd thought my eyes had deceived me until it did it again. Then I stared at the ice really hard.

And realized that the cave was perfect because it was the interior of a ship.

"It's a ship," I tell Vektal. Behind the thick layer of ice, I can barely make out a control panel of some kind.

His eyes narrow, and he shakes his head. He doesn't understand. *"Es sa-khui tokh."*

That doesn't sound like "spaceship" to me. Right. My big blue barbarian probably wouldn't know a spaceship if it bit him on his big ridge-covered nose. He wears leather, eats raw meat, and hunts with slings and bone knives. Big guy's probably never heard of a space heater, much less a spaceship.

I pat his chest. "You know what? I got this. Don't worry." I take the blade of the knife I carry with me and use it to hack at the thick ice coating the walls.

Vektal stops me with a gentle hand. He points at the firewood pile in the fire pit, still unlit. Oh. Fire will melt things faster. He's right. I reach up and give him a quick, smacking kiss. "Clever man."

He doesn't know what I'm saying, but he's pleased by the kiss anyhow.

As I wait for the fire to start, I stare at the walls around us. I'm trying not to freak out. The ice covering the walls is thick. Vektal's familiar with this place, and it's set up like a camp as the other caves are, which tells me that this has been here a long time. It looks nothing like the cargo hold the other girls are currently camping out in. The odds of it belonging to the same aliens are slim, I tell myself.

I still worry, though. That's why I have to see that control panel for myself. I have to know what it is we've found.

It's either a frying pan about to go into the fire . . . or a ticket home.

Or neither.

I need answers. No matter how tired I am, I won't be able to sleep without answering some of these questions.

When the fire is stoked and burning brightly, Vektal takes up a lit stick of wood and hands me the safe end. It's like a crappy makeshift torch, and I carry it carefully to the wall and then hold it near the panels, watching the ice glimmer and then melt. It takes a long time to thaw away the layers of ice, but as I do, more and more instrument panels become uncovered. I look over at Vektal, and he seems unnerved by this discovery as well.

It looks different than the sleek, bare walls of the alien ship I crashed in. Granted, I didn't see much outside of what I assumed was the cargo hold, but this has an entirely different feel to it. The panel I've uncovered is upraised with hundreds of buttons, and the blips of light flick regularly. It reminds me of when I've set electronic devices on standby in the past, and I wonder if that means everything is functional.

I wonder if this means we can go home.

I steal a look at Vektal. His brutishly handsome features are pulled down into a frown, as if he's not entirely sure what to make of this. He's been wonderful to me. And the sex? Okay, the sex is mind-blowing. But this place sucks. It's cold and horrible, and I don't know if I want to stay here when there's a ride home.

If there's a ride home, I remind myself. *If.*

I return my sputtering torch to the fire and examine the panels again. I see a lot of buttons and one blinking light but no screens. Am I wrong in hoping this works? I lean forward and examine the now-uncovered panel. The blinking light is actually a button with a strange squiggly character on it. I move forward to press it, then pause.

Is it dumb to press a strange button on an even stranger spaceship?

Yes, yes it is.

Do I have many options? I contemplate all the different things this button could be. It could be a distress signal. It could arm a security system. It could be nothing at all. Do I want to chance it?

I look at Vektal again.

Actually . . . I don't want to chance it, I realize. I'd be just as happy turning around and going out of here with him. I know I'm safe with him. I might even be able to be happy with him. But the other women don't have the same option as I do. They don't have a big, wonderful alien treating them like gold and catering to their every need.

So I suck in a deep breath and punch the flashing button.

It clicks.

Nothing happens.

Well that's . . . disappointing.

Then a slow whine starts, like the hum of something coming online. A smooth, androgynous voice says something in a fluid language that's unlike mine. Lights appear and begin to flash. There's a noise and then a hiss like central air was just turned on.

Vektal grabs me and hauls my body behind him, pulling out one of his blades to protect me.

I'm chicken enough to hide behind his back for a long moment. Then I pat his arm again and push forward. "It's okay," I say. "I think stuff is just . . . uh, booting up." I approach the panel.

As I do, the voice speaks again. This time it raises its voice at the end, almost like a question.

It's . . . asking us something? "I don't understand you," I say aloud.

There's another whirling, chirring sound. A picture of Earth appears in midair, three-dimensional. "Query," the voice says. "Language: Earth English. Is this correct?"

I gasp. "Yes! Yes, that's correct! You know English?"

"This ship's artificial intelligence is programmed with over twenty thousand common languages. Do you wish to change language selections? If so, say—"

"No," I say quickly. "Stay on English!" I point at the picture of Earth, spinning in midair. "That's my planet!"

"Settings accepted. Please wait for system to come fully online before requesting a query."

"I . . . all right." I look at Vektal with wide eyes. He seems equally as astonished as me. He puts an arm around my shoulder and pulls me in close, prepared for a just-in-case sort of scenario. It's strangely comforting.

The computer hums for a moment longer, and then I feel a gust of warm air brush my face. "Environmental controls online. Ideal habitat temperature for humans is 22 degrees Celsius or 72 degrees Fahrenheit. Ideal habitat temperature for modified *sakh* is 3 degrees Celsius or 37 degrees Fahrenheit. Which shall I program?"

"Modified sakh?" I ask.

"The male at your side is a sakh life-form, modified for habitation on this planet."

Oh. "Is he not from this planet?" Is Vektal a stranger here, too?

"Sakh originate from a planet that they call *Kes*, or 'home' in their language. It is approximately 3.2 million parsecs from your planet Earth. This planet is 5.8 million parsecs from your planet Earth."

That sounds . . . far. I feel faint. I have so many questions. I don't know what to ask first. "I . . . what is this place?"

"This planet has many names depending on the language. Your species has not discovered this solar system yet. Our current location is the second planet in this binary sun system. This particular world completes an orbit around the suns every 372.5 days and rotates on its axis every 27.2 hours. The current temperature is—"

"Cold. Yeah. I know." I wave a hand because none of this information is helping me out any. "So if he's not from here," I say, pointing at Vektal, "how did he get here?"

"This vessel was originally a sakh pleasure cruiser," the ship continues in a melodious voice. "Due to a solar storm, the crew was forced to shelter at the nearest habitable planet, which you are currently on. They experienced technical difficulties."

"Technical difficulties?" It sounds so absurd. "Really?"

"This ship is keyed to a specific pilot. The pilot experienced congestive heart failure, and a secondary was unavailable to pilot the ship. A distress signal was launched but malfunctioned. No further signals were sent."

So Vektal's people are stranded here, too? "When was this?" I ask, feeling a little faint at this new tidbit of information.

"This event occurred 287 years ago. Please note that when this system references 'years,' they are calculated based upon the orbit of this planet versus the planet Earth."

And the years were longer here. Jesus. I look at Vektal with wide eyes. He's looking at me curiously, impatience stamped on his features. I know he has questions, and my conversation with the computer is probably just giving him more of them.

But I still have more questions, so I'm selfish for a little longer. "How many of his people crashed here?"

"Logbooks record sixty-two passengers and one pilot. Many also died before accepting the symbiont."

That catches my attention. "Symbiont?"

"The definition for 'symbiont' is an organism that lives in symbiosis with another organism."

I'm starting to get creeped out. "Wait . . . Vektal has an . . . organism in him?"

"This planet has an element in its atmosphere that is toxic to humankind and also to sakh. It is a gas element similar to nitrogen that has not yet been discovered by humans as it does not exist in any form on Earth. Your body is not equipped to filter it out of the air. Once you reach toxic levels of the element, your body will slowly shut down. The sakh at your side exists in mutualistic symbiosis with a creature they refer to as a khui."

"Khui," Vektal says, suddenly speaking up. He asks the computer a question, and it immediately answers him. Then he nods and looks at me.

"I told him I am explaining to you how the khui functions in the atmosphere," the computer tells me.

I rub my forehead. "I'm not understanding. So you have to have this khui thing inside you or . . . you die?"

"The khui enhances the body of its host and makes subtle changes in order to allow it to thrive in an otherwise hostile environment. Those who originally found themselves stranded on this planet lasted eight days without the symbiotic relationship."

Eight days? All I have is eight freaking *days*? "M-modifies it?" I ask weakly. I feel sick. I either get a . . . parasite or I die?

"The khui modifies its host. Genetically modified khui-symbionts are altered to perform at lower temperatures and to filter the chemicals from the air that the body cannot process. It improves the host's recovery from wounds and sickness, and it ensures procreation of viable offspring."

Oh God. So I get a cold-resistant tapeworm, or I get to die. "What if I get this khui thing for now, and when I leave, have it removed? Can I do that?"

"Once implanted, the khui and host are dependent upon each other. The khui cannot exist outside of its host for longer than a few minutes, and the host will need a replacement khui in order to survive."

And here I thought staying on Not-Hoth with my sexy barbarian was the better option than waiting for the little green men to come back. If I choose to stay here, I can't ever leave again. It'll just be me and my parasite . . . forever.

Ugh.

But if I don't get the parasite, I only have days left to live. Not even a week, now. The green men must know that we humans can't survive on this planet for long. That means that either they aren't intending to pick us up again . . . or they're going to be returning very, very shortly. I suck in a breath at that.

The odds are not looking good. I have to get the others out of there, and fast.

I want to ask the computer more questions, but the welfare of the others takes priority. One step at a time—we have to rescue the other women, and then we'll figure out the khui thing. I turn to Vektal. "We need to talk."

He touches my face, glowing blue eyes tender. *"Sa-akh mevolo."*

"Shit. You're not understanding me." I turn to the computer. "Can you translate for me?"

"That is one of the functions of this unit," it says in an amicable tone. "Would you like to learn the sakh dialect he is speaking?"

"You . . . you can teach me?"

"I can perform a one-time linguistic upload. Would you like to do this?"

"God, yes." I want to be able to hold a real, honest-to-goodness conversation with Vektal. "Please."

A small red circle appears in midair. "Please step closer to the marked location." When I do, it gives me additional instructions. "I will perform a retinal scan. When I do, please do not blink or attempt to move. This can interfere with the transfer of information. It will be connected in three . . . two . . . one . . ."

A low hum starts. I freeze in place, trying not to blink as a red laser shines into my eyes.

"You may experience some discomfort as your brain processes the information," the computer tells me, just before a rush of symbols crashes through my brain and my head feels like it explodes.

Vektal

My mate collapses, and my khui slams against my chest in protest. I grab her before she can sink to the ground. "Georgie!"

"Please allow several minutes for recovery," the strange voice coming from the walls intones.

I snarl at it, at the air. I don't know where this faceless voice is coming from, but if it's hurt my Georgie, I will tear this place down to its strange-looking rocks and scatter the pieces to the icy seas. I cradle my mate against my chest, unable to breathe out of fear. I place a hand over her heart, where she has no protective plating. She's too soft and vulnerable, my poor human.

But it thumps steadily in her breast, and I exhale in relief. I press my lips to her strange, smooth forehead and hold her against me as the room becomes uncomfortably warm.

The disembodied voice speaks again. "Standby. Please indicate if you have questions for this unit. Otherwise, I will return to hibernation mode."

I hold Georgie against me, stroking her hair, her face, her

cool skin that cannot retain enough warmth for her to be comfortable. I ignore the strange voice, even though it's now speaking my language. When Georgie jabbered at it in her tongue, it sent a red beam through her head and knocked her unconscious. I do not want it to do the same to me, so I narrow my eyes at the flashing lights and wait.

Georgie's sleeping face turns to my chest and she nuzzles me. "Mmm."

"Georgie?" I ask, touching her cheek. "Are you well?"

Her eyes blink open, and the pale, ugly white with a weak blue circle in the middle is the most beautiful thing I've ever seen. "Oh. I hear you," she says in my language. "Your words. They're . . ." She thinks for a minute, and then a smile breaks across her face. "Wondrous."

"How did you learn my language?" I ask her, shocked.

She tilts her head, her nose scrunching adorably for a moment. It's as if she's considering something. Then she smiles again. "The words are a bit different than the ones in my head. Maybe it's the *die-ha-lekt* that the *kom-pu-tohr* has." Some of her words aren't mine. They make no sense.

"Kom-pu-tohr?" I ask.

Georgie gestures at the air. "The voice. The ship. It taught me."

"Magic?" I ask dubiously. The only magic I know of is khui-magic, and it does not teach languages.

She giggles, the sound bright and glorious. Then her eyes grow a bit dull again, and she rubs her forehead. "Not magic," she says. "Learning. I probably do not explain it right." Her eyes close again, and she curls against my chest. "My head hurts. Will you hold me for a bit longer?"

"Always," I tell her and cradle her close. My khui throbs in my chest, and for the moment, I am content. Full of questions and wonder, but content.

"Eat," I urge my mate, offering her my rations.

Georgie makes a gagging noise and shakes her head. "That stuff burns my tongue. Even now, it's making my eyes water."

I peer at her small face, and she's right; her pale eyes are weeping and glossy. Curious, I sniff the travel rations. They have a slightly spicy taste to them, but it's meant to be pleasant, not choking. "Humans have weak tongues."

"Gah!" She gives me an exasperated look. "We do not."

"Weak tongues, weak eyes, weak bodies," I murmur, enjoying the look of irritation on Georgie's face. It's such a pleasure to be able to speak to her—really speak to her—and to tease her. "Weak in many, many places . . . but a delicious cunt."

Her face goes bright red, and she bats my arm with her good hand. A hint of a smile curves her mouth. "You are always thinking about sex, aren't you?"

"It is difficult not to when my mate is so soft and beautiful." I brush a finger down the curve of her cheek.

She looks sober at my words. "Vektal . . . I'm not your mate."

"Yes, you are. My khui has chosen you. When you receive a khui, it will thrum for mine. Wait and see."

She shakes her head. "Humans choose their mates. I haven't chosen anyone. Not that you aren't nice," she tells me, giving me another soothing pat to the arm. "And not that I don't care about you. It's just that . . . mating should be a mutual decision."

A mutual decision? Is she mad? Are humans mad? "It is not a decision. The khui chooses. It always knows."

"But I don't have a khui."

"We will remedy this soon enough," I tell her. "Once we return to my tribe, we will organize a hunt to take down one of the great sa-kohtsk. They carry many khui in them. We shall provide enough for you and your tribeswomen."

"Vektal," she says, her face unhappy. "You're not listening to me. I . . . I don't even know that I want a khui."

My heart turns to ice at her words. "You must. It is a death sentence—"

"Only if I stay," she says softly. "I'm not sure. If there's a chance I can go home . . ." Georgie drops her gaze and looks away. "I just haven't decided yet, all right?"

"And where is your home, if it is not here?" My heart starts to pound a slow, unhappy beat. Georgie talks of leaving me as if she does not feel as I do. As if her heart is not torn apart at the very thought of being separated. My khui brought us together, but I am proud to have her as my mate. I want no other. Not now, not ever. It is unthinkable.

She lifts a hand, points at the cave ceiling. "In the sky. A really, really long way away from here."

My eyes narrow at her. I do not understand.

"Like in this *ship*," she continues. "Your ancestors came here in this thing from another place."

"This is the cave my ancestors came from," I agree slowly. "But it does not fly." I imagine a flying cave, moving through the skies like a bird. The thought is ludicrous.

Georgie makes a frustrated sound. "It's a *ship*. Do you know what a *ship* is?" When I remain blank, she drums her fingers on her lip, thinking. "It's a craft that floats through the stars, Vektal. You know I'm not from here, right? I don't have a khui. So I can't be."

I nod because I know this to be true. But the thought of her coming from . . . the stars . . . is strange and bizarre. Unfathomable. But there are things I cannot answer. Her strange language. Her clothing. Her lack of khui. "You . . . wish to go back to the stars?"

Her expression softens into something sad. Her pale eyes gleam for a moment, wet with unshed tears. "I don't know. I think I hate not having a choice more than anything."

So it is not me she hates. My khui begins to thrum in my breast again. I press a hand to it. "Then I will go with you."

Her tears vanish, and she gives a soft chuckle. Then she moves close and squeezes my arm with her good one. She lays her cheek on it and sighs. "I wish that you could."

I trace my fingers down her soft cheek. Does she not realize? Anywhere she goes, I will gladly follow. She is my heart, my resonance, my soul. My mate. It grieves me she is so miserable here, with me.

"Even if I wanted to stay," she says softly, "I cannot make that decision for the others. If there's a chance we can go home, I have to let them decide that for themselves."

My mate is noble. I grunt my understanding, though the animal side of me wants to drag her back to a hunting cave and keep her there, naked and pink, until it is out of the question.

But then my Georgie might die, because she has no khui. And the other girls will certainly die with no rescue. And all of my tribesmen who have no mates—Dagesh and Raahosh and Haeden and so many others—will never know this pleasure. Like Georgie, I cannot be cruel.

"We must go and rescue your friends," I tell her. "If we travel swiftly, we will make it to my tribal caves tonight. We can collect the best hunters and return after them in the morning."

"Let's do it, then," she says, determination steeling her voice. "Every moment that passes is another moment I feel guilty."

"Guilty?" I ask her, cupping her small face up so she can look me in the eye. "Why guilty?" Why does my mate carry such burdens?

Her cheeks pink again. "Because I'm here with you, and I'm warm and happy and fed, and they're not."

Ah. My thumb strokes over her full mouth. "And because my cock makes you cry out with such pleasure?"

The pink deepens, and she ducks her head. "*Ohjeez,*" she says in her language. Then in mine, "Let us keep such talk between us."

I am amused. Is my mate shy? Is this what the pink of her cheeks means? A sa-khui woman gets a flush at the base of her horns when she is embarrassed, but Georgie has no horns. "It is but talk between mates, my resonance."

She tilts her head. "Resonance? What is that?"

I take her small hand, her good one, and press it over my chest. My khui responds, thrumming a content beat inside my chest. "It is this. Only you call to it. Only you make my khui hum in my breast with happiness. It is a sign that one's mate has been found."

Her lips part, and she looks up at me, startled. "I thought you were *purring*."

"Prr-ing?" I am not familiar with this word.

"Like a cat."

"Cat? A snow cat?" I think of the ugly creatures with whiskers and tufts of fur all over. I don't recall them ever purring. They are tasty eating, though.

Georgie giggles. "You know what? Never mind. We should get going."

She gets to her feet and straightens her clothing. We have eaten, and all is ready to go, except I find myself strangely reluctant to continue on. If I do, I am acknowledging that I might not get to keep my Georgie.

The thought staggers me with misery. I press my face to her stomach and hold her against me, seeking a measure of peace. To think that I might lose my sweet resonance so soon after finding her. I cannot bear it.

"Oh, Vektal," she says softly. Her hands stroke over my horns, a tender caress. "I wish it was just me that I had to think for. Then this would be easier."

"It is easy," I tell her, pressing my face to her leather-covered body. Even through her coverings, I can smell her wonderful scent. I long to taste her again. "Accept the khui. Accept me."

She's silent, but her hands continue to touch me and smooth over my skin and stroke over my horns in what feels like a loving embrace. She must care something for me. She *must*. But she only says softly, "Something has to be my choice. So many things have been taken from me. I need to claim something for myself. For now. Grant me that."

I look up at her, at her sad face. "You know I can refuse you nothing."

Her smile is sweet. Sad. "I know."

Georgie

I ponder my choices all day as Vektal plods relentlessly through snowdrift after snowdrift, carrying me on his back.

Even though I am doing my best to deny it, it's entirely possible that we're never going to be able to get home. If Vektal's ancestors were stranded here, then we probably can't get home, no matter how hard we try. Our other option is to wait for the little green men to come back and try to hijack their ship and force them to take us home.

Or we can leave the ice planet when they return, taking our chances as cattle.

Or we can get the parasite—excuse me, symbiont—and make the best of things here with Vektal and his people.

I feel like if I were making an individual choice, it would probably be an easy one. Though the thought of leaving Earth and friends and family behind hurts me, a life with Vektal could be sweet and full of pleasure. I already am starting to look forward to the sight of his smiles, the feel of his skin against my own. I love the rumble of his laugh.

I love knowing what he's saying now.

If it were just me? I'd definitely be Team Vektal.

But I feel like the humans have to make a decision together. I don't want to influence the others. I lucked out and got Vektal, but if we stay here, we might be condemning ourselves to a life of hardship and snow, and who's to say that the others in Vektal's tribe—the sa-khui, as he calls them—will treat everyone as wonderfully as he has me?

And who's to say that the little green men wouldn't sell us to someone on a nice Tahiti-like planet full of sexy men who want nothing more than company while drinking mai tai cocktails? No one can say for sure. The odds are likely against that . . . but it's another reason not to influence the others. Whatever we decide, we'll decide as a group. We'll be making decisions not just for the six of us remaining but the six still tucked away in the wall, slumbering.

Before anyone decides anything, we need to talk it out.

If they want to stay, we'll figure stuff out together. If they want to fight the aliens for control of the returning ship, we'll need weapons and a plan.

My bad wrist aches and throbs, reminding me that we're all battered and wounded from the crash. Taking over anything seems like a horrible idea. Maybe that's just me being negative. I shake the thought away. I'm with my girls. If Liz, Megan, Tiffany, Kira, and Josie want to fight for our freedom, the least I can do is join the cause. Staying back and rolling in the furs with my big sexy alien seems disloyal after everything we've been through together.

"There," Vektal says, rousing me out of my dark thoughts. "Home is just ahead."

My arms tighten around his neck, and I peer through the

drifting snowfall. There's nothing ahead but another rocky cliff, this one barely peeking out of a deep thicket of the eyelash-like pink trees. "In there?"

"The entrance is hidden and guarded to prevent metlaks and other predators from entering. Do not worry. We will be safe and warm there." He pats my arm. "No one would dare harm you."

Am I tense? I must be tense for him to throw out a comment like that. It's just that for so long, it's only been Vektal to have to worry about. Now I'm about to be dropped in to meet thirty-odd others. My arms tighten around his neck. What if they all hate me? What if they all think I'm gross looking? What if—

"Ho," a deep, sonorous voice calls out.

Vektal raises a hand high into the air in response. I cling to his back, worry thudding through my body as another big body appears in the distance.

"That is Raahosh," Vektal tells me in a low voice. "He must be back from his hunting treks."

The other male jogs through the snow toward us, churning a path through the drifts. The pink, flimsy trees wave overhead, and the entire scene looks ludicrous. I try not to stare at Raahosh as he approaches, but, well . . . I'm staring. Where Vektal's horns are big and thick but sleek, Raahosh's horn-crown is a busted mess. He has one that juts out and then arches back, jutting high above his head. The second is broken off, a mere jagged stump. As he gets closer I see scars covering one side of Raahosh's broad face. His skin, er, pelt, er, whatever is a deeper gray than Vektal's . . . like dark smoke. And if I thought Vektal was fearsome looking, Raahosh takes things to a new level.

He grins and raises a hand as he jogs out to meet us, and then his steps slow as he sees me. "I thought you were burdened with the hunt, brother. I was about to come and relieve you."

"I have much to tell," Vektal says, and I can hear the pride in his voice as he gently lowers me to the ground. His chest starts to vibrate with a loud, incessant purr.

Raahosh's eyes go wide, and he looks at Vektal, then at me. "Her?" He gazes at me up and down. "What . . . what is she?"

"She is Georgie, a human and my mate." Vektal's arm goes around my shoulders, and he tugs me against him. I can feel the purr moving through his body, so strong that he's practically vibrating. Resonating, as he calls it.

Raahosh stares at me for so long that I feel uncomfortable. He considers my face, my hair—no doubt looking for horns—and then the rest of my smaller, shivering form. I'm wearing someone else's jumper, and I haven't had a comb in weeks, and I probably look like hell. This is the first time I've felt it, though. Vektal always makes me feel . . . pretty. Like I'm the sexiest thing to ever grace his presence and he can barely keep his hands off me. I've been taking for granted how wonderful it feels to be special to someone.

My hand goes to Vektal's waist, and I slide it down his back until I encounter the bump of his tail base. I circle it and caress it absently.

At my side, Vektal stiffens and the thrumming takes on an even more urgent beat. He reaches back and gently removes my hand, then nuzzles my ear. "Wait until we are in private, my sweet resonance. I know you are not comfortable with public displays."

Oops. Did I just give him the sa-khui equivalent of a public handy? A hot flush covers my cheeks, and I nod. I don't look at Raahosh, though, because then I will be completely and utterly embarrassed.

"Hu-man?" Raahosh says after a moment, the word swallowed and thick in his throat. "Her eyes—"

"She has no khui," Vektal says. His hand goes to my hair, and he combs through it with his big, thick fingers. I feel pretty once more. He still can't stand to take his hands off me, and, okay, I kinda adore that. "We will fix that problem soon."

I nudge Vektal with my elbow. "We'll talk about it."

"We will talk about it," he amends.

I sneak a glance at Raahosh, and he's still staring at me. But it's not a look of disinterest or revulsion. Rather, I see a yearning as he looks at me. Not in a sexual way. Instead, it's as if his best buddy just showed up with the Christmas present he'd been wishing on for years.

"You are lucky," he says finally, his voice thick, "to have found your resonance."

"The luckiest," Vektal agrees, and his fingers stroke my neck. "But my mate needs the healer."

I want to protest about the mate thing since I haven't said yes yet, but my wrist gives a pathetic throb, and I realize how much it still hurts. "Healer sounds good," I say faintly. "Food, too?"

"Food, yes," Vektal says and nuzzles my brow. "And warm clothing. And you shall sleep in my furs tonight."

I blush because I feel like that is an obvious way of saying "we're totally doing it" to his buddy, but Raahosh doesn't blink an eye. "Come," the new alien says and gestures for us to follow. "There will be many questions."

"I am ready for them," Vektal says.

"I'm not sure I am," I chime in. The thought of being quizzed by dozens of staring aliens makes me feel exhausted, and we haven't even entered the cave yet. "We're still going after the others in the morning, right?"

"Others," Raahosh says, and there is more than casual interest in his gaze.

"Georgie has arrived with five other humans," Vektal says. "They are in need of rescue."

"Five other humans?" Raahosh asks, his glowing blue eyes going wide. "Do you speak truly?"

"All female," Vektal says in a low, almost reverent voice.

As I watch, Raahosh staggers. "Truly?"

"Truly."

I'm starting to get worried, and I haven't even told them about the six other women in the hibernation pods. "Is this a problem?" I ask. "Vektal, you said your people would help mine."

"It is not a problem," my alien says in a grave tone. He caresses my cheek. "It is a blessing. There are only four adult females in our tribe, and all of them are mated."

"Do they resonate?" Raahosh asks in a harsh voice.

"They have no khui," Vektal says. "But I resonated for Georgie. Others might resonate to a human female."

I stop in my tracks. "Wait, what? This isn't open season on human ladies! I thought we were getting rescued, not playing matchmaker."

Raahosh simply stares at me like I'm insane. My words probably don't make sense in their language. I don't care. I'm trying to get help for my friends, not hook them up with alien boyfriends. I think back to Vektal's "greeting" of me in which he just grabbed me and initiated sex. Sure, I orgasmed a few times, but that didn't give him the right to make the decision to *mate* me, nor did it give him the right to decide the others got mates without their say-so.

"No one is being mated without their agreement," I say, crossing my arms. Then I wince because I keep forgetting my one wrist is total shit.

"It is agreed, my Georgie," Vektal says. He caresses my cheek again. "I am the chief. They will listen to me. Any male who wishes to mate a human woman must have her agreement."

I relax a bit at that.

"Agreement?" Raahosh sputters. "But resonance—"

"Doesn't happen for humans," I say sweetly.

"It is something to be argued about later, when my mate is not cold and hungry," Vektal says, breaking in before Raahosh protests at me again. He puts a protective arm over my shoulders. "We have traveled far, and we will be traveling far again in the morning."

"Of course," Raahosh says stiffly. He turns and heads back to the trees, and Vektal and I follow him in.

The trees thicken, and as we approach the cliff, I see the entrance to an extremely large cave. The mouth of it is enormous and wide, bigger than any human or sa-khui—even if I stood on Vektal's shoulders and tried to touch the ceiling. It narrows down further in, and this is where Raahosh and Vektal lead me. I cringe at the thought of spending endless hours in a deep cavern. It doesn't strike me as safe.

But as we make our way through the winding tunnel, the air gets warmer. Noticeably so. It feels like we're going down, so shouldn't it be getting colder? I'm puzzled by this until the cave opens up into a larger chamber and the faint smell of rotten eggs touches my nose.

And then I'm just stunned.

The hill the sa-khui live in is hollow. The cave opens up into an enormous cavern that reminds me of a gigantic hollow donut. It's circular, and the center is composed entirely of a large, incredibly blue pool. Another heated spring, I realize with wonder. That is why it smells so strongly of eggs.

I pinch my nose and look around in surprise. There are people bathing in the pool, a tiny child with nubs for horns splashing in the water as a man holds it and a female laughs nearby. The cavern walls round upward, and the roof has a hole in it, almost like a sunroof. From here, I can see snow drifting in, but it melts in the presence of the warmer air and drips down harmlessly.

The edges of the cavern "donut" are riddled with caves, most with ledges and walkways built from additional rock or woven reeds of some kind. A reed-like bridge spans one side of the donut's ceiling over to the other. There are aliens everywhere, too. Some sit in the entrances of their cave-homes. Another pair weaves baskets in the distance. Off to one side, an alien with enormous, arching horns and pale skin scrapes a hide stretched over a frame.

"Vektal is back," a voice calls out happily. Exclamations of joy and chatter erupt in the cave . . . and all heads turn toward us.

And then everyone's staring at me.

It feels weird to be the center of so much attention. As more heads turn and people stand, others approach. And there are a lot of men. A lot of them. Some are dressed only in loincloths due to the warmth of the cave. All of them are muscular, tall, and good looking for sa-khui kind, I'm guessing. And they're all staring super intently at me with a mixture of curiosity and longing.

"My mate," Vektal says proudly. "A human."

"Mother, why is its face so ugly?" a tiny voice asks. Voices raise to hush it.

Raahosh looks chagrined or choked. I can't decide which

one. Vektal growls low in his throat and takes a step forward, clearly insulted on my behalf.

I giggle. To think that these weird people think I'm ugly. They're the ones with horns, tails, glowing eyes, and a downy suede over their bodies. They're the ones with ridges all over their foreheads and noses and, um, other interesting body parts.

Vektal drags me against his chest in a possessive grip, and I suddenly find myself pressed against one rock-hard, vest-covered pectoral. "This is my mate. I resonate for her." As if on cue, his chest starts to vibrate, the thick, steady purr jiggling my cheek. "She is beautiful to me. Different, but beautiful nevertheless." He brushes his fingers through my hair. "I have seen her bravery, her spirit, and her will. She has trusted me when she has no reason to. She has given me her body when she has no khui to compel her. And it does not matter what any eyes think of her but mine . . . and to me, she is the most wonderful, most attractive, and most compelling of creatures."

My eyes prick with emotion. Okay, for a barbarian, he's pretty good at making a romantic speech. I'm totally giving him a handy for real when we get alone again.

"What is a huu-mehn?" someone else asks.

"Are there others?" says another voice.

"He says there are five," Raahosh says in that low, rumbly voice of his. "All female."

I wince at the awe and wonder that fills the voices in the cavern. Fuck a duck. These guys are going to think it's straight-up mating season if this continues. Especially if there are only four adult women in their tribe. That is a lot of unfulfilled sexual need. And what's going to happen when they find out there are six women in stasis in addition to the six who are awake? "Vektal,"

I murmur uncomfortably. As the other aliens get more excited, I get more nervous.

All eyes turn on me at the sound of my voice.

Vektal tugs me tighter against him. "There will be time to answer questions later. My mate has survived an ordeal. She is hungry and tired and needs the healer. Where is Maylak?"

"Here," says a sweet voice. A woman with curling horns and long, flowing dark hair steps forward. She holds a child to her breast, and her belly is rounded with another. Her glowing eyes watch me with fascination.

"Good," Vektal says. "Come with Georgie and me to my cave."

She nods and hands her child off to another man. "Let me get my healing basket."

My alien takes my hand and pulls me along after him. The others follow, and I don't blame them for staring. More whisper as I turn my back to them, and I hear comments about my missing tail. I glance around, just in time to see Raahosh sink into the shadows, a spear gripped in his arms. He watches me intently but not in a creepy way. If I had to place bets, I'd say that Raahosh is going to lobby hard for a human mate.

The thought makes me uncomfortable. It's got to be hard in a tribe full of single, lonely men . . . no pun intended.

Vektal takes me through the labyrinth of caves to one of the back ones along the edge of the donut. There are a few feathers and what look like decorations on the outside of the door but nothing to mark it as a chief's lodge. It looks just like any other cave to my eyes. Inside, though, it's warm and cozy. Furs spill over a plush nest in the corner, and there is a shelf made out of rock that holds a few household implements. There's a fire pit in the corner, not in use, and what looks like a reed net hanging on one wall. I give Vektal a curious look. "Fishing?"

He grins, the look boyish. "I wanted to see if we could catch one of the great fish in the salt lake."

Salt lake? Are we near a sea? I have so many questions.

"This is my cave . . . and your home now, too, Georgie." After a moment, he adds, "If you accept me as mate." He sounds uncertain, unhappy, and I feel a twinge of sadness that my indecision is hurting him.

The pile of furs looks inviting, though, and I can't help but move toward it. I sit on the edge and moan with pleasure as I sink backward. This is by far the nicest, snuggliest bed I've had since I got here. "I'm looking forward to curling up in this," I tell him.

His eyes light up, and I hear the thrum in his chest start.

Oh. He's taking that as a come-on. I should correct him. Instead, I luxuriate in the furs a bit longer, thinking of his sweet words earlier about how beautiful and strong I am. I arch my back so my breasts jut out. His attention goes there, and I see the look in his strange, glowing eyes grow heated.

"Shall I enter?" says a female voice.

Vektal rubs a hand over his face. "Yes. Come, Maylak." He moves to my side and presses a kiss to my hair. "I shall go and talk with my hunters. Maylak will take care of you."

I want to pout, but my wrist hurts, and if Maylak's got food, she's my new favorite person. "All right. Don't be too long?"

"Never," he says fervently, and his fingers trace my jaw. "If you are asleep, I shall wake you up by mating your mouth."

A scorching blush colors my cheeks. "It's called a kiss, Vektal." Saying it like that makes it utterly filthy. And I'm perverted enough to be completely aroused at the thought.

He simply gives me a roguish look, presses his mouth to mine, and then bounds out of his cave. I'm admiring my last glimpse of his tight ass in his leggings when Maylak steps through the entrance a moment later, parting the door hangings. She carries a large basket in her hands and smiles at me, flashing dainty fangs. "May I join you?"

I nod. I watch her as she glides into the room, all fluid steps, and note the difference between her and a male of Vektal's tribe. Her horns are smaller and more delicate, though it seems horns are like noses for these people in that some are huge and some are just smaller and less twisty. It probably has more to do with heredity than testosterone. Her features are as strong and heavy as Vektal's, but her eyes seem to be bigger and longer-lashed, and her mouth is full and pouty. Her breasts are small, and her entire body seems more wiry than soft, but she moves in an utterly sensuous way that makes me jealous. Her hair is long and gorgeous, rippling in a dark waterfall to her waist and tail.

She's dressed curiously, too. Her leathers seem more intricate than Vektal's, with interesting little designs worked into the soft hide that remind me of embroidery. The designs edge the artfully jagged hem of her neckline that crisscrosses over her broad shoulders and drapes loosely over her belly. It's knotted high on one hip, revealing leggings covered with more of the woven embroidery dotted through the leather. Her feet are bare when she sits next to me, though, and I'm surprised. It's warmer in the caves, granted, but it's still chilly to me. But Vektal's people seem to be wearing clothing as if it's a summer's day.

I'm rather envious of that. I'd like to be warm for a change.

In one fluid motion, Maylak sits in front of me, cross-legged. She sets her basket down on the cave floor next to the bed and places both of her hands, palms up, on her knees. "May I heal you?"

"Um . . . yes?" There's no word in their language for "okay."

She takes my bad hand gently in hers, pulls back the leathers, and then unwraps the bindings that Vektal put on it. My wrist is still bruised and swollen, and as the bandages are removed, it throbs with renewed pain. To my surprise, Maylak closes her eyes and cradles my wrist, as if waiting for something.

Er . . . okay. I wait, since it seems impolite to ask what the hell she's doing.

After a long moment, she opens her eyes and frowns at me. "You have no khui. I thought perhaps Vektal was mistaken."

"No," I say with a faint smile. "He's right. I don't have a khui." The word feels strange in my mouth.

She sets my wrist down gently. "Strange. I cannot do much for you, then. My khui is a special one," she says, touching her breast and then extending her hand outward. "It can call upon your khui and encourage it to work stronger."

"Ah." Well, at least she isn't offering to rub crystals or pack mud on me or something barbarian-like. "It's all right, really."

"I can rewrap it for now," she says, reaching into her basket. "Once you have taken on a khui, then I can heal it for you."

I say nothing. I haven't exactly decided that I want a planetary parasite, though the odds certainly aren't looking in my favor at the moment. "Can I ask something?"

"Of course." Her big, glowing eyes look up at me.

"Do you remember getting your khui?" Is that why all these people are so blasé about having a tapeworm?

Her eyes widen, and she shakes her head. "Our children are born helpless, with no khui. They are vulnerable until they have passed four days of age. Then, we hunt the great sa-kohtsk and transfer a khui to the child."

"Why wait four days?"

"The child must be strong enough to accept the khui," she

says. "Otherwise it is death for both child and khui." Her hands
are gentle as she takes bone splints from her basket and works
them into my leather wrappings, supporting my wrist.

"Does it hurt?"

She shrugs her graceful shoulders. "I do not know. I was very
young when I accepted mine. It is very rare that a khui dies and
a new one must be found for a sa-khui. It has only happened
once in my lifetime."

This isn't doing much to help my worry at the thought of
taking a freaking symbiont into my body. "Do you feel it moving? Do you know it's there? Does it like . . . talk to you?"

"Talk?" Her eyes widen, and she laughs until she sees how
very serious my face is. Then her laughter dies. "No, of course
not. It does not speak. It is like having a heart or a lung or a
stomach. You have a khui." Again she shrugs her shoulders.
"Some go their entire lives without feeling resonance. That is the
only time the khui awakens. Then, it makes its presence known
fiercely."

"With the purring."

"Prr—?"

"The sound," I correct, then try to imitate it in my throat. "It
makes you purr near your mate, right?"

"It is more than just that," she says, tying down the last of
the bindings around my wrist. Her hand goes to her breast.
"One feels an intense surge of urgency when the khui comes to
life. It is like . . . a rush of spirit." It's clear she's struggling to
describe it.

"Like adrenaline?" I guess, then add, "Like running down a
hill really fast? Or during a hunt?"

She nods slowly. "More than that. It is . . . possessiveness, too. Your mate is yours, and those who wait to claim their mate find the feeling intensifies over time. It is difficult to describe. It is more than feeling. It is knowing."

This worries me a little. I imagine Vektal and what he must be going through when he resonates with me. He hasn't seemed all jacked up, though. Possessive, yes. But content. Maybe it's different for different people.

"It is part of our lives," she says gently. "The khui chooses the mate, and the khui is never wrong. It brings greater pleasure than any can imagine when one resonates against one's mate."

"And were you happy with the mate it chose for you?"

Her smile curves sweetly. "My Kashrem? No, at first I was quite angry. The khui does not always pick who we think we want in our furs. Kashrem is a tanner, not a hunter. I was young and drawn to one hunter in particular who I shared furs with." Her long lashes flutter, and she turns to her basket and pulls out clothing. "I brought you these. Vektal says you are frequently cold, so I hope these shall help keep you warm."

I'm sensing a conversation change. "Who did you share furs with before you, er, resonated?" I ask, wondering if it's taboo to bring it up.

But her expression is guileless as she looks up at me. "Why, Vektal of course."

I'm stunned at the stab of jealousy that shoots through me. This is my alien's lover? My alien who lived a life of bachelorhood before resonating for me? I picture the scenario: Maylak and Vektal rolling around in bed. Him licking her like he does me. Then her getting up and running to another man just because she resonated for him.

Then my jealousy dies away, and I'm filled with sympathy for my Vektal. How that must have disappointed him. To have a lover when there were so few women must have seemed like a gift. Then to have her taken away—it must have been a very dark time for him. Maybe that's why he's so stinking happy to have me. I feel a surge of affection for the big guy.

Totally getting a handy tonight.

Vektal

The men have endless questions, as I knew they would. Will the women resonate for them? How many are there? What did they look like? Do they have mates of their own? Are the humans shaped like sa-khui women? "The differences are minor," I tell them. "They have no tails, and their mouths are small, and they do not have fangs. They cannot eat meat fresh. They must cook it until it has no flavor."

Someone makes a gagging noise.

"But . . . you resonated for her? She is small. Can she take you?" Salukh asks this, the biggest of our hunters. No doubt he's picturing himself next to tiny Georgie and trying to fit himself into her. The thought makes me curiously angry. I know it is an innocent question—Salukh has never had a mate to share his furs. He keenly wants one.

I should share the information I have. Tell them that sliding into Georgie's tight, wet cunt is like a dream. That she convulses and clenches around my cock when she's feeling pleasure, just like our women. That her nipples are tipped with soft, textured skin and that they're pink like her tongue. But it seems too intimate. As I look at Salukh's avid gaze, though, I know he is hoping that one of the human females will make his khui resonate. Then he will be able to claim a mate and have a family, his greatest desire.

So I give them a few grudging facts. "She has fur in one other spot on her body. On her sex." At the exclamations, I add, "And a third nipple."

"Another nipple?" Raahosh asks, his voice curt. Disbelieving. "For young? Where?"

"Between her legs."

He snorts, clearly finding this ridiculous. "She is deformed, and yet she will not accept the mating? She should be lucky to have you."

His words infuriate me. I rise to my feet. "You speak out of bitterness, Raahosh," I tell him. "You are jealous that I have resonated and your own khui remains silent after all this time. My mate is perfect in every way. It is not her fault that she comes from a place with different customs. In her land, they choose their mates."

Someone mutters at this strangeness.

"Georgie will take a khui soon," I tell them. She must. I cannot bear the thought of her declining it and leaving me to go back to her strange planet. The thought stabs me like a knife, and I fight back the agony it brings. "When she feels the khui within her resonate, she will know what it means to be mated. Until then, I court her with caresses and affection. Just because she does not resonate for me does not mean I shall treat her any differently."

"Probably a good thing that she resonated for you then,

Vektal, and not Raahosh. He'd have found her lacking," Aehako teases.

Raahosh's nostrils flare. He shoots me a cold look and then storms away from the gathering of men.

I rub my face wearily. I am glad to be home amongst my tribe, but my body aches for Georgie. I am eager to join her in bed. "I need hunters and supplies in the morning," I tell them. "We go to rescue the other humans. Who will join me?"

Soon, I have a good group of hunters that have volunteered. It does not surprise me that they are all unmated males and young. The elder ones might be used to their solitude, but the others, like me, hunger for a mate. Young, brawny Salukh will go. Laughing Aehako. Quiet Pashov and his sibling Zennek. Hotheaded Rokan, who has a quick tongue but even quicker senses. Skilled Zolaya and grim, unsmiling Haeden, whose sad history serves as a lesson to others. I suspect that, come morning, Raahosh will show up and join us. He is an excellent hunter, for all his bitterness.

It is a good party. Maylak will want to go, but Kashrem worries that the trek is too far for her while carrying her kit. She will stay behind.

Once the hunters have been finalized, I give orders to find rations—blandly cooked and not spiced. Waterskins for the human women. Warm foot coverings. Extra leathers. Blankets, as many as the men can carry. We will head straight from the humans' strange cave-ship to a sa-kohtsk hunt. There we will get the women their khui.

Then, my Georgie will resonate for me. She will be safe, her life unthreatened by khui-sickness. Both she and our child will be protected from harm.

"Sleep," I tell the hunters. "We will leave at dawn of the second sun."

The men scatter, though I doubt any of them will be able to sleep. They will be dreaming of flat-faced human women with third nipples and welcoming bodies.

My own body hardens at the thought of Georgie, waiting in bed for me. I sprint to my cave, eager to see my mate again. Aehako calls out a jest, but I ignore it; I don't care if I seem eager. Any unmated man would gladly trade his place for mine, and they know it.

The inside of my cave is dark and silent, no hearthstones uncovered for soft light. I don't need them; I know my small abode by heart. I move to the bed and hear Georgie's soft breathing, and my khui thrums again. My heart swells with love and desire for this soft yet strong-willed human. She is already everything to me.

I brush my fingers over her soft mane, and she stirs. "Mmm, Vektal?"

"Go back to sleep," I tell her, pulling off my leathers. "I will join you in bed."

She sits up, and in the pale bit of light, I see her hair tousled on her head. "I thought you were going to wake me with a mouth-mating," she says, and her voice is husky and full of promise.

I groan, my cock hard at her suggestion. "You are tired and must sleep, my resonance. We leave early in the morning."

"Then we'll have to be quick," she says, and her hands go to my breeches. I dare not move as her hands undo the laces of my loincloth, and she tugs the leather free. My cock is met by open air and then a moment later is clasped in her small, warm hands. Impossibly, I grow even harder. "Mmm, I've been daydreaming about this all day," she tells me in a delicious voice.

It seems too incredible to think about. "Have you?" My hands steal to her soft hair, unable to resist touching her. I stroke it off her brow as she wraps her hands around my cock and grips it tight. It doesn't feel as good as burying myself deep into her cunt, but I'm fascinated and aroused by her motions.

"Yes," she says, and when she speaks, her lips move over the aching crown of my cock. I suck in a breath, and my khui begins to vibrate—a hard, insistent pulse of need.

Then, I can scarcely believe it when she takes my cock into her mouth. I feel the head enclosed by a warm wetness, and I nearly spill my seed then. I groan, my entire body tensing in response. It feels like nothing I have ever experienced before. Her soft sucking mouth with its smooth, slick tongue feels like dipping into her cunt. It is only through strength of will that I don't push deep into her mouth. I don't want to choke her.

She flicks her tongue over the head of my shaft, and I clench my fists against the need to pump into her. I'm too fascinated by what she's doing. With little nibbling touches of her tongue and lips, she moves over my cock, down the shaft, and then licks her way back up again. Then she takes the head into her mouth and rolls her tongue against it. "You're too big for me to take deep," she murmurs, her voice sounding awed. "I can barely fit my fingers around you."

"Is that . . . good?"

She chuckles, the sound throaty and sexual. "For me it is." She swipes her tongue over the head of my cock again.

"Georgie," I rasp. The blood in my body seems to be pooling in my cock. My khui pounds against my chest. "If I am not inside you in the next moment—"

"Wait," she murmurs softly, and I hear her shift on the bedding. Then the scent of her arousal perfumes the air, and I hear the sound of wet flesh slicking. She moans. "Oh yeah, I'm wet."

It's too much. I groan again and push her back on the bed. I fumble at her clothing—it's all different. Why is it different?—until I find her slick, inviting core. I drag my fingers over her sex, and she's right, she's wet and ready for me. I grip her hips, push my cock against her entrance, and then surge into her.

She squeals, and I feel her cunt grip me, hard. "Oh," she moans. "Oh, Vektal. Again!"

My mate is loud, and others will hear her. I don't care. I pull back and thrust into her again, my cock pushing deep, the spur above sliding through her wet folds.

She cries out again, and I feel her clench around me. *"Imcomingllredee,"* she breathes in her own language. *"Gahdalmitee!"* I pause, worried, and her good hand slams down on my arm. "Again," she demands in my language. "Just like that!"

With a chuckle, I give my sweet, demanding mate what she wants. I pump into her, over and over, and my khui vibrates with intensity, so strong that I feel it in my jaw and in my cock. Georgie must feel it, too, because she's squirming underneath me, making aroused noises and panting. Her hands claw at my shoulders, and she chants "Again" over and over. I do as she commands, thrusting over and over again until she cries out with her pleasure. Her cunt clenches around me hard, and then I finally spill into her, releasing so hard that stars dance before my eyes. I weave for a moment, and when Georgie tugs me down on the bed next to her, I gratefully follow.

Cock still buried inside her, I turn and cup her body against mine, her back pressed to my chest. She squirms a little at this position. "I feel you pressing into my . . . backside," she says, struggling with the right word.

"My spur?" I ask, chuckling. I'm aroused by the thought of taking her from this way. It's not done with my people. Not when we have tails that get in the way. "Is it uncomfortable?"

She squirms again. "It's just . . . weird."

I run a pleased hand over her still-flat belly. "We will have time to discover our likes and dislikes together, my Georgie. Do not worry." Then my heart seems to still in my chest.

If she stays with me. *If.*

"Mm," she says, her voice sleepy. Then she makes a *huh* noise in the dark. "Your khui stopped."

"It silences for a time after a mating," I tell her. "It will not go away even when the kit arrives."

"Kit?" she asks, and I can hear the frown on her face. "What is this word? The mental picture I am getting with the word is a child."

"That is correct," I tell her and stroke my hand down her stomach again. "A kit is a child."

"Why . . . how can I have your baby?" she asks, her body utterly still against me. "I'm an alien. Actually, you are, but for the argument, let us say it's me."

Have I not explained this to her? "That is how the khui chooses," I tell her. "It determines offspring. A resonance mate is the only one who can bear children. Offspring only come through a khui-mating."

"Wait. Wait, wait, wait. Wait," Georgie moans, and then she's climbing out of bed. I feel a sense of loss as my body slides from hers. Already my cock longs to return to her wet warmth. But she's making anguished sounds. "Waiiiiiiit. Vektal, be straight with me."

"Straight," I repeat, confused by her use of the word. "You wish me to form a line?"

"No! Tell me the truth!"

"I am telling you the truth," I say, baffled.

"You . . . you vibrated—resonated—because your khui decided you could make me pregnant?" she asks, her voice raising in volume.

"Yes," I say, not sure where this is heading. "A khui always responds to a fertile female."

She moans again. "No. You can't make me pregnant. I'm not due for my period . . . oh *fuck*," she says in her own language. "*Fuck! FUCK!! I'm never late! FUCK!!!*"

"Fuhk?" I echo. "I do not know this word."

Georgie descends back to the bed, only to smack a fist against my arm. "It means I'm late! It means you could have gotten me pregnant, you *asshole*!"

"Ass-hole?" I do not know this word either.

"*Fuck!*" is all she says.

PART SIX

Georgie

It's hard to stay mad at a guy who doesn't know why you're so upset.

No, scratch that. It's easy to stay mad at a guy like that. It's really, really hard to stay mad at a guy who acts like you're the best thing since sliced bread, pampers you at every turn, and acts like the baby you're carrying in your belly is the only thing he's ever wanted in his life. Especially hard to stay mad as he and nine of his strongest hunters trek through thick snowdrifts in the bitter cold, carrying supplies for what they think are five more human women (and are actually eleven).

I haven't told them that part yet. One bombshell at a time. And if we decide to take our chances with the little green men, there would be no reason to wake them up and subject them to new and scary things. Like, big blue horned guys who want to potentially mate them and give them a bun in the oven.

I feel the urge to touch my stomach, even though I'm currently piggyback on Vektal through the snow, heading ever up the icy mountain to where I left the others. I might not have had a choice about the baby thing, but . . . I'm not upset. Which is weird to me. It's hard to be angry when you see so much joy on another person's face, and bringing Vektal that joy gives me a sweet sort of satisfaction, too.

Maybe I'm more crazy about the guy than I like to admit.

"There," Vektal says, voice nearly lost in the wind. There's a blizzard blowing, and it's making trekking uphill a nightmare. No matter how many furs I wear, I can't stay warm; even Vektal is bundled against the cold. I'm covered from head to toe, gloves cover my hands, and my teeth are still chattering. It's worrying Vektal, but when he suggested he leave me behind at the elders' "cave," I refused. I won't leave the others behind. I can't. I need to see them to make sure they're safe.

While we paused at the elders' cave overnight, a few of the sa-khui learned English through the brain-zapping. Their version isn't entirely right, but it's close enough that they'll be able to talk to the other women at least.

I didn't miss the fact that Raahosh was the first one to step forward for the zap. He was definitely planning on scoring himself some human booty. I told Vektal, too, and warned him to watch the hunter. He nodded, and we've been trekking close to Raahosh at the front ever since.

The black bit of ship in the distance is nearly invisible, covered entirely with snow. Worry strikes me anew, that I've left them all behind for so long. That was never part of the plan. I'm a shitty, shitty leader. "Oh," I say softly. "Hurry, Vektal. Please. If anything's happened to them . . ."

I let the words trail off into the bitter wind. I don't even want to throw them out into the universe.

Vektal pats my arm with a gloved hand. "All will be well, sweet resonance. Do not worry. We are here."

Strangely enough, his words are comforting. This isn't a rescue party of one anymore. It's a rescue party of eleven. I don't have to do this all on my own. These crazy aliens have my back.

Which is actually pretty darn nice.

"Ahead," Vektal calls out, and he picks up the pace, surging to the front. I cling to his neck for dear life and don't issue a peep of protest, even though his rough jog is killing my wrist. I have to know if everyone's okay. Have to.

Time seems to slow as we make it to the discarded cargo bay. The snow is almost to the gap in the hull, and I slide off of Vektal's back as the others surge to our sides.

"Let us go in first," Vektal says.

"Me first," I declare stubbornly, stepping forward.

Vektal steps ahead of me again with a shake of his head. "Let me. In case there is something dangerous."

I want to protest, but his hand goes to my stomach and he caresses it. Oh, shit. A baby on board totally changes the game, doesn't it? I nod mutely and touch my stomach as he unsheathes a bone knife and descends into the hold.

Stars flick in front of my eyes, and I realize I'm holding my breath. I exhale deeply, then have to concentrate on breathing. It's so quiet in there. What if everyone's dead? What if—

Vektal's head pops up through the break in the hull, and he extends a hand to me, glove removed. "Come below, Georgie."

I give a loud sigh of relief and gratefully take his hand. It feels strong and warm against mine, and again, I'm reminded how much Vektal has been here for me. I feel a surge of gratitude even as he helps me climb down into the hold again.

The stink of the interior washes over me. It smells of urine and poop and unwashed bodies, but not, thankfully, of dead things. "Guys?" I call out. The blankets are huddled in the corners of the cargo bay, unmoving. It makes my heart clench, and I stumble toward the mound of blankets. "Liz? Kira? Megan?"

I peel the blankets back to reveal Kira's sunken face.

She gives me a wan smile. "Hey, Georgie. You're back."

My eyes go wide at the sight of her. She's paler than before, her hair matted. Her eyes are hollow and dull, and she looks so weak that I doubt she has the strength to move. At her side, Tiffany sleeps on, her darker skin ashy and dry.

"Are you guys okay? Can you sit up?" I pull her against me, ignoring the protest of my hurt wrist. Somewhere in the distance, Vektal is calling for his men to bring food, water, blankets.

"I think it's the sickness," Kira says, voice exhausted. She seems to take forever to blink, and when she does, her eyes don't focus. "We're just weaker every day. Tiffany won't wake up."

I lean over Kira and press my fingers to Tiffany's forehead. She's burning up with fever. She doesn't stir at my touch, either. "Are the others still alive?" I ask Kira.

On the far side of the room, I see Raahosh stalk toward the blankets. He lifts one corner and then, ever so gently, lifts Liz and cradles her in his arms. He holds a waterskin to her slack mouth so she can drink.

Vektal pushes a waterskin into my hand as more warriors drop into the hull, looking around. They don't comment on the smell, which is good, because that would make me angry. Instead, they look curiously at the human women who are rousing. I hold the skin so Kira can drink. There's a strange tension in the air.

A faint, familiar purr sounds.

My head snaps up. "Who's that?" I ask. "Who's resonating?"

The aliens are silent. The purr dies away. I narrow my eyes.

Someone just resonated to one of the other humans—yet another problem we don't need—and is hiding it.

"Georgie," Kira says, dragging my attention back to her. "I'm so glad to see you," she says, her voice soft and happy. "You've brought help. You've rescued us."

I catch the faint sound of someone resonating again, and my heart sinks. I'm not sure if I've freed them or brought them a new set of problems. "We need to talk," I tell her. "All of us."

Two hours later, the girls are feeling a bit better after eating and drinking. They're still weak and listless, but even Tiffany has been roused by a meal of broth delivered by a sa-khui who calls himself Salukh. Warm clothing has been provided, and the men are practically fawning over the women, who view them a lot more warily.

Eventually, I give Vektal an exasperated look when yet another male hovers over an alarmed Megan and keeps trying to offer her bites of raw meat. "Can you clear this place out? We need space to talk amongst ourselves safely."

He looks as if he wants to protest and then bites it back. Instead, he nods, kisses my brow, and tells the men, "Come. We will hunt to feed the women. Pashov, Zennek, guard the entrance. The rest of you, come with me."

Eventually the men organize themselves and leave, though several longing glances are cast in the direction of the human women. Then we're finally alone again, and I grab a bowl of the hot broth and sit with the rest of the girls, huddled against one of the walls.

"So," I tell them. "I brought rescuers. They're both a good thing and a bad thing."

"The way I see it, it's a good thing," Tiffany says in an exhausted voice. "What's so bad about a bunch of big hunky aliens acting as babysitters?"

"There's more to it than just that," I hedge.

But Kira's giving me a suspicious look. "How did you learn their language so fast?"

So I tell them about the spaceship that Vektal calls the elders' cave. The language dump it shot into my brain. The whole "parasite" thing that seems to be a requirement for Not-Hoth living. The "Vektal's tribe only has four women, and they're looking at us to hook up and become part of the family" thing.

The women make no comment, except for a few horrified blanches at the thought of a symbiont. I don't blame them.

"If we stay here," I tell them, "we're committing to an entirely different life. It's not a choice that can be made lightly. We have other options. We can opt not to take in the . . . symbiont. We can fight instead."

Tiffany shakes her head. "But we're so weak right now. I can barely lift my arms." Others nod. I'm rather exhausted, too, just not as bad as the others because Vektal's been taking care of me. But in another day or so? I might be just like them.

"Not to mention, we don't know when the ship is coming back," Megan says. "Or if."

"I think they'll come back to get us," Kira says thoughtfully. "They're not going to want to lose such valuable cargo, and from what it sounds like, we're extra *extra* valuable."

"Goody," Liz says with a sarcastic tone. "So they'll be back."

"And we can fight, or we can make it so they can't remove us from this place," I tell them.

"I'm more than a little freaked out at the thought of getting a sym-thing," Megan confesses. "The cootie."

"Khui," I correct, then shudder. What if it does look like a cootie? "So we fight, then?"

"Girl," Tiffany says. "I can barely lift my eyelids. I cannot fight. I vote we go with the big guys."

"Here's the thing," I say, rubbing my brow. I have a headache that won't go away. I don't know if it's khui-sickness or the smell of the hold, but I'm aching and frustrated. "The khui picks mates. So if it decides that you would be perfect having babies with your worst enemy, you don't get a say in things."

"But it beats being cattle," Liz chimes in.

"Even if we do manage to somehow take over the ship, there's no guarantee we'll be able to get ourselves back home or that they'll take us. They could lie to us about it, and we'd be no wiser."

"What do you want to do?" Josie asks me. "You keep asking us. Tell us what you are thinking."

My hand goes to my stomach. "I'm kind of biased in one direction because . . . I'm pregnant. With Vektal's baby. He's resonating for me, and apparently it means that, despite the fact that we're not the same species, he can get me pregnant. So I want to stay."

The moment I say it aloud, I feel cleansed. Of course I want to stay. I'm coming to care for Vektal. I might even love the big guy. And I'm carrying his child. It's not his fault I was kidnapped by evil aliens and now I have to get a "cootie," as Megan calls it. He's done nothing but love me.

"Pregnant?" Tiffany repeats. "In a week? Seriously, girl?"

"Damn, girl, we can't leave you alone for five minutes," Liz says. "Dead serious this time. I feel like if you leave our sights again, you're going to show up with a litter."

A hot flush comes over my face. "To be fair, I thought he couldn't make me pregnant if it was interspecies sex."

"A Great Dane can still make a Chihuahua pregnant," Liz points out. "Guess which one you are."

I make a face at her. "I didn't want to say anything to influence you guys."

"Like, hey, someone buttered my roll while you guys were waiting for me to return, and he left a few crumbs behind?" Liz cracks.

Ouch. "I'm sorry. I—"

"Don't be sorry," Kira says, butting in. She touches Liz's arm before Liz can make another comment. "It's just been rough for us."

"Trust me, showing up pregnant was a surprise for me, too."

"So we're staying?" Josie asks.

I look at the tired, exhausted faces of my fellow captives. "If you guys are decided, yes."

"If a guy shows up with a hamburger, he can plant as many babies in me as he wants," Liz declares.

I hear shuffling outside and low murmured conversations. I sigh and look at Liz. "Did I mention that some of them learned English from the old ship?"

"The offer stands," Liz says with a grin. "Should we wake up our test tube ladies?"

I eye the wall and feel a bit of anxiety. "They're really going to hate us, aren't they?"

"Why?" Kira says. "It's not like we kidnapped them. We're giving them an out."

"An out that involves cooties and mating an alien," I point out.

"You're not complaining," Liz says. "If they treat us half as good as Vektal's been treating you, it's not a terrible thing. And it beats being cattle, doesn't it?"

I nod, then touch my stomach. "I guess we wake them up, then. Maybe we should warn Vektal and the others that there are eleven of us."

Around me, eyes widen.

"You haven't told them there are six more?" Josie asks.

"Oh shit, they're totally going to think it's Christmas around here," Liz says and starts to laugh. "I can't wait to see the looks on their faces."

Vektal

Just when I think my mate can surprise me no more, she brings something new.

"So, Vektal," she says, sidling up to me as I return with my men and a freshly slain dvisti for the humans to char into inedible food. "Can we talk for a minute?"

The other men shoot me envious looks as my mate touches my arm and my khui begins to hum. One of the men resonated earlier as well, but no one is stepping forward. I don't blame them. With the humans undecided as to if they will stay or go—a thought that is like a knife to the gut—no one is sure how to act.

But Georgie gives me an encouraging smile and pulls me aside. Her hand goes to my chest, and I hold it against my thrumming khui.

"So I have good news and bad news. Which do you want first?"

"There is bad news?" I'm staggered. The urge to grab my

mate and run off with her hits me like a palpable thing. "If it is bad, you must tell me now. I cannot bear it."

She looks a little alarmed at my response. "It's a human tease, Vektal," she says. "Don't get so upset. I don't know if it's bad news as much as it is startling news."

I exhale slowly. "I am ready."

"The good news is that we're staying," she says, a small smile playing on her lips. "We talked and *voted*."

I don't know what "voted" is, but the words she's saying fill me with utter joy. I crush her against me and press my lips to hers. She twitches, and a happy laugh escapes her. Then, she wraps her arms around my neck and kisses me back, and for a moment, nothing exists outside of my Georgie and her soft, sweet mouth. "My resonance," I murmur between kisses. "You fill me with joy."

She breaks the kiss, and there's a worried look on her strange, smooth little face. "You might not like what else I have to say."

I want to tell her that nothing else matters. Not as long as she is with me. But there's such anxiety in her strange eyes that I bite back the words. "What is it?"

"Your men are here to rescue five women," she says, her fingers fiddling with the laces on my vest. She won't look me in the eye. "But there are six more of us. Hibernating."

I study Georgie for a long moment. Her words don't make sense. Perhaps she still has not grasped all of our language. "The word you say, it means . . . sleeping? Did you mean something else?"

"No, I mean hibernating," she says again. Her smaller hand grips mine, and she pulls me toward the wall with the strange panels and the lights, much like that in our elders' cave. When we get to the wall, she touches it with a pat of her hand. "They're asleep in here, and they have no idea what is going on."

I am astonished. "Asleep in the walls of your cave?"

"Yes," she says, her expression sad. "We were afraid to wake them." And she tells me an incredible story of being taken from her home while she was sleeping and finding herself in the belly of the cave-ship. "We are the extras. These in the wall are the original cargo."

I don't understand her words, but I understand what she is telling me. "Your numbers are twice what they seem."

"I hope you're not mad?" Her face is worried.

Mad? I am ecstatic. That there are five women who are young, healthy, and mate-able seems a gift from the gods. Six more is an unthinkable bounty. I want to press Georgie against me and crush her in a hug for saving my tribe from what feels like certain destruction. Instead, I must remain calm. "Six more females . . . And they will be frightened and confused and will need to be treated carefully."

She nods. "Your men will need to be careful around them. They haven't been held captive like us. As far as we know, they might still think they are at home, sleeping in their beds. This is all going to be very strange and very frightening to them." She squeezes my hand. "We didn't want to wake them when we weren't decided. Do you understand what I'm saying?"

I do. Georgie's telling me that however reluctant the humans are to join our tribe, these women might be even more so. That it will take time and patience to bring them into our tribe. "I understand."

"Some of them might reject the . . . khui," she says, her mouth struggling to form the word. "That must also be their choice."

It's not something I comprehend, but as long as Georgie takes the khui, I care not what the others do. I press her palm to my mouth. "I shall leave it in your charge."

She nods, a grim look on her face. "I'll get the others, then."

The men retreat, a little awed by the newest revelation that there are yet more human females. I see eagerness in their faces, and they want to stay behind to be the first to lay eyes on the new females—in the hopes of resonating to one. But we know the women will be hungry when they awaken, and a sa-khui male's instinct is to feed and tend to his mate. So the men set off hunting, and Georgie and her women get to work prying open the compartments. I watch from a distance, unable to let my mate leave my sight. She and her women are weak and listless, and I am worried that the khui-sickness might be too much for them.

With Kira's help as translator, they manage to open the strange wall, revealing six long tubes with floating, naked women. Georgie is right. Six more women, all so similar to my Georgie that it makes my heart clench uncomfortably at the thought of her being trapped inside one of those tubes.

One by one, the women are freed from the tubes. There's confusion at first, followed by sobbing. The others wrap the new female in a warm fur and take her aside to answer questions she might have, feed her, and clothe her. Some of the women stare blankly as Georgie and the others explain. One is furious. There is one with flaming orange hair and orange specks all over her strange pale skin. She sees me and chokes back a little scream, only to be comforted with small pats from Georgie and the other women.

My mate is right. It will take some time before these women

are comfortable, and it's time we don't have. Georgie and her women cannot last much longer without a khui.

As the women share clothing and chatter together, I head out to check on the men who were exiled from the hold to give the humans time to acclimate. A few of my hunters have stayed behind to guard the hold while the others search for more food. Amongst them are Aehako and Rokan.

Aehako presses a hand to his chest. "I do not know if my heart is beating fast with excitement or if it is resonance."

I clap him on the shoulder. "You will know when you see your female's face. Until then, do not worry."

"I have longed for a mate all my years," he says. "Now I cannot stop wondering if it is one of the human females. To think of having a family after so long." There is an ache in his voice I well understand. Before my Georgie, I felt the same. Now my life feels almost complete.

When she takes the khui and her life is no longer in jeopardy, I will know total contentment.

"When can we look upon them?" he asks.

"Soon," I tell Aehako. "The humans are scared. This is all new, and we are strange to them. Give them a bit more time to adjust."

"It is difficult to be patient," Rokan says. He seems to be calmer than Aehako, but the hands that grip his spear are white-knuckled. "To know that there are mate-able females so close by . . ."

I nod, but my gaze is on the men in the distance. The hunters are returning, and there is haste in their steps. I watch them approach, and when Raahosh arrives at the head of the hunting party, he is out of breath but jubilant. "A sa-kohtsk is near. A large one."

"Then we will bring our humans to it in the morning." My

own blood thrums with excitement. The sa-kohtsk are lone wanderers. To find one so close to the human encampment is a sign. I decide it's time to sit back no longer. Entering the human cave, I ignore the startled looks the new humans send my way and call Georgie to my side.

She comes, all kisses and smiles. I suspect that's for my benefit as much as the wary humans'. "Hi," she says in a cheery voice. She looks tired, though. All of the humans do.

I take her hand in mine to kiss her palm again, and she gives me another tiny sigh of pleasure. I can smell her arousal bloom at my touch, and it's making my khui hum in my chest. But I cannot take her tonight. She needs her rest. "Tomorrow, we leave here."

"To go to your caves?"

"To go hunt the sa-kohtsk. We seek khui for you and the women."

She flinches a little but nods. "If we must, we must."

"We need more time," the mouthy one called Liz says. She looks weaker than the rest, thin and wan. But she's got a stubborn set to her flat mouth. "Not all of us are sold on the idea." She puts an arm around a new human's shoulders, and the woman trembles and leans into Liz's caress.

"You may not have much more time," I begin, but I'm interrupted by a high-pitched whine. In the background, Kira claps a hand to her ear and collapses. Georgie claps a hand to her own arm, wincing.

"What? What is that?" I ask.

Her mouth opens in pain, and she pulls her hand away from her arm even as the whine dies down. There's a light blinking in her arm, just under the skin, an angry, glaring red.

"The aliens are coming back," she tells me. "We need to leave."

Georgie

We're a sad, sad little party as we set out from the cargo bay a short time later. The new girls are weeping and confused. They want more furs than we have to go around. They want better shoes. They're hungry, cold, and tired. Maybe it's exhaustion, but I'm frustrated with them because we're doing the best we can and they just keep crying. I know this is new and scary for them, but I find myself wishing they'd catch up and get with the program already.

The women also want to avoid the men, who are giving them longing looks. Someone keeps purring, though no one will step up and admit things. It's probably for the best, because I'm guessing that the girls can't handle the thought of taking on an alien boyfriend right now. Not with everything else going on.

My upper arm throbs. It's freshly bandaged, but it still stings like the dickens. Once the sensors went off, we set into action, readying to leave the camp. Before we did, though, we had to take care of matters. If the sensors were trackers, we had to get rid of them, and fast.

Out came the knives, and five minutes—and a lot of tears—later, the trackers had been removed. Pashov had been sent to dump them into the nearest metlak cave. Let the little green men take *them* if they want captives.

Now, the rest of us trudge through the snowy dusk, except for Josie, who is carried by a big male called Haeden. We're trying to ignore the bitter cold, in search of something Vektal called a sa-kohtsk. It would have the khui we needed, and it, he told me, would save us.

I am all for being saved at this point. Exhaustion is making it difficult for me to keep up, and Liz is so weak that Raahosh decides to carry her slung over his shoulder like a sack of potatoes.

One of the scouts appears, waving his spear overhead. "Sa-kohtsk," he calls into the driving wind. "In the valley. Hurry!"

Vektal puts an arm around my waist. He is now carrying Tiffany, who's too exhausted to lift her feet. "Come, my resonance," he tells me. "Not much further."

"I'm good," I tell him, plodding ahead. "I—"

The ground shakes under my feet.

"What was that?" I ask, stopping. Terror ripples through me as it happens again. Even the snow at my feet vibrates.

"That," Vektal says, urging me forward again, "is a sa-kohtsk."

Oh, shit. I'm a little terrified of what we're about to find, but we've come this far. Vektal and his men press ahead, so we have little choice but to keep up. "Have you hunted these a lot?" I ask him.

"Not often," he tells me. "Only when a khui is needed. They are too fierce otherwise."

"Great," I say dryly.

204 • RUBY DIXON

"This will go well," Vektal tells me and gives me a comforting pat on the arm, which only sends a flare of pain through my new wound again.

At least when I get a khui, Maylak will be able to heal me. At this rate all she's going to have left are a bunch of Georgie-shaped pieces. I ready the knife I carry with me.

"What's happening?" one of the new girls asks, shivering in her furs. Her name's Nora, I think, and she's one of the stronger newbies.

The ground thumps again, and Vektal points at a copse of pink feathery trees ahead. "Take the women there. If the creature comes for you, hide amongst the trees."

"By climbing them?" I look at the other women. "I don't think they can climb."

"You won't need to climb," Vektal says. "He cannot get to you through them." I wonder at his words, but there's no time to talk. He presses a kiss to my forehead and then passes Tiffany off to me. She's so weak that she clings to me, and I have to drag her over to the trees with Nora's help.

It feels a bit sexist to have all the women huddling under the trees as the men go off to fight, but I look at the women around me and feel a little despair. We're weak, exhausted, and not used to all this cold. If the little green men showed up right now, we'd be helpless to fight back against them, even if we outnumbered them.

The ground shakes again, and at my side, Kira clutches a spear while Liz moans unhappily. "What the fuck is that *Jurassic Park* shit?"

"I don't know," I tell her. But I ready the knife I carry with me.

Something gives a high-pitched roar, and the hairs on the back of my neck stand up. It seems close, really freaking close, and the ground shakes again. Megan chokes back a sob of fright, and the other women are whispering. I hiss for silence because I want to know what the hell is going on, damn it. The thought of Vektal out there with some huge monster frightens me.

What if he gets hurt? What if he . . . dies? My heart clenches at the thought. In such a short period of time, I've come to care for him more than I like to admit, even to myself.

I don't want to be here if Vektal is not.

A gigantic head rises over the trees. I suck in a breath, staring in horror. There's a thing with four glowing blue eyes, two sets stacked on top of one another. It's got enormous tusks and is covered in long, grayish shaggy fur. It gives another high-pitched roar and lumbers forward, the ground shaking. It's taller than all the trees, and as it moves past, I see long, twiggy legs with wide feet pushing through the snow. An alien hunter hangs off of one side, clinging to a spear sticking through the creature's flank.

"Holy shit," Liz says. "What the hell is that?"

"I think it's a sa-kohtsk," I say, feeling faint. It looks like a Macy's Parade float with legs. And they're going to kill that thing? Dear God. *Be careful, Vektal,* I send out quietly. More of the men run past, chasing after it with spears. I try to pick out Vektal in the group, but I don't see him. He doesn't carry a spear, only knives and a sling, and the thought fills me with dread.

"I wish I had a bow," Liz says as we stare at the creature lumbering past.

"That's random," Kira comments, her tone awed. We can't take our eyes off the sa-kohtsk.

"I was a champion archer when I was a teenager," Liz comments. "Though I don't know if I could shoot that thing."

"Huh," is all Kira says.

I stride forward through the snow as the creature lumbers

away from the trees, the hunters chasing it. Where is Vektal? Where? I follow behind in the distance as the men harass it with spears.

The creature bellows again, and his head swings low, dipping toward the ground. An alien grabs one of the jutting tusks, and as the creature jerks his head back, the man goes flying onto the creature's head, barely holding on. I suck in a breath as I recognize the graceful movements and the long, fluttering black hair. Vektal. My hand goes to my mouth, and I press my fingers against my lips so I don't scream in fright.

Please don't get killed for me, I think. *Please.*

I watch as he gracefully flips to his feet atop the monster's head. It swings back and forth, trying to dislodge him, but Vektal's holding on tight. He pulls something from his vest—a bone blade, I think—and raises it high into the air.

With a battle cry, he plunges it downward, and the creature screams and writhes in pain. Behind me, a few of the women choke out cries of their own. I'm breathless as Vektal raises the knife and slams it home over and over again, driving it into the creature's eye.

With a final gurgle, the creature staggers. It takes one step forward and then collapses. The ground shudders with the force of it, and I can't help but rush forward to Vektal. I push through the thick, knee-high snow, ignoring my exhaustion. I have to get to him, to know he's all right.

When I do, I see he's covered in blood and gore from the creature, wiping his face clean on one edge of his vest. He grins at me, and it's so boyish and did-you-see-me that I choke back my sob and fling my arms around his neck. "You scared the shit out of me," I babble in English, not caring that he's getting my new clothing all gunked up.

"Georgie?" he asks, patting my back. "Are you well?"

"I am now," I answer in his language. "That was scary as hell."

"They are strong," he admits. "But not so strong that I would not bring one down for you and the humans."

"Just as long as this is not a regular occurrence," I tell him.

His hand touches my belly, and there is warmth in his shining eyes. "We will need one for our kit, and I will gladly do so."

"All right, all right," I grumble. "So what now?"

He presses a kiss to my forehead. "Now, we get the khui. Gather the women."

My stomach drops at the thought, but I force myself to nod. If they risked their lives to get us the symbionts, the least we can do is hold up our end of the bargain, since it's for us anyhow.

I go to Tiffany's side and help her walk, trying to seem more confident about this than I really am. If I freak out, so will the other humans. I need to be cool, calm, and collected about things.

I manage to remain cool, calm, and collected for all of five minutes as we gather nearby. The men are watching us avidly, hope and hunger both in their eyes. I ignore them, focusing on the gigantic fallen sa-kohtsk. The long, spindly legs are splayed, and the fat belly of the creature sticks out. I look for something that resembles a remora—*please, please don't look like a remora*—but the thick, bushy coat of the creature hides anything that might be living against the skin.

"Where are the khui?" I ask, since the men seem to be waiting for the humans to say something.

"Inside," Vektal says. He moves forward and touches my jaw. "Are you ready, my Georgie?"

Oh God. I don't know that I am. I swallow hard. "Let's do this."

He nods and pulls his longest, thickest blade out of the sheath at his belt. I brace myself as he sets the tip of the blade against the creature's belly. In a swift motion, he sinks it deep and then begins to cut. Blood gushes and dribbles out of the wound, and someone behind me makes a choking sound. There's a sickly, coppery smell in the air, and I force myself to ignore it.

Two of the warriors move forward, and they peel back the creature's wound, revealing a mass of bloodied organs.

"Just like skinning a deer," Liz breathes at my side in a curiously blank voice. "No big deal. No sweat."

Vektal moves to the rib cage of the creature and steps on one side, then pushes against the other. His big arms strain, and then there's a snap like a tree falling in the forest, and the ribs split open.

"Really, really big deer," Liz says.

Vektal makes a few cuts, the sound wet and overloud in the quiet evening. He pulls out a giant organ that must be the heart, still pulsing. It's glowing from within, the light dappled and shining a pale blue. With one slit, he opens it, and the light spills out.

There are dozens of thin, wriggling gossamer worms in there. Worms.

Oh God.

One of the warriors approaches Vektal, and he hands off the heart before gently pulling one of the glowing filaments from it.

"I think I'm going to be sick," Kira says faintly.

I think I am, too. But I force myself to remain in place as Vektal reverently frees the long, coiling strand of light and comes toward me with it cupped in his big hands. It's wriggling and writhing against his palms. "They cannot live long out in the cold," he tells me. "We must make an incision in your neck and give the khui a safe place to reside."

His eyes are speaking volumes. In this, I must be a leader. In this, I must trust him.

I swallow hard, looking at that long, wormlike glowing thing. "What . . . what if it goes to my brain?"

"Like that's any better than your heart?" Liz sputters.

"The khui is the essence of life," Vektal tells me, even as he cups the snakelike thing in his hands. His gaze is on my face, and there is a mixture of emotions there. If I turn away now, I'm turning away everything he and his people are offering. I'm turning away a life here and love, all for the potential of a Hail Mary rescue.

"In the neck, huh?" I say, my voice faint. "Will it hurt?"

"I do not know." Vektal approaches me, and I can hear the thing in his hands flicking and making a purring sort of sound.

"Fair enough," I say. The thing is pressing against his hands, looking for a way to burrow into his skin. I feel faint at the thought of voluntarily letting it inside me . . . but what choice do I have?

I made my choice. I chose Vektal . . . and our child, who might even now be inside my womb.

"Do I need to make the cut?" I ask him. "Or will you?"

"I can," he says and offers his cupped hands to me.

I take the khui with a small grimace. It feels like a sticky strand of spaghetti, impossibly warm despite the cold, wintry wind blowing around us. The light flickers faintly as it's transferred to my hands, and I experience a moment of worry. What if khui can't bond with humans? But Vektal has pulled out a new, clean blade, and his hand has gone to the back of my neck, cupping it.

And then there's really no going back.

"Are you really going to do this, Georgie?" Kira asks, sounding ill.

"I really am." I look into Vektal's glowing eyes as he leans in. He presses a kiss to my forehead, and I'm struck again at how wonderful he is. "I love you," I say softly.

"You are my heart, Georgie," he murmurs. I feel the cool press of the knife against my throat for a quick moment and then a sting as he nicks me near my collarbone. Not deep, but enough that the blood crusts up and freezes against my skin.

Vektal takes the khui from my hands and lifts it, and as I see his hand with that weird, glowing filament approach my bared neck, I think, *No, no, wait, I changed my mind.*

But it doesn't matter.

The moment the khui touches my skin, it begins to burrow, seeking warmth. I suck in a horrified breath as I feel it push through my body. It's like ice water moving through my veins, and I can feel the thing climbing toward my heart and *oh shit.*

Oh shit.

Everything's going dark.

Vektal's face is blurring in front of mine.

This is a mistake, isn't it?

But then there's warmth.

So much warmth.

And humming . . .

And then darkness.

My eyes snap open at some point later. It's curious because I can feel the wind blowing and snow falling around me, but I'm not cold anymore. Warm fingers brush over my cheek, and I look into Vektal's handsome face. I feel a little stiff and achy overall, but I don't feel as weak as I was before. I lick my lips. "How'd it go?"

"Your eyes are a lovely shade of blue," he tells me, voice warm with happiness.

"Oh?" I sit up with his help and look around. Not much time has passed, I think, since I took in the khui. There's thunder in the distance, and the skies are black with night. I blink and look around. I feel . . . the same. There's no weirdness. No oh-my-God-there's-a-tapeworm-in-me feeling. Everything is quiet.

As a snowflake lands on my arm, though, I look around in surprise. "I'm warm?"

"The khui will keep you warm," he says, his hand brushing over my skin. He's touching me everywhere, as if he can't quite believe I'm all right.

"Wow, okay." I glance through the camp, and the men are helping the women to their feet. "Did they all take it? The khui?"

"Everyone," he says, a proud note in his voice. He helps me stand, though I don't suppose I need the help anymore. I'm just fine, oddly enough. I feel . . . good. "You were brave and led the way."

"I have a lot to live for." The sound of the thunder increases, and as his hand touches mine, I feel . . . strange. Aroused. It's weird because all he's doing is touching my arm. I look at Vektal in surprise. I fight the urge to kiss his hard mouth, to climb him like a freaking tree, and to drag him into the snow and make sweet, sweet love to him.

Good lord, what is going on with me?

The thunder rumbles louder, and I look behind me.

Vektal chuckles and presses a hand between my breasts. "You hear it?"

"What is that noise?"

"It is you," he says. "Your khui sings for me."

I press a hand to my chest. Sure enough, the rumble's coming from me. I'm *purring*. "Oh." Heat pools between my legs, and my pulse starts to thrum as if he's touched me in naughty ways, just from his fingertips on my chest. "Oh man, I feel . . ."

"I know," he says, and his eyes glow with a mixture of need and amusement. "I can smell your need, mate."

"Oh boy," I say faintly. "Can . . . can anyone else?" If they can, I might die of embarrassment.

"My senses are attuned to you. The others are too busy helping the humans. Look around you," he says, pulling me against him.

God, he's warm and big and delicious, and I want to shove my hands in his pants and take his cock in my grip. It takes me a moment to focus, and I cling to his vest as I try to get a grip on myself. Is this what resonating feels like? I mean . . . wow. But good lord. I don't know if I can stand being this sensitized around Vektal constantly.

Then again . . . the orgasms are going to be mind-blowing.

My gaze focuses on the women in the distance. Tiffany's on her feet, which is wonderful, and a sa-khui male dotes on her. Almost every woman seems to be escorted by a man of Vektal's tribe, and the sound of faint purring fills the air.

"Are they all—"

"Not all," Vektal says. "But some." At my worried look, he adds, "They will approach things slowly. This I promise." Then he grimaces. "Except for one."

"One?" I look around at the sea of faces and notice that one familiar, lippy one is missing. "Where is Liz?"

"Raahosh has slunk off with her like a metlak with a kill." Irritation clouds his features. "He will answer to the tribe when he returns."

My entire body tenses. "Is he going to hurt her?"

"Hurt her?" The look Vektal gives me is incredulous. "He takes her to mate her. Harming her is the last thing on his mind."

Boy, I almost feel sorry for Raahosh. He doesn't know what he's gotten himself into by taking Liz. She's not about to let an alien run roughshod over her. "I'm sure Liz will have a few things to say about that."

He gives a wry smile. "I am sure she will, too."

I wouldn't be surprised if Raahosh brought Liz back, I think to myself. She's a handful. "Can we go after them?"

"Raahosh is the best of my hunters. If he does not wish to be found, he will not be found. We can simply wait for them to return."

"Let me guess," I say dryly. "Barefoot and pregnant?"

He looks puzzled at my words. "Why would her feet be bare?"

"Never mind." I pat his chest and then find myself utterly fascinated with the play of his muscles. "Oh, wow. Vektal, I feel very . . ."

"In tune with your resonance?" he asks. Under my hand, he begins to thrum louder, and that makes my nipples prick as my own khui responds.

I nod.

He clasps me against him, and I gasp because it feels . . . amazing. "Shall we go somewhere private then, my mate?"

"But . . . the others . . ."

"The men will take care of them for the night," he says and traces a finger down my cheek that leaves me shuddering with need. "They will keep them warm and fed while they adjust to their khui. And in the morning, we shall all start the journey home."

Home. After weeks of being captive, it feels so nice to think of a place as home. "Where can we go?" I ask him, lacing my fingers in his. "Lead on."

But he hesitates. "Do you feel well, my resonance? Do you want to rest? To sleep?"

"Right now, I want to tear your clothing off and put my mouth all over you," I tell him, and the purring in my chest increases. So does the wetness between my legs. If I had panties, they'd be soaked.

Vektal's nostrils flare, and he stifles a groan in his throat. Before I can react, he throws me over his shoulder and begins to storm off into the darkness. "We will return at daybreak," he calls to one of his men.

"Enjoy the resonance," the man calls back, and there is envy in his voice.

I wiggle with excitement on Vektal's shoulder. God, I should not be so aroused, but I am. The khui humming through my system is making me feel warm and good, and the intense arousal feels like a bonus. Why was I so against the thing? I touch my breastbone and feel it humming happily underneath. If this is all it takes to live at Vektal's side for the rest of my life, I'll take it.

I mean, there aren't any toilets, but living as a barbarian? Not so bad when you've got a big, sexy barbarian male with you.

Vektal tromps through the snow for several minutes, and just when I'm about to shove a hand down my own pants and take care of business, he stops. "Here is far enough."

He sets me down, and I look around with a frown. We're in the middle of nowhere, a few scattered trees nearby. There's a large flat rock here, about waist height, and the sight of it arouses me because I picture Vektal mounting me from behind and fucking the daylights out of me. My thighs tighten again. "Here?"

His hand goes to my neck, and he pulls me against him in a brutal, possessive kiss. "Here we are far enough away that when they hear you scream with pleasure, they will not think to come and rescue you."

I blush at his words, but they make heat pool in my veins. "You are one sexy beast, you know that?"

"All I know is that I am yours," he says to me. His mouth captures mine again, and I feel the scrape of his fangs a moment before his tongue swipes against mine, the bumps playing against my own tongue and sending a spike of fierce desire through me.

I moan and slide my hands into the laces of his leggings. "I want your skin against mine," I tell him. "All of you, against me." My khui hums an agreement. A moment later, my wandering hands brush against the head of his cock, and I feel drops of pre-cum against the crown of his cock. I lift one to my mouth and moan at the taste of him. It's like nothing I've ever tasted before: sweet, musky, and delicious. He tasted good pre-khui, but now . . . I drop to my knees in front of him. "God, I really want to suck your cock."

"It is said that the taste of a resonance mate is like no other flavor," he murmurs, his hand brushing through my hair. "I know there is no finer thing than your dew on my tongue."

Dew? We'd have to talk about love words in the future. I smile up at him and pull at his pants until his cock is freed from his lacings. I take him in my hand and moan my pleasure at the hot, throbbing length of him and then lick the droplets beading on the crown. Each one is delicious. My hand steals to my own thighs, sliding into the leggings that Maylak gave me so I can rub myself as I touch him. I'm absolutely wild with lust, and I need him right this moment or I'm going to lose my mind. All the while, the khui is humming and throbbing a tune in time with Vektal's.

It feels amazing. I sink a finger into myself and moan. It's not enough.

"On your back for me," my mate breathes, his hands caressing me. "If you must be filled so quickly, let me be the one to do it."

I don't need any convincing. I'm so wet, so slippery that I know I can take him. Feeling naughty, I get up on the stone and press my belly to it, my hips in the air. "Let's do it from behind, Vektal. Remember? That night in your cave? You said you'd never done it that way."

He growls, and I feel his mouth press to my back. "Never . . . tails . . ."

"But I have no tail," I say and wiggle my ass at him.

Vektal grips my hips, and his hands rip at my leggings. I'm trying to help him, too, and then my ass is exposed to the chilly air and my pants are around my knees. I feel the hard press of his cock against my hip, and I spread my thighs wider—as wide as my clothing will allow. "Yes," I breathe. *"Please."*

Then my mate pushes into me, and he's so big that a gasp catches in my throat. I feel every ridge of his cock as he enters me, I'm so tight. But God, it's so freaking good that I cry out. My fingers claw at the rock, desperate for something to hold on to. But there's nothing. There's just Vektal and his cock pushing into me.

He pushes even deeper, and then I feel something push against my bottom, feel the prod of that hard spur against the bud of my ass. That sends an entirely new set of sensations shooting through me, and I practically leap off the rock. "Again," I cry out when he pulls back. "Oh fuck, do that again!"

Then he thrusts into me, and instead of rubbing against my

clit, the spur pushes against the entrance of my ass. It feels weird and tight and oddly arousing. "We're definitely going to have to add doggy style to our repertoire," I tell him, panting.

"My sweet resonance," he grits out. "You—"

Something bright flashes in the sky. I freeze under Vektal, and we watch, breathless, as a spaceship, swimming with lights, hovers in the skies over the mountain. It circles and then hangs in the sky over the spot where the old cargo bay was left behind.

Where *we* were left behind.

I can't move as I watch the sky, waiting to see what happens. Over me, cock-deep inside me, Vektal is frozen as well.

The ship seems to hover for forever. Then the lights blink off, and it lifts up, winking out of the atmosphere.

I gasp with relief. "It's gone?"

"It seems they do not want metlaks," Vektal says, amusement in his voice. "And you, my sweet human, are now forever part of this world."

I touch my breastbone, and then I begin to thrum anew, my purring matching Vektal's. "I'm yours forever, aren't I?"

"Forever," he says, thrusting deep once more. He pumps into me over and over, until I'm crying out with my release. It's swift and rough, just like how he's taking me, and Vektal's own release is but moments behind. This time, when his seed spurts into me, I don't feel the heat of it. My body temperature's warmer now, like his. I'm not sure how it's possible, because a fever can damage humans, but I suspect the khui is busy inside me, rewriting all kinds of genetic things to make sure that I have a long, healthy life on this new planet.

Vektal lifts me off the rock and pulls me into his arms, and he can't stop kissing me. I laugh and kiss him back, and then we fall into the snow together, our pants down.

I huff, exhausted but still humming from within. I stare up at the night sky, checking for more spaceships, but all is quiet.

For better or for worse, we're here. I'm thinking it's for better. In fact, I know it's for better because the man next to me pulls me against him and begins to lick and nibble at my earlobes. "I'm pretty sure we're going to have to do that again," I tell him breathlessly. "My khui doesn't seem to be calming down much."

"I'm told it's most intense during the first few days of resonance. After that, we should be able to walk normally," he teases.

Well, thank God for that. "And then what comes next?"

"Home. Our den together." He touches my stomach. "Our kit." His fingers caress my flat stomach. "Hopefully the first of many human and sa-khui matings."

That . . . sounds pretty good to me. I push him onto his back, noticing that even my busted wrist doesn't hurt much anymore—the khui at work, maybe? I smile down at my mate. "Just as long as you don't go resonating for anyone else."

He shakes his head somberly. "One resonance mate. We mate for life."

I like the sound of that, too.

BONUS EPILOGUE

GEORGIE GOES HUNTING

Georgie

Nights might just be my favorite part of being on this planet with Vektal.

Don't get me wrong—it's all amazing. But the days are busy ones. If Vektal's not off hunting from dawn to dusk, he's leading his tribe. There are hunters to organize, advice to be doled out, and someone inevitably has an issue with something that needs arbitration of some kind. As chief, Vektal is team coach, office boss, and judge all at once. But at night? At night we can relax in our cave together and just . . . hang out. We don't have to do anything or guide anyone. It's understood that we're going to be in our cave, acting like newlyweds—or newly-mates—and people leave us alone.

That's why nights are my favorite.

Tonight Vektal is sprawled on the furs. He wears a loincloth and nothing else, and I'm playing with his big, weird feet as we talk about leather, of all things. We need a lot of it to make clothes for all the humans I brought with me, and we've nearly wiped out the tribe's supply they had in storage. More animals will need to be hunted, and there are certain ones that make better, softer leather than others. Or so he tells me.

I'm listening, but at the same time, I'm toying with his toes. This is our time alone together, and my thoughts almost always quickly turn to sex. Things are still new after a week and a half of being at the caves, and maybe it's the resonance having some lingering effects, or maybe it's that Vektal's just really, really good in bed, but I'm always eager for him to touch me, day or night, anytime, anywhere.

But Vektal's thoughts seem to be on leather, so I play with his piggies. Except they're not really "piggies." That term implies that there's a daintiness to things, and Vektal's feet are anything but. He's got three large splayed toes at the front and a weird, slender, hard heel, and like . . . that's it. I shake his feet, looking for a hidden toe somewhere, but there's nothing.

Vektal wiggles one of his toes at me when I touch the underside of his foot. "You are fascinated with my feet this day."

"Where's your toe? That's what I'm trying to figure out." I smile up at him, loving how relaxed he looks. He's got one arm under his head, and the other is on his belly. His eyes are heavy-lidded, and he looks . . . content. I love that. He's only like that with me. Around others, he has to be the leader, the one in charge, the one with all the answers. He's constantly "on." But with me? He can relax . . . and even be a bit silly.

He chuckles, moving his foot in my grasp. "What do you mean? All my toes are right there."

I shake my head, releasing his foot and crawling up his body to grab the hand he has resting on his belly. I hold his wrist and point at each finger. "One, two, three." And then I tap his thumb. "Four. Right?"

"Very good. You can count. I am truly proud." His firm mouth twitches with amusement.

I return to my seat and pull his foot into my lap again. I point at each toe. "One . . . two . . . three. Where's the other?"

He puts both arms behind his head, avoiding his horns. "I am amused that you think I need more."

"You have one less on each foot! It's weird!" I'm sure it has something to do with that oddly prominent heel of his, but I'm no biologist. Besides, I like teasing him.

"Weird?" He snorts. "You have a nipple between your legs. I think that, perhaps, is weird."

I choke on my laughter. "I what?"

Vektal's eyes gleam with a mixture of amusement and arousal. He pulls his foot out of my grasp and gets up on all fours, a predatory look in his gaze. My heart pounds and I get to my feet—or try to—only to have him pull me back down into his arms. We wrestle for control, but seeing as I'm practically half his size, I lose. I end up flat on my back in the furs, my mate looming over me with a triumphant smile on his face.

"Let me show you," he murmurs. One big hand tugs up my tunic, shoving it to my neck and revealing my breasts to the open air. Vektal gazes down at them as my breath hitches, and when he caresses my nipple, I bite back a moan. "One." He moves his hand to the other and gives it a teasing touch. "Two."

"Very good. You can count," I tease back, using his words against him. It sounds breathless and turned on when I say it, though.

He slides that big hand down into my pants, cupping my pussy and then slipping a finger through my folds. "Three." He brushes it over my clit. "A very perfect three."

I arch against his hand, gasping. "That . . . that's my clit." I cling to him, desperately wanting him to keep petting me there. I'm already aroused and wet with need, and squirming against his touch. "It's not a nipple."

"It is the sweetest nipple," he tells me stubbornly, and continues to circle it in soft, teasing strokes, just the way I like. Vektal leans in close. "And when I suck on it, I make my mate come."

I rock against his hand, frantic for more. "You know you are a very infuriating man." I pant the words out, and they don't sound frustrated in the slightest. They sound like a caress. "My very, very infuriating, big, handsome man." He dips a finger lower, stroking it into my core, and I melt. "With the best hands."

"And mouth."

I moan at that. I absolutely want his mouth on me. He leans down and gives me a hungry kiss, then slides his hand out of my leather pants. When I whimper a protest, Vektal pulls on the drawstring to my pants, loosening them, and then tugs them down my thighs. When they're halfway down my legs, he yanks them off and tosses them aside, and then pushes his big head between my thighs. He wraps one massive hand around my leg, holding me in place as he licks and sucks on his favorite spot.

I don't care if he calls it a "clit" or a "nipple," as long as he does this to me on a regular basis. I move against his mouth, grasping his horns and holding on for dear life as he eats me out with hungry enthusiasm. He knows just how to make my toes curl, to bring me to the brink of climax in no time at all, but instead of pushing me over the edge, he pulls back, lowering his head and then teasing his tongue at the entrance to my core as I writhe pitifully, wanting the orgasm that's been denied me.

He loves remaining between my legs. I think he could lick me out for hours on end. I've never been with anyone quite so . . . generous with his mouth.

And tongue.

And lips.

Pretty much everything, really. I squirm as he lavishes attention on my core, then nuzzles his way back up to my clit. "Vektal," I pant as he drives me close to the edge again. "I'm so close. Want you inside me. Don't make me come without you."

"Never," he murmurs between kisses on my mound. "Never."

He surges over me, and I'm greedy as I clutch at him, at his big shoulders and warm, muscular chest. At the skin that feels like the most incredible suede under my fingertips. Vektal pauses to kiss my mouth oh-so-gently, and then he rises over me, big and hulking and beautiful, and thrusts deep.

I gasp at the awareness of him piercing me—it never grows old. I feel every ridge as he plunges, the sensations battering through me in brutal succession. He sinks in and then flexes his hips, grinding his spur against my clit in a way that makes my entire body light up with fierce arousal. I hitch my legs around his hips, holding on tight as he claims me for himself. Every stroke feels like he's claiming me all over again, and when my orgasm thunders through my body, I'm not at all surprised to find that my khui is purring with satisfaction.

Even though we've fulfilled resonance, it still purrs when I'm around Vektal, especially when we're making love. It's like it knows how happy I am and it's telling me that it's happy, too.

Vektal moves over me, seeking his own release, and I whisper soft words of encouragement as he rocks into me, and when he comes, he shudders, a laugh huffing out of his throat as he collapses, spent. I wind my arms around his neck, pressing kisses to his skin everywhere I can. He's addictive, this big alien of mine. I'm no longer thinking that I'm screwed, being stranded here on this inhospitable planet.

I feel . . . lucky. Because I get to be with him, always. I love that.

I love him, too.

Vektal rolls off of me too quickly, getting a bit of fur scrap to clean up. He wets it and takes care of me, his fingers lingering between my thighs as a look of pride settles on his face. It's like seeing my well-used body makes him proud. A caveman-esque "I did that to her" moment. When he's done, he settles onto his back and pulls me against him. I curl up next to him, my hand on his chest, feeling the low thrum of his pleased khui as it hums to mine. I smile, pressing a kiss to his warm skin and tangling my feet with his legs. "So what was that laugh for?"

He covers the hand I put on his chest, and his paws seem huge compared to my own. I'll never get over our size difference. "What laugh?"

I flick his nipple. "You laughed when you came. It was cute, but I'm wondering why you laughed."

"Because I am happy." He shrugs, then wraps an arm around me, pulling me closer. "Sometimes I cannot believe it."

I'm not the most sentimental of women, but Vektal's making me feel all kinds of things. My heart pounds as if it's going to burst with love for him, my khui singing happily. I smile against his skin, kissing him again. "I'm happy, too. Is that bad?"

"Why would it be bad?"

I think of everything we've been through. Of weird green aliens kidnapping me and the other human women from Earth, enslaving us and hurting us, then abandoning us in a snowy place where we thought we wouldn't survive. Yet we did, and Vektal's people took us in. It's been a big adjustment for some of the girls. A few resonated right away, like me and Vektal, and they seem content. Others . . . well, others are still coping.

It's a lot. I understand that it's going to take time. "Some of the others are having difficulty settling in. It makes me feel a little guilty to be so happy."

He rubs my shoulder. "You are the chief's mate. You set an example for the others. If you are happy, maybe they will see it is all right to be happy, too."

My sweet, darling, innocent mate. I don't point out that it's going to take a lot more than a few smiles to get some of the women through their trauma. In his way, he's trying, though. I pat his chest. "Maybe so. What are you doing tomorrow?"

"Hunting." Vektal presses a kiss to the top of my head and squeezes me tight. The only thing better than the great sex might be the intense cuddling that comes after. He can't get enough of touching me, and I eat it up with a spoon. "I will stay close, though. I do not wish to leave my mate for long. I do not want her lonely."

As if I'd be lonely. There are forty-plus people living in the same cave system. All I have to do is step out of our private cave and be surrounded by the tribe. But it also wouldn't be the same as being with Vektal. I'll miss him when we have to spend a night apart. I know that day is coming soon, but I'm not ready for it quite yet. I'm still happily in the clingy phase of early love. I think about him leaving in the morning, and it makes me sad. There's so much that pulls at his attention that I feel selfish for wanting to spend more time with him. If he's not busy leading the tribe, he's got hunting duties or has to help with one of the other bajillion tasks that must be done by hand.

There's plenty for me to do. I know there is. Hemalo has

started showing me how to tan leather that Vektal brings back, and there's cooking and sewing and gathering herbs. There are baskets to be woven from hardened hide strips and roots to be dried and so many things that I took for granted back home. Did I want to grab a morning coffee and a donut? Here I'd have to grow and gather the beans for the coffee, grind them myself, then kill an animal for its leather, sew and treat a waterproof pouch, create a tripod out of animal bones to hang the pouch over the fire . . . which I'd also have to make, along with a mug made out of animal bone to hold the drink.

Don't even get me started on the damn donut. The sa-khui don't seem to have a thing for sweets.

It's an overwhelming amount of work, and I don't mind doing my fair share. I really don't. Everyone pitches in, and I love that the little tribe, between gossiping and laughing, makes things as pleasant as can be by working together and sharing the load. But . . . hunting is work, too.

I consider going to hunt with Vektal. Earlier today, I saw Farli, the young teenage girl sa-khui, holding a spear and talking with one of the alien men. She had been gesturing at the snowy hills and had a dead rabbit—no, a hopper, I remind myself—strapped to her belt. She'd been hunting. If a teen girl can go hunting, surely I can go with my mate? I haven't yet. After my initial journey here, I was too exhausted and overwhelmed by the new world to even think about venturing out of the cave. But I've been here several days now, and I'm feeling a little more settled.

Maybe Vektal's right and I should set an example for the other human women. I can go hunting and start tackling this world. I can show everyone that just because we're human, it doesn't mean we have to cower in the caves and be afraid of this new life. That it can be as beautiful and grand as we make it. We just have to put in the effort.

"Georgie? My mate?" Vektal runs his fingers along my jaw, gazing down at me. "Did you fall asleep? You are quiet."

"I'm awake. I was just thinking." I sit up, letting my hair spill over my shoulder, and give him a sultry smile. I've still got my bulky tunic on and my hair is tangled, but I feel sexy and pretty whenever I'm with him. When his eyes light up at the sight of me, I know I'm utterly delectable in his eyes. "I'm going with you tomorrow."

Vektal looks at me in surprise. "I thought you did not know how to hunt."

"I don't." I reach down and poke his chest. "You're going to show me how. We're going to set an example for everyone else, just like you said. I'll learn how to hunt, and maybe I can even double how much you bring in. If there's two of us working, it should go quickly, right?"

He blinks at me and is quiet for a long moment. "I do not think it will be quicker if we work together," he says slowly. "You cannot learn to hunt in one day."

"But it's a skill I should learn, isn't it?" I give him a bright smile. "And you'll show me how?"

Vektal pulls me down against him and brushes my hair back from my face. "My lovely mate, you know I would do anything for you. I would eat fire if you asked me to."

I lean in and rub my nose against his, teasing. "Then it's a good thing that I don't want you eating fire. I'd rather you eat me."

Vektal

It feels disloyal . . . but I am not looking forward to hunting with my mate.

I keep these thoughts to myself, because they would hurt Georgie. She is determined to be as capable as any other hunter. She is smart and clever, and I have no doubt she will pick things up quickly.

She is just . . . small. And fragile. I try not to watch her too closely as we rise before dawn and dress to hunt. Humans are not nearly as hardy as sa-khui, and this worries me. She is my mate, and I feel very protective of her. The moment she puts on her boots and clumsily laces them up, I want to push her hands aside and do it properly for her. I want to put another layer of furs on her when she dresses, because the winds tear at fragile human skin.

Sa-khui instinct tells me to protect her. But as her mate, I know it will only make her sad and upset. I know Georgie. I know how she thinks. She is determined and strong-willed and wants to be as useful as any other sa-khui hunter.

She will hunt . . . and so I must teach her to be the best hunter possible, so she can be safe, so she will know how to take care of herself in the wilds. Bringing Georgie into danger goes against everything I am as a newly mated male, but I want to please my mate more than anything, so I swallow my worries. "Are you ready to go out?" I ask her as she settles a fur cape over her shoulders.

"I think so!" Her eyes are shining with excitement, her cheeks flushed pink. "Am I good? What do you think?"

I take the hood of the cloak and pull it over her head, unable to stop my protective instincts. "Are you hungry? We should eat something hot first, in case the weather is foul."

"Do you normally fill up before going out?" Georgie asks, curious. "I thought you skipped breakfast."

But I am not you, I want to say. You are my precious, soft mate, and I must look out for you. "This day I am hungry," I declare. "It will not hurt to eat before we journey."

"All right. I'll go see what's for breakfast." She glances over at me, then leans in. "What's the name of the woman by the fire? The one with the looping braids?"

"Sevvah," I remind her.

Her smile is brilliant. "Sevvah. Thank you." She grabs my hand and pulls herself up against me, tilting her head back and pursing her lips. I know this movement. I am to kiss her. I lean in and press my mouth to hers, expecting her pink tongue to flick against mine, but she just gives me a smacking kiss and releases me, then rushes out of the cave, heading for the community fire, where there is always a hot meal waiting and ready.

I walk out of our private cave, too, but I head for the entrance. There, along the wall, we keep a ready supply of freshly sharpened spears, and I pick through them, looking for a

232 • RUBY DIXON

weapon small enough to fit my Georgie's slender, five-fingered hand.

"Did you break your spear?" a voice asks, and a hand thumps my shoulder in greeting. Harrec—one of the younger hunters in the tribe, and one of the louder mouths, too. He grins at me, his long face bright with interest. "That spear you are holding does not look big enough for those mighty hands of yours."

"It is for Georgie," I admit. "She wishes to learn hunting, so I will teach her."

Harrec gives me a look of surprise, then laughs. "Shorshie? To hunt?"

His amusement irritates me. "Yes."

"Did you not pluck her out of a trap when you found her?"

Harrec is good-natured and clever most times, but I find that when it comes to my new mate, I do not have a sense of humor. I stare at him, frowning. "Are you saying a human female cannot hunt?"

I ignore that I had the same worry a short time ago.

"All females can hunt." Harrec shrugs. "I am just saying, perhaps giving that one a spear is a bad idea."

"I will mark your concern," I reply dryly. His words have made me more determined than ever to show my mate how to hunt. I do not like anyone thinking less of her. She is strong and brave and good. Just because she stumbled into a trap does not mean she is a fool. She has told me that such traps are not common where she is from, just like the heavy snow. It seems odd to me, but if this is true, of course she does not know these dangers. I study the spear in my hands. Light but with a good, sharp point. It must be one of Farli's.

Harrec moves a few paces away, waving an arm. "Warrek! Come here! Listen to what your chief has planned for today."

I bite back a groan. My tribe is full of nosy, nosy hunters. "Do you not have traps to check, Harrec?"

"Soon." He grins, then races over to the taller, older hunter. Warrek is the opposite of Harrec in every way—he is tall and quiet, his mane a flowing waterfall down his back compared to Harrec's tangled, chopped mess. His gaze is solemn and patient as he regards me. Sometimes it is hard to believe Eklan raised them both.

Warrek looks at the smaller spear in my hands and then at me. "Training?"

I nod.

"Shall I take her out on the kit trails?" Warrek's question is somber, and it is not an unreasonable one. Warrek teaches all of the kits how to hunt, how to read tracks, how to learn their surroundings. Naturally, he would offer.

Just the thought of Warrek spending all day with my mate bothers me, though. I imagine him guiding her hands, showing her how to hold a spear. I picture solemn Warrek sharing a secret smile with my mate as they look for tracks and . . . I do not like any of it. "I will show her."

"He is growling like a cornered metlak," Harrec jokes, taking a step back as if afraid. "Do not get between a newly mated hunter and his female, my friend."

Warrek only blinks at me, ever calm. "Remember to be patient, my chief. A newly fledged hunter requires patience."

"So does Harrec," I grit out. "And I have not killed him yet."

Harrec just laughs, and Georgie comes over with a bowl in her hands for us to share as the two hunters finally leave me alone. She looks up at me with curiosity, and I merely touch her chin. Sometimes just touching her settles me. "Everything all right?" she asks, holding the bowl up so I can have a taste. "You look annoyed."

"I am better now," I promise her, and take a sip. I make sure to put my mouth on the same spot where she drank from, because even the smallest taste of her is perfection. "Shall we get going?"

She nods with enthusiasm.

It goes . . . poorly.

I take my eager mate out into the snowy hills. Almost immediately, she strains to keep up. I have forgotten that humans have much shorter legs, and their weaker bodies cannot wade through the snow as easily as the sa-khui's can. I hate to see her struggle, but she will not let me carry her. Georgie insists she can walk the trail, and so I slow down my steps to keep pace with her.

We do not make it very far, and when we do reach the good hunting grounds, my mate is panting and loud, her breath rasping and her feet crunching through the snow. She does not know how to move silently, and it seems cruel to demand silence when she is gasping for breath.

"Perhaps a spear is the wrong choice," I suggest to my mate after her footsteps scare a pair of fat birds out of a nearby shrub. "Perhaps a different weapon is wisest."

Something that will allow my mate to hunt from afar, because she will never get close to her prey at this rate.

Leaning heavily on the spear, she looks over at me. Her face is sweaty and she pushed the warm hood off long ago. Her cheeks are bright pink, and so is the tip of her nose. She looks exhausted. "Maybe your sword, then? I guess I could try that."

"Not my sword," I say as kindly as I can. "It is little more than an oversized knife. You would need to get very close with it, and I do not want you in danger."

"From birds and rabbits?" She looks at me strangely.

"Those are not the only things we hunt. I want you to be prepared for anything."

She nods, a hand on her hip as she catches her breath. "Why do you use a sword anyhow? No one else does."

I shrug. "It is how my father taught me, and his father taught him. I do not only use a sword, of course. As chief, though, I need to show my tribe I can hunt in many different ways."

"So it's to show off?" Georgie chuckles. "All right, then. What do you think I should use?"

I consider this for a moment. What would keep my Georgie at a safe distance from the creatures she hunts? I imagine her chasing after a herd of dvisti and frown because they are large animals and their hooves can be sharp when they kick. Snow cats are out. Two-teeth are out, because they could bite her. Quilled beasts, too. I do not want her wounded.

I am not even sure I like the idea of her fishing, because the waters hold just as many dangers as the snow.

But there must be something . . . "How good are you with a bola?"

Georgie blinks at me. "I don't think I've ever used one. Can you show me how?"

I nod. For the next while, I show her how the bola works. It is two rock-filled leather sacks at the ends of a long length of cord. I show her how to swing them around, and when she spies a bird or a hopper, she can fling the bola forward, tangling her prey and bringing it down for the kill. Her movements are clumsy as she lifts it, but Georgie seems excited to give it a try. I take it from her and demonstrate the bola for her one more time and then hand it over. "We will practice," I say, pointing at one of the distant pink twigs jutting from the ground. "See if you can hit that tree."

She squints at it. "How come that tree looks different than the ones in the mountains? It looks . . . kinda weak and puny."

"The ones in the mountains are hard and strong. These are weaker, with bulbous roots." I tap the spear I am holding. "We make our weapons out of bone because it is foolish to go to the mountains just for wood."

"And that's why we burn dung chips," Georgie says, nodding. She toys with the bola in her hands, testing it. "So how come we don't live in the mountains with all the wood?"

"Because there are far too many metlaks and our cave here is much, much nicer."

She sighs heavily. "I'm dreaming of a nice hot bath after this, I admit."

"You are doing well. Come. Try the bola."

Georgie nods, that stubborn look of determination on her strange face. I love the sight, and I know she will give this her all. Nothing will keep my Georgie from something she wishes to accomplish. She lifts her arm, swings it around just as I've shown her—

The end of the bola—a heavy, rock-filled bag—slams into Georgie's delicate face.

My mate crashes to the ground.

I roar with terror.

Georgie

Vektal's bellow of agony keeps me from bursting into tears.

I clutch at my face, groaning, flat on my back. My nose feels as if it's been pushed in, and everything throbs with intense, fiery pain. Fuck, fuck fuck fuck. I should have known that it looked too easy, that my shorter arms can't swing Vektal's long bola like he can. I just pummeled my face like an idiot.

He's immediately at my side, pulling me into his arms. *"Georgie!"*

"I'm okay," I manage, holding on to my face. It really does feel flattened. "I'm okay. I swear. I was just . . . surprised."

I'm suddenly squished against Vektal's big chest, and he holds me tight. At first I think he's resonating again, but when his khui is silent, I realize he's just shaking. He's terrified—for me.

That makes me push my pain aside, and I tap his chest. "Lemme up, honey. I promise I'm fine."

"I do not like this," he grits out. "You are fragile."

"Okay," I say, trying to soothe him. "Let's bring it down a

notch. I'm just not used to your weapons, that's all. It was a simple mistake. Here, look. I'm fine." I reach out and touch my nose, and even though it hurts like the dickens, it seems to be all in place. "I didn't even hit myself hard."

Vektal cups my face in one of those giant mitts of his and studies me so intently I know he's looking for injuries. "Your nose is swelling," he says accusingly. "You are hurt."

"It's fine," I reassure him.

"It is not fine." The look in his eyes is almost frantic. "I will not teach you hunting if you will just hurt yourself."

I stiffen at that and try to push out of his clinging arms, but he won't let me go. "Hang on a moment. Do you have a problem with me hunting because I'm a girl?"

"No, I have a problem with you hunting because you are my mate, and you are carrying my kit, and the thought of you being hurt tears my heart out of my chest." He runs his hand down my arm and then across my belly, as if making sure all of me is still whole, even though all I did was sock myself in the face. "Georgie, we cannot do this. I cannot bear it."

"So it's not because I'm a girl?"

He clutches me tighter to his chest. "I do not care if all the other females hunt. But you must not. I cannot handle it."

Okay, that makes me feel better. This is just Vektal being overprotective; it's not a gender issue. I relax a little, stroking his arm. "Babe, it's okay. Really. I'm fine. I just wanted to help out, but I guess I'm not being very helpful." I keep rubbing his arm until he stops shaking and the terror leaves his face. "What if . . . what if you show me how to set down traps instead?"

"Traps," he echoes, and then nearly squeezes the life out of me. "Yes. Traps. Perfect. We will do traps."

"Great." I breathe a sigh of relief and touch my nose again.

It throbs, but I'm pretty confident it's all fine. "I'm not bleeding, am I?"

Vektal's eyes go wide with alarm, and then my head tilts back and I have the world's biggest alien staring up my nostrils.

Perhaps I should have thought this through before volunteering to go hunting. I knew I wouldn't be great at it, but I've clearly underestimated Vektal's protective nature. It's sweet, though. It's just going to take some getting used to. So I pat his hand and then give him a smile, even though it makes my face ache. "Help me get up, and let's work on this trapping thing."

Vektal watches me like a hawk as he shows me how to set traps. I suspect he's waiting to see if I show the slightest bit of pain, and if I do, we're going to head home. I ignore my throbbing face and concentrate on what he's demonstrating, determined to get this right. I'm not exactly setting a great example for my people so far. There has to be something I can do. I don't like the idea of the others feeling trapped in the cave. If they want to hunt, I want to show them they absolutely can hunt. I want everyone to be free to choose how they contribute to the tribe.

As for me? It's quickly becoming clear that I'm not a huntress. I can't help but think of Liz, who'd probably rock this. I hope she's safe with Raahosh and he's treating her well. She'd probably laugh at me beaning myself with the bola, and it wouldn't feel like such a big deal. I glance over at Vektal, and he's watching me with those fervent, worried eyes.

Right. I gesture at the trap he's showing me. "Can you go through it one more time?"

He does, demonstrating how it works. It's all about bending one of the willowy pink trees and setting a snare in the snow.

The trap is anchored with a twig, and the braided leather twine is set to create a loop. A few dried berries are tossed into the snow nearby to entice a hopper in, and once it triggers the trap, the snare tightens and catches the creature. It's then disposed of with a kind knife to the throat to put it out of its misery.

It takes me forever to get the snare to set, because it keeps popping off of the branch. When I finally accomplish it, though, I feel proud. Relieved. I give Vektal a happy smile and he hugs me against his chest, his big body practically swallowing mine. "You have done very well, my resonance."

Finally. Something I can do well. "So do we come back and check this tomorrow?"

"No, we set more snares." He gestures along the cliffs, toward the distant stream we passed some time ago. "This is a popular game trail. More snares nearby will be wise. The more you set, the more likely it is that you will catch something and bring meat home." He hands me another length of cord. "Come. We have more to do."

I try not to droop at that. More? But I nod, determined to show I can keep up.

We set three more traps, each one a fair walk away from the others. So the game does not smell anything that might be caught, Vektal tells me. By the time we're done, the twin suns are high in the sky and I'm utterly exhausted. My hands are shaky as I hold the spear I'm using for a walking stick, and I manage a brave smile for my mate. "Okay. What now?"

Vektal cups my chin, running his thumb along my jaw as he studies me. "You look tired."

"I am, but I can keep up. Are there more traps?" Please, please don't let there be more.

He shakes his head. "We will return for now." He strokes my

jaw again, looking at me thoughtfully. "Would you . . . May I carry you?"

I hesitate. I'm so tired that the thought of him carrying me back to the cave makes me want to cry with sheer joy. At the same time, I don't want to seem weak or helpless. "Will you think less of me if I say yes?"

"Never. It would bring me joy to take care of you." He drops to his knees in the snow and gestures at his broad shoulders.

I climb up and hook my arms around his neck, and I'm reminded of our journey through the mountains. He carried me on his back all the way to his home, and he did so without breaking a sweat. He hefts me once I'm settled, getting to his feet, and his arms go around my legs, holding me against him. He turns his head, nearly taking my eye out with one of his horns. "Good?"

"Good," I agree, hunching a little so I can tuck my head against his shoulder. "This remind you of anything?"

"Last night, when you wrapped your legs around me and begged for me to go deeper?"

I blush, smacking his shoulder. "No! Of when we first got together."

"When I greeted you with my tongue on your cunt?"

I roll my eyes, because clearly someone has sex on the brain. "Never mind. I give up."

Vektal chuckles, adjusting me on his back with a slight bounce. The spears are pressed between us, tied to his back, but overall, it's comfortable and pleasant, and I snuggle against my mate, happy that he's so damn strong.

"Are we far out from the cave?" I ask, yawning. "We must be a pretty good distance. I feel like we've walked over every hill out here."

He is quiet.

That deflates my spirits a little. "We're not far at all, are we?"

"Will it wound you if I say no?" Vektal hesitates a moment longer and then continues. "We are on the kit trails."

"Kit trails?"

"Where Warrek takes the young when he teaches them to hunt."

"Oh." Well, that's embarrassing. "I guess . . . should we check the traps before we head in?"

"Do you want to?"

I swallow. "Honestly? I don't know. Today has been a lot, and the thought of discovering a creature in my trap kinda makes my stomach turn. I know I'm trying to learn how to hunt, but . . ." I trail off. I think about finding some hopper-rabbit or, worse, one of those pony things, and me having to kill it to bring it in as meat. I never killed anything bigger than a spider back home, and the thought is a rough one. "I'm not sure I'm ready for the killing part of the hunt."

Vektal pauses. "So you would leave it to suffer in the trap all night?"

Fuck. I didn't think about that. "No." I feel dangerously close to tears. Not just because this new life means I sometimes have to kill my own food to survive, but because I feel as if I'm disappointing Vektal, the person that I've come to rely on and love. I want him to be proud of me, and right now I don't feel like someone to be proud of. "Let's go check them, then. I don't want to leave anything to suffer."

"It is a good choice, my mate."

Vektal

This is harder than I thought it would be.

The traps are empty, and I do not know who is more relieved, myself or Georgie. We head back to the tribal caves, and my mate is quiet. As we approach, I see Warrek outside with Sessah, crouching in the snow and studying tracks. Georgie seems to shrink down against me, and she is utterly silent as we pass them.

I know she is comparing herself to Sessah, who is small but already shows signs of being a great hunter.

I should have known this was too much for my mate. She comes from a place where she did not need to hunt to survive. She has a soft heart and does not like to eat raw meat, fresh from the kill. Of course she will struggle with hunting and killing her own food. I know she wants to be strong and to contribute to the tribe, but this is not how to do it.

I am failing her as a mate.

I carry Georgie inside the main cave, but instead of heading to our private quarters, I walk to the pool in the center. It is warm and comforting, and will help ease her exhaustion. I nod at the others who watch us come in, but I do not talk to any of them. They know the look on my face.

"Oh, Vektal, I'm not sure I want to swim," Georgie protests, her voice tired. "I just want to go to bed."

I set her down gently by the edge of the pool. No one else is bathing at the moment, and I am glad. It will just be us. I turn to my mate and peel off one layer of leathers, then another. "This is not swimming. This is your mate taking care of you."

She shakes her head. "You don't have to—"

"Hush," I say softly. "It is a male's duty to ensure his mate is comfortable and happy. I will wash your mane for you and rub soapberries on your skin, and you will listen when I tell you how brave you are and how proud I am of you."

My mate bites her lip and looks ashamed as I undress her. "Vektal . . . I don't know if I'm cut out to be a hunter."

"Have I asked you to be one?"

"No, but it's important that I be able to take care of myself," she says desperately. "I don't want to be a burden. None of us do."

As if she could ever be such a thing. As if the mere sight of her in my furs does not fill me with so much joy it is unbearable. As if she and the other females have not brought hope back to our slowly dying tribe. "How can you think yourself a burden? Because you did not bring back fresh meat?" When she gazes up at me miserably, I pull off her last layer, enjoying the sight of my mate's naked body. She is still a little shy when it comes to disrobing, but I pull my clothes off, too, so she will not feel foolish. I strip down, then take my mate by the shoulders and turn her around so she can look at the rest of the tribe. "What do you see, my resonance?"

"A lot of people with clothes on," she mumbles.

I gesture to the fire. "You see Sevvah and Oshen, cooking food for the hunters that return." I point at Kashrem, who rocks his daughter and talks to Maylak as she sorts through her medicinal stores. "You see the healer and her mate, neither of whom hunts, but they still provide to the group." I do not see Hemalo, but old Eklan has a skin he is working on stretched over a frame, and I gesture at him. "You see those that work hides to help out. There are many in our tribe that do not hunt, and no one forces them to." I turn back to my mate, cupping her small jaw in my hand. I cannot help it—I love to touch her. "I am happy you wish to contribute, my resonance, but not if it hurts your spirit."

Her eyes fill with tears. The stubborn look returns to her face, and she swipes at them, irritated. "I'm not upset. I'm just . . . I wish I could be stronger. I always feel as if I'm not strong enough."

"Foolishness." I slide into the water and then hold a hand out to my mate, inviting her to join me. She follows me in, slipping between my thighs, her back to me. I grab the soapberries and pulp them in my hand, then slather her shoulders generously with their juice. "There are many kinds of strength, my mate. Hemalo and Kashrem do not hunt, because they have gentle hearts. Farli loves to hunt, because it brings her joy, but if she did not wish to, she could stay in the caves, like Asha, and sew and skin or cook or make weapons. Whatever pleases her." I rub Georgie's shoulders, wishing I could work my words into her head the same way. "If it does not bring you joy to hunt, let your mate do so for you."

She touches my slippery hand, bringing it to her face and rubbing her cheek against it. "You're not disappointed in me?"

"Never." I lean in and nuzzle her neck, wondering if anyone would notice—or care—if we mated right here in these waters. I know my people would not, but Georgie's are still new and skittish. They—

"Georgie!" cries a shrill human voice. It is one of the females with a pale, shorter mane. She bursts into tears as she hurries toward my mate. "There you are. I've been looking everywhere for you."

"Oh no." My mate squeezes my thigh and then swims forward in the pool, moving to the edge of the water. "What's wrong?"

"I. Got. My. Period!" the female cries. "If I have to use a leather tampon, I am going to lose my fucking mind! I need help!"

Georgie gives me an apologetic look, and I just nod at her, indicating she should help her friend. She climbs out of the pool, wraps my cloak around her naked body, and heads off with the crying female to solve the problem of a period, whatever that might be. She is the chief to her people, who all look to her. No wonder she wishes to succeed at everything. If she feels comfortable, they are comfortable. If she is miserable, they are miserable. I make a mental note to show her small tasks around the cave that can be easily taught but are still useful, and she can show them to her friends. If she is busy, she will not fret over hunting.

I relax in the water, thinking about my lovely mate and enjoying the warmth. A few of the other hunters come in, and I talk with them about the weather and hunting. When Georgie returns, she smiles at me and tosses my fur aside before slipping back into the water and swimming over to me.

"Miss me?" she asks, straddling my hips as I sit on the rock ledge. This time she faces me, and her teats are enticingly wet and gleaming. My cock stirs at the sight.

"I always miss you," I tell her. It is the truth.

She chuckles, settling her arms around my neck and leaning against me. "Well, crisis averted. Just call me the Paleolithic maxi-pad wrangler." At my confusion, she merely shakes her head and cuddles up against me. "Never mind. Long story. Sorry if I interrupted things."

"Interrupted?" I lazily run my hand down her back. "How so?"

"You know, in case things were about to get sexy." She brushes her thumb over my nipple. "But I wanted to make sure she was okay."

I hold my mate close, debating if I should pick her up and head back to our cave or finish bathing her. Which does Georgie want more? Mating or bathing? "I do not mind. You are the chief to your people. If they need you, you must be there for them."

"Just . . . not in any sort of hunting capacity." She sits up, watching me.

"Not if it wounds your spirit. Leave it to others. I would change nothing about you, my Georgie. I do not care if you hunt every day or if you never hunt again. If there is something that hurts your spirit to do, then let your mate handle it. All I care about is that you are happy."

She flings her arms around my neck. "I love you so damn much."

I kiss her everywhere I can, her brow, her cheek, her mouth. "Do you want to wash, or do you want your mate to lick your cunt?"

Georgie giggles, wriggling over me and making my cock grow hard. "I like my choices here. Let's go with the second one."

And that is why we are perfect for each other. Truly, my khui has chosen wisely.

ICE PLANET HONEYMOON

VEKTAL & GEORGIE

AUTHOR'S NOTE: While this novella completes Georgie and Vektal's main story, chronologically it occurs after *Barbarian Alien*, Liz and Raahosh's story. Therefore, this might contain a few spoilers about their story.

Georgie

I wake up to find Vektal watching me sleep. Again.

I yawn, rubbing my eyes, and give him a sleepy smile. "Hey there. How long have you been awake?"

The big alien shrugs, his face inches from mine. I'm snuggled under the furs in the cave that's now my home. As with every morning, I wake up with Vektal beside me, and he's always watching me. It's kind of cute. He reaches out and runs his big, blunt fingers through my tangled hair, pulling it forward over my shoulders and then sliding his hand down my arm. "I have been awake for some time. It is my custom to wake up before dawn."

"Oh." I grimace, because I'm guessing it's later than that. "Am I keeping you from something?"

"No." He touches my hair again.

"Then why are you staring?" I ask him with a chuckle as I settle back into the blankets, closing my eyes again. If we're not being kept from something, maybe I can steal a few more minutes of shut-eye.

"Because I like to watch you sleep," he says in that delicious, deep voice of his. "It is bad to watch you?"

"Not bad, no. I'm just not used to it." I smile and slide a little closer. "Then again, I'm not used to sleeping with someone. Or this planet. Or any of this, really."

Vektal wraps big arms around me and hauls me against his chest, tucking me against him and then stroking my hair. "Does this make you unhappy?"

I open my eyes, frowning into the pre-dawn darkness. That's . . . a strange thing to ask. "Unhappy?"

"You do not smile like the others. You do not laugh with delight. I want to hear you laugh more, my Georgie." He says my name carefully, doing his best to pronounce the hard *g* sounds. "Is something bothering you?"

Bothering me? Only a small something, really, and I feel too selfish to ask for it. So I just smile against his stomach and snuggle closer, looping an arm over his chest and tucking my cheek against his skin. I love to cuddle against his big, brawny chest. I don't mind the thick plating that makes parts of him less snuggleable, because the rest of him is suede-soft over rock-hard muscles.

I sigh with contentment and close my eyes, listening to his heartbeat and his khui as it hums gently in his chest. I'm a little sad that the sound of it changed. It took me a bit to notice it, but the sound of his khui changed a few days after I first got mine, and when I asked him about it, he told me that resonance had truly been fulfilled, and both our khui were sated. It was surprising to me because I'd thought he'd gotten me pregnant right away, but I guess not. Sometimes I miss that wild, crazy beat of his khui, but I like the contented purring of today, too.

Vektal's hand steals to my hair and he strokes it again. "Do you wish to stay in the furs this day, my mate?"

"I'm just being lazy," I tell him, tracing a finger along his chest. "Give me a few more minutes and I'll wake up for real."

"Take as long as you like." He strokes my back. "I enjoy holding you."

Oh, I know he does. He's by far the handsiest man I've ever met. He's constantly touching me or caressing me, as if he needs to reassure himself that I'm here and I exist. I understand it. After learning what I have of these people and of how few females there were until we came along? No wonder he's so protective. I suspect if he didn't have to go hunting he'd just sit around all day and watch me.

The thought of the big, fierce-looking Vektal sitting in a corner of the cave and watching me sew clothing by the fire as if it's the most fascinating thing ever makes me smile. It's been a few weeks since we arrived here, but I'm not sick of him in the slightest. I worried that being the object of such attention might get tiresome, that he'd grow used to me or I'd get irked by his hovering, but if anything, we're closer by the day. I love how attentive he is. I love how he's fascinated by everything about me, as if I'm some sort of unique unicorn of a human instead of just an average-looking girl from Florida.

I'm not tired of him, either. Not in the slightest.

I press a kiss to his skin, running my fingertips along his sculpted abs. "So you've been awake for a bit?"

He grunts agreement.

"Any new resonances?"

Vektal chuckles, and I can hear the sound as it moves through his chest. "You ask that every day."

"It felt like it was happening every day," I admit. We're up to five now—mine, Liz, Marlene, Nora, Stacy, and Ariana. Most of them happened right away, but I've seen how the guys watch the girls and I know it has to be on their minds as much as it is on mine.

Vektal rumbles with laughter again. "It is a rare thing, this I promise."

If he says so. Doesn't seem all that rare to me so far, but he's the expert. I run a fingertip along the dip of his navel just because I like touching him. He shudders underneath my caress and I decide I like that, too. "Everyone settled in this morning? No crying?"

My big alien makes a disgruntled sound in his throat. "There is always some crying."

"There is," I admit. "It's to be expected."

"You did not cry." He wraps a curl of my hair around one finger.

My smile falters. "Maybe I just haven't cried yet," I whisper. I'm the unofficial leader of the humans, after all. I've had to be strong ever since we got here, because I was the one with the plan to attack our captors, I was the one that went out to find help, I was the one who resonated to Vektal, the strong, capable—and yummy—chief of the alien tribe here. Everyone's viewed the humans here as my tribe, and me as their chief, and even us humans have kinda fallen into that way of thinking. They come to me when they're worried or scared, as if I'm in charge.

Sometimes, it feels like a lot. I'm the same age they are, but I don't get to be the one that cries about our fate, or the one that stays in bed all day. I have to be a responsible leader, even when I feel just as overwhelmed and helpless as they do.

But I won't focus on that right now. I wouldn't change anything that's happened since we arrived on this planet, right from the very first time I met Vektal and he was feasting between my thighs as if he'd never tasted anything so good. I squeeze my legs together at the delicious memory. "Who was crying this morning?"

"Air-ee-yon-uh."

Ah. "Is Zolaya with her?" If her mate is out hunting, I should probably go see what's bothering her, do some damage control. Some of the girls here aren't being very welcoming to her and most of the aliens are puzzled by her constant tears. Her mate is a sweetheart, though, and I'm so glad he dotes on her like he does.

"Yes, and Mar-lenn too."

"Then she'll be okay."

He grunts. "I heard that Bek has been sneaking off with one of the humans, as well."

"That would be Claire," I admit. I've heard this too but said nothing because Claire didn't want me to. "Is it a bad idea?"

"A pleasure mate? No." Vektal shifts as I tease his belly button again, and I realize he's ticklish. How have I not known this after being with him for weeks now? It makes me want to tickle more, even though we should probably be getting up. "It is just that . . ." He pauses, choosing his words. "Bek is a very strong-minded hunter."

I know what he's saying, what he's thinking. Claire is a sweetheart, but she's also not a very strong-willed personality. I worry she's going to get steamrolled by a guy and it'll end up being a messy, volatile situation. I know a lot of these guys are coming to terms with the fact that there's now a bunch of single women in the tribe, and they're overzealous in their eagerness to impress. "You think I should tell her to stop seeing him?"

"Why?" He sounds genuinely confused.

"So he doesn't get the wrong idea and force himself on her if she says no?"

I can feel Vektal's body stiffen underneath me. "No male would do such a thing, my sweet resonance. How can you think that?"

I sit up, looking into his eyes. He's shocked. I've shocked my darling Vektal. It truly has never occurred to him that someone would want to hurt a human woman. But since we just got out of an ugly situation, that thought's on my mind far too much. I think of Dominique, dead in the snow, and the ache I constantly fight returns. I smile at Vektal, patting his chest. "Of course he wouldn't, babe. I'm sure your hunters are as noble as you are."

There's something sweet and innocent about Vektal. Despite his ferociousness and the harsh world they live in, he's charmingly naïve and adorable for it.

I hope he never loses it and becomes as jaded as I am.

Vektal

My Georgie is distracted.

It has been only hands of days since she and the humans arrived and changed our lives forever. In those hands of days, though, I have learned the deep breaths she makes as she sleeps, the way she shivers and jumps when she bathes herself in the morning, and the way her smile lights her eyes. She smiles this day, but her eyes do not shine with the same amusement, and I wonder what is wrong.

For me, the day has never been so full of promise and joy. My mate—a thought which still staggers me—sits by the fire with two of her humans, sewing tunics and chatting. In her belly, she carries my kit. My khui rumbles a low, pleasant murmur at the sight of her, and I rub my chest absently, watching her from afar when I should be sharpening the point of my spear. I must go check traps soon, but I cannot bring myself to leave the cave, not when Georgie sits next to Jo-see and Ki-rah and gives her mane a little toss before leaning over her sewing once more. The curls of her incredibly soft mane rest against her shoulders and invite touching. I think of them, and how her mane feels when it spills over my thighs when she puts her mouth on me in that human way of hers that upends my world and makes me see stars.

I know all this about her. And I know when she is distressed over something. It is in the way she takes a little longer to answer each question, in the small furrow between her brows when she sews, the way she stares at the fire a little too long.

She says that she is happy with me, but . . . is this a lie? Am I not enough for my beautiful human? Because she is everything to me.

Georgie looks up from her sewing, and her gaze catches mine. The smile she sends in my direction is genuine and full of affection, and I am even more pleased when she puts a hand to her mouth and purses her lips. This is called "blowing kisses" and it is meant to mimic a mouth-mating from afar. I do the same, putting my hand to my mouth, and then I lick it long and slow so she may know exactly what parts of her I am thinking of mating.

Her cheeks flush bright red and she ducks her head, but she is smiling. Whatever it is that troubles her, it is not our mating, then. Pleased, I pick up my spear and get to my feet. Time to hunt.

Nearby, Haeden looks at me with disgust. "Did you just lick your hand?"

"It was for my mate," I tell him, as if that explains everything.

He just grunts, shaking his head at me.

He does not understand what it is like to be freshly resonated to such a female. He never will, and for a moment, I feel pity for him.

But pity will not fill my Georgie's belly, so I go hunting anyhow.

That evening, after my traps have been cleared and reset, the game cached and a fresh kill brought home and (disgustingly) cooked for my Georgie, we retreat to our private cave. I immediately put the privacy screen up, and my mate just cocks an eyebrow at me in that strange human way.

"You going to wash up?"

"No. I am going to mate my sweet human's cunt with my tongue," I tell her, dragging her into my arms and pulling her close for a mouth-mating. I kiss her, teasing her with tiny licks and loving the little sighs of need she makes as I hold her. "It has been far too long since I have tasted my mate."

Georgie laughs. "You tasted her just this morning."

"Far, far too long," I agree, dropping to my knees in front of her. I pull on the laces of her leggings and then notice that she has another pair of very short leggings on underneath. "What . . . what are these?"

"Those are leather panties," she says proudly. "I made them myself."

"But . . . why?" There is a drawstring at the waist and they end just below her hips. "They do not seem warm at all. Are these parts of you cold?" I look up at her in surprise. Is this something new I must worry about for my mate? That her cunt gets chilled easily?

"Um, because that's what you wear under pants?" She shrugs, her expression embarrassed. "It's kind of like the breast band."

Another thing I have yet to understand. But this is distracting her away from the mating, so all I say is, "Ah. May I take them off of you?"

"Of course." Her hands go to my face and she caresses my jaw. "I missed you today."

"I was not gone long." Even so, I missed her, too. "Soon I will have to go out on a longer hunt. It will be my turn."

"I know. I'm just trying to prepare myself." She runs a finger along my lower lip. "Until then, we have fun, right?"

"When I come back, we will have so much 'fun' you will not be able to walk straight for days." I undo the strange laces on her short leggings and slide them down to reveal the delicate tuft of curls between her thighs. "Ahhh. I am home."

Georgie chuckles. "Is that your home now, babe?"

"Why would it not be? My tongue fits here perfectly." I wrap an arm around her hips and lick the seam of her cunt. "My fingers fit here perfectly. My cock fits here perfectly. Where is this if not home?" I look up at her. "You are my home, Georgie. Wherever you are, that is where I want to be."

Her expression grows soft. "I love you."

Humans always say such things, as if speaking the words aloud somehow makes them more real than actions. "I love you, too," I say back, because I know she values hearing such things. For my Georgie, I can pleasure her body for hours, tend to her every need, and share my most secret thoughts with her . . . and yet she must still hear the words. It is something I am learning to say aloud, because I do not like the look of hurt on her face if I forget. "I love all of you."

"But certain parts more than others?" she teases.

"No," I say solemnly. "I love all of you equally. There is no part I would rather have than another." I press another kiss to the tuft between her thighs. "Lie down so I may taste all of the parts of my mate that I love."

She tugs her tunic over her head and lies back in the furs, her eyes shining. I love the sight of them, so bright with life, so bright with her khui. It is so different from my first sight of her, when her eyes were dead and without color. But she is strong with khui now, and my kit is rooted into her belly. We will have a family eventually. The thought is humbling.

I press a kiss to my mate's soft belly first, where our kit awaits. "I love this," I tell her. "So soft here."

Georgie squirms under me, her hands going to my horns. She loves when I touch her all over, but she is always impatient, my mate. She wriggles underneath me like a hopper caught in a snare, and I move higher, because I want to see her teats jiggle. Even though she is not nursing a kit, they are large and full, and I love the sight of them.

"You are even softer here," I murmur, pressing a kiss to one dark pink tip.

She sucks in a breath. "They're getting sensitive."

"They are?" I am fascinated. "Should I not touch them?"

"No, it's okay," she says, and then squirms again. "Just . . . sensitive."

I lean in and lick the tip of one and she moans, arching. "Better?"

"Oh God, yeah." A whimper escapes her and she clings to me. "I love you, Vektal."

I growl low in my throat, utterly pleased to have her coming apart in my arms so quickly. Her arousal perfumes the air around us, and I drink in her scent, thick and sweet. It calls to me, and I lick her other teat before sinking between her thighs.

"I love your cunt," I say, parting her lips and revealing her mysterious third nipple tucked in the folds. "I love the dew it creates, just for my mouth. I love how soft you are. I love your scent." I lean in and rub my nose along her folds, teasing her nipple with the tip of my nose. "You are the only taste I need every day."

She moans, arching her hips in anticipation. "Vektal," she pants, holding on to my horns. "Make me come."

"Soon," I promise, and then tease my tongue up her folds. She whimpers, and I enjoy how she squirms. "First . . . tell me what troubles you."

Georgie pants, her fists tight on my horns. "W-what?"

"I must know," I say, lifting my head to meet her gaze. "There is something you are not sharing with me, and I will hear it before I make you come."

Her eyes go wide. "Can we talk about that some other time? Later?" She pushes at my head, trying to make me lick her again.

Normally I would never refuse such a request. But my Georgie is keeping secrets from me, and I do not like that. It worries me. I need to hear from her lips that she is happy here, that she will not become one of the humans that weeps endlessly at her fate. So I just watch her, waiting.

"Vektal," she says again, frowning at me. "There's nothing wrong—"

I lean in and let my breath fan over her cunt, my fingers still holding her open for my tongue.

She moans, a shudder rocking through her. I can see more of her sweet dew forming, and my mouth waters to taste her again . . . but I must know her secret first.

"Tell me and I will make you come so hard you will scream, my sweet resonance," I murmur, lowering my mouth again. I do not taste her, not yet. I simply wait.

"Nothing's wrong!" she cries, arching her hips. "I swear!"

"Georgie."

She puts a fist to her smooth brow, her breathing raspy. "Ohmigod, I cannot believe you're doing this."

"I want to lick your cunt, my mate. You do not know how bad I want it," I growl. My cock throbs with need, and I want to seat myself deep inside her . . . after I have tasted her sweetness on my lips. But this secret hangs in the air between us, and I do not like it. "I need you to trust me. To tell me whatever troubles you. You know you have all of my heart, my mate—"

"It's . . . it's not you, okay?" She presses her hands to her face. "It's just me being silly."

"I do not think you are silly," I say, taking my hands from her cunt. I move over her and lie down next to her in the furs, cupping her face and pulling her close. "What troubles you so, my heart? Say it, and if it is in my power to grant it, I shall."

She looks over at me, wariness in her eyes. "I don't want you to think I'm crazy."

"I would never think such a thing."

She bites her lip. "I . . . want to leave."

I blink. "Forever?" I rub my chin, considering. "If we leave, we must appoint a new chief. Tell me your thoughts on who would be best for the role. Salukh? Zolaya? Haeden is too hot-tempered and Bek even worse."

Georgie sits up on her elbows, her jaw dropping. "No, I didn't mean—wait, you'd leave with me? Just like that?"

I shrug. "I would be sad to leave my people behind, but you are my mate. You come first in all ways."

Her eyes grow soft. "You big silly thing. God, I love you." She leans forward and gives me a quick kiss, then brushes her fingers over my mouth. "That wasn't what I meant, though. I meant just . . . leave temporarily. On a trip."

"Like a hunting trip?" Georgie has not shown much interest in hunting thus far, and I am surprised. She has too much to deal with in regard to her humans and their needs to take on a hunting role, but I am happy to teach her.

"No, like a honeymoon." Georgie smiles at me. "It's a human tradition. Newly married people take a trip together, just the two of them. It's bonding time."

"I see." A trip alone. "What do newly married humans do on such a trip?" She has told me before that "married" is the human word for "mated," so this I understand.

"Well," she says, and there is a playful note in her voice as she taps a finger on my chest. "They have lots and lots of sex."

"Mmm. Do we not mate all the time already? I do not see why we have to travel to do so." I grin at her. "We can mate right here. I can take you from behind just as you like, let my spur press into your bottom—"

Her fingers press to my lips, silencing me. "Vektal, babe. Please. I just . . . I want to go. I need to go, okay?"

I study her face. There is such worry in her gaze, as if I will refuse her request. This means a lot to her . . . and I suspect there is something she is still not telling me.

But I nod. "Very well, my sweet resonance. We will go on this honey-moons."

"Really?"

"Really." If this is all she wants, it is easy to give. "If a trip will make you smile, then we will go on dozens and dozens of trips."

Relief shows on her face. She bites her lip again. "You're too good to me, Vektal."

Her heart does not seem as light as I want it to be, but it is a good start. We will do this human tradition and I will show her that her mate will give her anything her heart desires . . . she has but to ask.

"Does this make you happy?" I ask, letting my breath fan over her dew-slick cunt once more. When she moans and nods, I put my mouth on her sweetness once more, tasting her. Georgie gasps and clings to me as I mouth-mate her cunt, licking and sucking at her tender folds and the nipple there. She arches against me, her movements growing more insistent as I move lower, spearing my tongue into her heated core. She is wet here, and I want to be seated deep inside her. I sit up and move over her again, dragging her legs around my hips.

She locks them around me eagerly, her nails digging into my shoulders as I settle my weight over her. I sink into her heat, groaning at the delicious pleasure of it. She clasps my cock so tight and it feels so good, but even better are the little sounds she makes. Georgie whimpers and breathes my name, her expression full of rapture as I push deep.

I have mated with another, but it never came close to the pleasure I feel with my mate. Not once.

I caress my Georgie's face, touch her mane, and then lean in and give her a kiss even as I surge into her. She moans, clinging to me as I begin a rhythm, rocking into her. My spur rubs against her third nipple with every stroke, and it does not take long before my mate is squirming under me, on edge.

"Make me come," she pants, arching her hips to meet my thrusts. "Make me come, Vektal."

There is nothing I want more. With a low growl, I redouble my efforts, taking her harder, faster, deeper. I can feel when she goes over the edge—her cunt tightens and ripples around me, as if she's sucking me deeper. Her eyes close and she gives a low cry even as her folds flood with more dew and my thrusts into her are wetter. Slicker. She is clenched all around me, tight as a snare, a look of utter joy on her face.

I know I can make her come twice. So I keep driving into her, not stopping until she gives another shuddering cry. This time, when she clenches around me, I allow my own release to take flight. With her name on my lips, I pump into her roughly, letting my seed spill into her depths. I fill my mate, my strokes erratic and slowing until I am completely spent. Then, I press my mouth to hers in a hungry kiss before rolling onto my side and pulling her with me, our bodies still joined.

She snuggles against me, a happy sigh escaping her throat, and I run my fingers through her mane. "If all you wished for was a trip, my Georgie, all you had to do was ask," I tell her.

Georgie makes a little sound in her throat and holds on to me, content.

Georgie

"I can't believe you're leaving. Didn't we just get here?" Claire gives me a worried look. "Liz just got back, too! I thought we were all settling down."

"It's just a honeymoon of sorts," I say, keeping my tone light and cheery. "To celebrate our marriage. Or mating. Whatever you want to call it." I put the finishing stitches on a new set of mittens as I smile at Claire. "We won't be gone more than a handful of days. I promise. It's just time to reconnect."

"We hear you guys reconnecting every night," Josie says, giggling. "You're almost as loud as Nora and her mate." She stabs her needle into her leather with enthusiasm. "I get it, though. A honeymoon is so romantic. I don't see why we can't carry on some of the Earth traditions here. You may not have the white dress and the veil, but I don't see why you can't have the honeymoon trip." She gets a dreamy look on her face.

I wish my motives were as pure as Josie's interpretation. I grin, tying off my stitch and then pulling a glove over my hand. It's turned so that the fur is inside to keep my fingers warm, and the fit is just loose enough that I can grip things. "It's just for a few days," I say again. "We're coming back."

"I just wish you didn't have to go," Claire says uneasily. "I still feel really unsettled here, and now our leader's leaving us behind." Her mouth pulls down into a frown.

"It really will be all right."

"Of course it will," Josie chirps. Her expression brightens. "Maybe by the time you guys come back, some more of us will resonate. I'd love a soul mate." She clutches her leathers to her chest and sighs. "I just love the way Vektal looks at you, Georgie. The way he touches your hair. The way he watches you all the time with this expression that says, 'I'm the luckiest man alive.' I want that." She looks utterly wistful. "Hopefully it's coming."

I didn't plan on getting a "soul mate" like Josie says, but now that I have Vektal, I can't complain. He really is amazing. "The right person for you is here somewhere, Josie. I'm sure of it."

"I hope so." She begins to sew again. "So where are you guys going on your trip? To see something pretty? A sexy little cave somewhere remote?"

"Nowhere in particular," I lie. We haven't talked about where we're headed tomorrow morning when we go out, but I do have one spot in particular I want to go back to.

Need to go back to.

If nothing else, for peace of mind. But I don't want to tell the others because I worry it'll become a big deal. Claire is fragile right now and Josie is a chatterbox. I'd talk to Liz, who has a good attitude about things (and a smart mouth), but she's off with Raahosh, working on his "exile" penance for stealing her away.

It's best if I just keep it to myself for now. So I put a cheery expression on my face and lean closer to Claire. "What are you working on? Is that fur trim?"

Claire nods and holds it out to me. "Do you think it's too much?"

"We're on an ice planet. I don't think such a thing exists anymore," I tease. "Show me how you're handling the sleeves? I always have trouble with mine."

She scoots closer to me to demonstrate her sewing and my trip is forgotten.

I check in with all the girls that day to make sure everyone knows we're going on a quick "vacation" and we'll come back very soon. No one is envious of our trip—they're all quite content to stay in the warmth and safety of the home cave. The only one I don't get to talk to is Liz, who's out with her mate, but Kira reassures me that she'll let Liz know the situation when they come back again.

We pack bags that evening, Vektal throwing extra blankets and fur wraps and food into his pack because he wants to "take care of his mate." I've seen how light he travels, so it feels a little silly to bring so much gear, but he's also the expert. If he thinks I'm going to be freezing my butt off, I believe him. We go to bed early and Vektal wakes me up with a kiss before dawn so we can get started on our day.

It feels a bit like sneaking out as I dress in thick leathers and a cloak and we head toward the entrance of the cave. Hardly anyone is up except for a few of the hunters, who raise a hand in greeting but don't stop us. I don't see any human girls, and part of me wants to go cave to cave, waking them up and checking in on them one last time before I head out, but that's just me being overly protective. They're fine. They're adults surrounded by other adults and no one will let them starve, or freeze, or have anything bad happen to them.

I don't know why I feel utterly responsible for all the women, but I do. I can't mother them since we're the same age, but I do feel like a team leader who's leaving her team completely behind.

Pretty sure that's not what you do with a team.

Then again . . . isn't that the heart of this? I'm doing what I need to do for my team, all of them. I bite back any worries I have and smile at Vektal when he puts his hand out for me.

"Time to go?" I ask, and he nods.

We head out into the snow and I can tell immediately it's going to be another hard walk. I'm reminded of before, when we were in such a hurry that Vektal carried me on his back because the snow was so thick that it was an effort for me to walk through. He says he didn't mind, but I always worry I'll be too heavy, because toting another grown human being around on your back isn't really done back where I come from. The occasional piggyback ride? Sure. Hours on end through the craggy hills and valleys of this new, snowy place? Not so much.

As we get away from the cave, Vektal turns to look at me. His hand still clasps mine, his tail flicking behind him as we walk. In his other hand, he carries a spear, and he's wearing his vest o' knives again today. My man is bound and determined to keep his lady safe, and it should probably look alarming. Instead, I just think he looks handsome. He watches me, waiting, and when I don't speak, he finally says, "Where do you wish to do this honey-moons?"

"You're letting me pick?" In truth, I've had an idea of where I want to go all along, but I thought I'd have more time to ease him into the idea, maybe after a little playful sex after we were already out on the road . . .

But he's looking at me expectantly, waiting.

I guess now's the best time to ask. I suck in a deep breath, steeling my nerves, and then tell him the truth. "I want to go back to the ship."

His mouth firms as if he digests this. "The cave of the ancestors?"

"No," I admit. "Though that's a good guess. I want to go back to the ship we arrived in. The one where you guys rescued all of us." Almost all of us.

Vektal frowns at that. "Up the mountain?"

I nod.

"I do not like that place. It is dangerous."

"I know—"

"There are metlak burrows all over the mountain, and it is colder there. The snow is thicker. It will be difficult on you."

"I know," I say again. "But I need to go back." I lick my dry lips. "Please. It's important to me."

He turns to me, stabs his spear in the snow, and then takes my other hand in his. Both of our packs are on his big, strong back, and I'm only in charge of myself, so my hands are free. "Georgie," he says. "I do not hesitate because I feel your request is foolish. I only worry over my precious mate. I do not want to endanger her days after she has come into my world. Not when she carries my kit in her belly. Not when she is my reason to breathe." He shakes his head at me. "I wish to understand why you want to go back. You have been hiding secrets from me for many days now, and I need to know the truth of it. All of it. You can trust me with everything. Do you think I will judge you?"

I swallow hard. He's right. I'm being far too secretive. "It's just hard for me to rely on others. I'm used to doing things on my own. I'm used to being the one that tries to fix things." I take my hand from his and gesture at the cave. "Even here, I'm trying to do the best I can for everyone."

"I am your mate," Vektal says, deep voice gentle. "If you cannot turn to me, who can you turn to?"

He's right. Even though I feel my request is a strange one, I know he's right. "I want to go back to the old ship because Krissy and Peg and Dominique died and we didn't give them a proper burial. Everything was so crazy that we didn't have time to give them a proper send-off and I feel like I failed them." I swallow hard, trying to prevent the knot determined to form in my throat. "I need to give them a real farewell."

He doesn't laugh. He doesn't say I'm crazy. He just watches me with those too-knowing eyes. "This is important to you?"

"Very." They were my responsibility and I let them down. The least I can do is bury them.

"Then we will do this. We will have a good honey-moons. We will bury the dead, and then we will retreat to a cave and mate feverishly until you smile once more."

I laugh. Strangely enough, I already feel a little bit lighter. Sharing this with him was good. He didn't act like I was crazy for wanting to travel several days up a mountain into dangerous territory all to bury a few strangers who are long dead. "Thank you for understanding, Vektal."

The look he gives me is intense. My big alien moves forward and cups my cheek. His fingers are warm despite the drifting snow and chilly wind. "You do not need to thank me, my sweet resonance. You are my mate. There is nothing I will not do for you."

He's such a good man. I'm really the luckiest of women.

From the moment I met him, I've never felt so safe and protected. So understood—even when we had a language barrier. Our cultures are different, our planets are different, but somewhere out there, someone in the cosmos decided we should be together forever.

I'm eternally grateful for that. I smile at my handsome alien and squeeze his hand. "Shall we go?"

Vektal

A FEW DAYS LATER

I kiss my mate's bare shoulder to wake her up. "Georgie, my resonance," I whisper. "It is dawn."

She groans and rolls over in the furs, burying her face against my chest. "Five more minutes."

I grin, holding her close. She can sleep for a few more moments if she wishes. This is our honey-moons after all, a special trip for just the two of us. I stroke her back, tracing the curve of her spine as she drowses against me.

It has been a hard three days for my Georgie. If it was me alone, it would not take this long to make it back to the humans' flying cave, but there is no reason to hurry with my mate at my side, so we stop at a hunter cave each night and sleep on a bed of furs and eat fresh food. That part has been nice, though she has been too tired for mating. I do not mind as long as I get to hold her, but it is not a very good honey-moons by human standards, I think. But this is what my mate wants, and I can refuse her nothing.

She has walked resolutely in the snow next to me as much as

she can. Sometimes she grows tired and her feet begin to drag, and I carry her in my arms like I would a kit. She grumbles about it but holds on to my neck, relaxing, and when she presses little kisses against my skin? It is worth everything.

Georgie yawns and rubs her eyes. "I'm up."

"Clearly," I tease, tapping the tip of her small human nose. "Let us eat something before we go."

We dress and then sit by the coals of the fire as we eat our morning food. She still does not like the taste of kah, wrinkling her nose at the spicy flavor. Lately we have been making it blander for human tongues, but I did not think to grab it when I snagged kah from the stores. I was distracted, my thoughts on my mate.

"I will catch you something to eat later tonight," I promise her as she takes a big mouthful of water.

"This is okay. I'm getting used to it. Slowly."

"You are a bad liar," I tease.

"The worst." She wrinkles her nose and grins. "It's really not that bad, I promise. I'm just being extra dramatic. I've never been a fan of spicy food, even human food." As if to prove she is fine, she takes another big mouthful and washes it down with more water. "Should we get going?"

I nod, then clean up the cave, straightening the supplies and packing things away for the next hunter to come in this direction. Georgie bundles up in her layers, and when she pulls on her mittens, I tug the hood of her cloak over her pretty face and then steal a kiss. "We will be at your flying cave later today."

Georgie takes a deep breath. "Okay. And Dominique? The red-haired human?"

"She is much closer." I still remember the heart-stopping sight of her, frozen in the snow, and how for a moment I thought it was Georgie. How my heart had thumped with panic. Just the memory of that makes me uneasy and I pull her against me. I want this day to go well for her, I think, as I press my mate to my chest. I try not to think of all the bad things we can find, if metlaks or other predators have gotten to the corpses first.

"We'll take her and bury her with the others, won't we?" Georgie asks in a quiet, subdued voice.

"Of course." It is important to her, and I will deny her nothing. Even so, I do not want her to be surprised if what we find is not . . . whole. "My mate, I do not want to fill you with worry, but it is possible others have gotten to them before us."

"I know," she says, and I breathe a sigh of relief. "Trust me, it's been going through my mind constantly. But whatever we can do to put them to rest, it will be enough." She looks up at me, her eyes bright with khui-blue under the hood. "Thank you again."

"There is no need for thanks," I say again.

"Right. Of course." Georgie smiles tremulously up at me. "I suppose we'd better tackle the day, then."

But her eyes are filled with dread.

We walk, and she tells me of human burial customs. They are far more ornate than those of the sa-khui. Poems are read, prayers sent, and monuments in stone carved for those that have fallen. We have no such things to give these dead females, but Georgie says it is fine. It is the thought and effort behind it.

I tell her of sa-khui customs, the few that we have. Sometimes if someone does not come back from a hunt, there is no body to be found. Sometimes it is left behind for scavengers, only knives and personal possessions passed on to the family.

Horns are etched and cut to show grief, snow poured over the head and the mourner keening their loss. The tribe celebrates the life of the one that has passed, and then . . . the world goes on. When there are dead, they are taken to an unused cave, dressed in their finest leathers, and then the cave is collapsed so they may sleep eternally. My father—and many others—sleep in such a cave thanks to the khui-sickness.

Those were bad times, and I do not want to dwell on them more than I must.

We find the red-maned female's body a short distance from a cave I once shared with Georgie. I remember the spot, remember covering her with snow and marking a nearby rock so I would know the place to show her later. I dig in the snow, with Georgie watching nearby. Once we find the red mane, it does not take long to dig out the rest of her pale limbs. She is frozen solid, and I wrap her in a large sa-kohtsk hide I brought for such a thing. I heft the corpse into my arms and look to my mate.

Her arms are crossed over her chest and her face is paler than usual.

"I can walk," she tells me, moving close. She looks very small, very fragile.

"Stay near," I tell her, even though the words are unnecessary. "This is metlak territory."

Georgie nods. "I remember what happened before, when I fell into their cave and you rescued me. I'll stay close." Her mittened hand slips into my belt and she holds on to me.

We travel farther up the mountain, and I deliberately keep my steps slow so Georgie can keep up. It makes for a very slow pace, but eventually, I spot the black hull of the flying cave that brought my mate and the other humans to this world. She said it came from high above in the sky. Now, it is covered with newly fallen snow, the top of it pristine save for the jagged hole that lets fresh air in.

I turn to my mate. "Where should I put the human?" I try to say the words delicately, because I know she is fragile in this moment. Her expression is distant, her eyes big in her face as she looks at the cave, and I know she is lost in recent memories. They were not kind to her, those that stole her away, and I want to hurt all of them for daring to touch my Georgie.

After a moment, her gaze focuses on me and her hand tightens on my belt once more. "Is it safe if we leave her out here? I'd like to bury her and the others outside."

"We can do that." I set the dead female gently in the snow. "Do you want to go inside or shall I do it?" She hesitates, and I turn to my mate, a protective feeling sweeping over me. "You do not have to go, Georgie."

"I do." She shakes her head. "I need to."

"There is nothing in there for you."

She shakes her head again, biting her lip. "I need to remember, so I never forget, Vektal. It's important to me. Please help me climb up there?" She gestures at the opening at the top. The snow packed around it has given way to ice, and it will be a slippery climb for her.

I hate that she insists . . . but how can I refuse? I frown at her for a moment, hoping she will change her mind, but Georgie only raises her chin and meets my gaze steadily. There is no shaking my mate from her course. This is important to her . . . and so I must allow it.

I sigh and kneel into the snow. "Climb onto my back."

"You're the best man ever, you know that?" She gives me a kiss on my brow before moving to put her arms around my neck and lean against my spine.

"I am the most tolerant of mates," I grumble, but her slight chuckle makes me feel better. I pat her hand before getting to my feet, and then wrap her legs around my waist from behind. "Hold on to your male." Finding handholds on the strange, cold surface, I begin to climb.

It is a short drop inside, made shorter still by the pile of snow under my feet. It has drifted in here, creating a soft landing spot, and when my boots thump onto the floor of the cave, it is muffled. The interior is dark and still smells of many things. I catch the faint hint of smoke from our fires when we rescued the females, and the stink of their forced habitation here. They were trapped in this small, strange cave for two hands of days and near death when we were able to bring them to the tribe. Keeping a cave clean and fresh was not a priority.

I kneel again and Georgie slides from my shoulders, stepping forward. She clutches her cloak to her neck, her eyes wide and glowing as she looks around the dark interior. "It looks smaller than I remember it," she whispers. "Darker, too."

I grunt, glancing around. At the far end of the cave, near the wall where we pried six females from their sleeping pods, I see the two lumps of the carefully covered females. We were to bury them for the humans but were forced to flee quickly when their captors threatened to return. I look to my mate, waiting.

She is lost in thought, staring around her. Her eyes are shiny with unshed tears and she licks her lips. "It's so cold in here."

It is warmer than outside, because there is no wind, but I say nothing.

"I left them here with no clothing because I went to get help. They had no food, no nothing, and I wandered off into the snow and met you. While they were shivering, we were flirting." She swallows hard and then swipes at her cheeks. "I should have tried to get back to them faster. Maybe if I had, Dominique would still be alive."

Did we come here so she could blame herself? I hold back the words, but this is not like my Georgie. If there is a problem, she is the first to offer a solution. She does not like to dwell on the past. But there is something about this place—and these dead females—that she cannot move on from. "You did the best you could. We could not speak, remember?"

"I could have tried harder." She swallows, looking around at the cavern. "I could have left your side and come back here—"

"And been eaten by metlaks. Or snow cats. Or ended up dead in the snow yourself."

But she only shakes her head. She wanders about inside the cave for a bit longer, touching the dirty walls or staring at the floor. She pauses over the two covered bodies, silent for so long that I worry about her. Then, she takes a deep breath and turns to me. "Can we move them outside? I don't think they'd want to be buried in here. They'd want to be . . . free." Her voice wobbles on the last part. "Under the skies."

I nod. "I can do this."

For the next while, we do not speak as I carefully take one hide-wrapped human corpse and haul it outside, then the next. Georgie is lost in thought, but when I kneel in front of her and gesture that she should climb on my back again so we can leave, she does so without protest. She holds tightly to me, burying her face against my mane as I climb back out and into the brisk air. I carry my mate back down to the snowy ground and then kneel again so she can dismount, and when she stands before me, I rise.

Georgie stares at the three bodies, her expression hollow. "They're together now."

"Tell me where I should bury them, and how deep." If she asks me to dig to the bottom of the mountain, I will. Anything to ease the sadness from her eyes.

My mate directs me, and I dig deep into the snow at the edge of one of the nearby cliffs. I dig as deep as I can, until the packed snow turns to ice. Georgie tries to help, but I growl at her and she backs off. I do not want her doing hard work, not with our kit so newly in her belly. I can do this for her. While I work, she wraps the skins tighter about each fallen human, making sure the body is tightly covered. She takes a piece of coal and writes strange symbols on the furs, and when I ask what she is doing, she says she writes down everything she knows about each girl so it will not be forgotten.

When that is done, she makes little crosses out of bone and decorates them with beaded thongs that I know Maylak gave to her. "I don't know what their religions were, but I'm hoping it's the thought that counts," she tells me as I hop out of the pit and move to her side.

Then it is time to lay the dead inside. I do so carefully, listening to her instructions as she tells me to lay them head to foot, as if they are all sleeping in a large nest of furs alongside one another. I turn to my mate when the last one is placed.

She is crying.

I am shocked. The other humans cry and weep from time to time, but my Georgie is always competent, always ready with a solution. Right now, though, her eyes are wet and shiny and her mouth trembles.

"Georgie?" I ask, worried. This is not like her.

"You can cover them now," she whispers, her gaze on the dead and not me.

I nod, and even though I am uneasy at her tears, I do as she asks. She sits beside the grave and cries silently all the while as I cover them, and then when the pit is filled once more, we both get small rocks and outline the graves. Georgie puts her crosses at the head of each grave and then moves to sit at the foot, her hands clasped together.

I sit next to her. It is clear she needs to say a few things. Perhaps this is part of the human burial ceremony.

Georgie stares at the crosses, her eyes wet, and takes a deep breath. "Krissy, Peg, Dominique . . . I'm sorry. I'm so sorry I failed you."

Eh? I turn to my mate, surprised. "How did you fail them?"

She swipes at her eyes. "I'm the reason they died. I couldn't keep them safe."

I shake my head, not understanding.

"I was the leader," she says, voice shuddering. "It was my idea to fight our captors. That fight helped us break free just as we were crashing." She bites her lip. "And I was the one that went for help."

"You saved eleven other females, Georgie. You saved Leezh and Ki-rah and all the others. You came and found me and convinced me to go up the mountain to save them. You have brought life back to our tribe. You have given the males of my people hope for a mate and a future. Would you choose differently if you could go back?"

She swallows hard and shakes her head. "No. I guess that's part of the reason why I feel so guilty." Georgie looks over at me. "I'm happy. I should be devastated that I left Earth behind and three of my people died, but all I can think about is you and our baby and the future."

I reach out and take one of her hands in mine. I understand now. It is guilt that drives her to tears, a chief's guilt when anyone in the tribe suffers. She feels responsible for these females. I understand. "You feel you should not be happy?"

"Sometimes I wonder."

"Do you think that they would wish for you to be unhappy? That they do not want any of the others to have good, long lives? Do you think they would not want them to be free?"

"No, I don't think that. It just feels strange to be so happy even after everything's been taken away from me, you know?" She holds my hand tightly.

"There is nothing wrong with finding joy in life, my Georgie. Nothing at all. I think your friends would want that for you, as well. You gave everyone freedom. These three might have died, but they did not die as captives or slaves."

Fresh tears spill down her cheeks. She nods. "You're right. I know you're right."

"Then why do you cry?"

A watery laugh bubbles up from her throat and she squeezes my hand so hard I am surprised at her strength. "Because it's a good cry. I think I needed to say goodbye before I moved on. And now that they're buried, I hope they find peace." Georgie looks at the graves again, still clinging to my hand. "We all need to move on."

I nod. She does not get up, and I remain at her side. For as long as Georgie needs to sit here, I will be with her. Eventually, her tears dry and her hand clenches mine less tightly. She looks over at me and her expression is less troubled than it has been in many days.

"I think I'm good," she says to me. "I needed this. They needed this." She gestures at the graves. "And now we can all move forward."

"Then what would you like to do now, my sweet resonance?"

"Go back to our cave?" She gives me a tired smile. "I'm suddenly exhausted."

It is because she is free of the weight of her troubles, I think. She has been carrying them silently for so long that now they are gone, she feels lighter—and she also feels tired. But I do not say that. I just smile and touch her belly. "The kit will make you sleepy. Shall we go back to the hunter cave for the night, then?"

She looks over at the flying cave with its strange, dark walls. "Absolutely. I don't want to spend another night in that hellhole."

Georgie

I feel . . . free.

It's a strange feeling, to wake up after crashing into a pile of furs the moment we got back to the hunter cave, and not feel the weight of obligation on my shoulders. I don't feel the intense guilt over the deaths of the three women, or the endless worry that I made the wrong decisions and caused their deaths. I don't feel that ache of sadness over leaving Earth behind.

I've left it all back in the graves up on the mountain, where Krissy, Peg, and Dominique have finally been laid to rest.

I did what I could, I saved myself and as many others as I could, and we have a new life here. It's enough. We buried our dead, and I've buried my past—Earth included. I'm free to move forward with my mate.

My wonderful, wonderful mate.

As if he knows I'm thinking about him, Vektal's arms tighten around me and he holds me closer. He's all warmth, entirely naked under the furs, and I love curling up against him. "It is early," he murmurs, stroking my arm. "Go back to sleep."

"I will," I promise, but I'm rather awake. My thoughts are buzzing and I feel free. I'm excited about what the day holds, what the month holds, what the future holds.

I touch my lower belly, wondering how long before I start showing. Before it puffs out with the baby inside and my breasts grow and everything changes. Is it weird that I'm looking forward to morning sickness? I want a sign that the baby inside me exists. I want some sort of proof, more than just a missed period or a change in the sound our khui make when we come together.

"Georgie?" Vektal murmurs, moving his fingers through my hair. "Are you all right?"

"I'm great," I answer him, and it's the truth. I feel like a wound has been lanced—a wound I didn't even know I had until recently. Now the bad things have been forced out and I'm ready for the healing to begin . . . actually, I already feel pretty healed. "I'm just thinking."

"About?"

There's a wariness in his tone, as if he expects to hear something sad or troubling from me. I don't blame him for that wariness—I promised him a sexy honeymoon and gave him a funeral instead. I snuggle up to my mate and put my chin on his chest, seeking out his glowing eyes in the dim light of the cave. "Thinking about our baby. Our future. The tribe. A bunch of stuff."

He grins, his eyes sleepy slits of blue light. "I like these thoughts."

"Me, too." I skate my fingers over his abdomen and brush them over his sides, loving the way he tenses. Ticklish. "I wanted to talk to you about things, too. About the graves. Let's not tell the others what we've done, all right?"

"You think they would not want to know? Or that they would not approve?"

"I think they would approve," I say. "But I also want them to move on, to move forward like I plan on doing. I feel like if we bring it up it'll just remind them of our losses. If someone asks, we'll share, but if they don't ask, I don't want to be the one to volunteer it. We all need to start fresh."

"Very well."

"If they ask, we just had a sex-filled honeymoon where we barely left the furs."

"So we . . . make up stories?" He grins down at me.

I wince. That was my original pitch to him, wasn't it? That we'd run off together and just fuck like bunnies until the cows came home. This has to be a disappointing trip for him even if it was a necessary one for me. "I'm so sorry, Vektal. This wasn't a very good trip for you, was it?"

"You needed this trip. I have no regrets. I am just glad the sorrow is gone from your eyes." He runs a finger lightly down my cheek, then traces my jaw. "I knew my Georgie had something troubling her, and if this is what it took to fix it, then I am very happy."

"It was exactly what I needed," I agree. I'm feeling . . . curiously frisky, too. I run my fingers along his side, tickling slightly, and love that he squirms and his tail thumps against the blankets like an irritated cat. "You know . . . we're still alone. We don't have to go back just yet. We can still make this a sexy honeymoon."

He chuckles. "Not if you are not feeling it, my mate. I am content to wait." He brushes his fingers over my cheek again in the gentlest of caresses. "We have all our lives to mate. It does not have to be now if you are not in the mood."

Sweet Vektal. He's totally misunderstanding me. "When did I say I wasn't in the mood?" I give his chiseled stomach a kiss.

He's got washboard abs, rippled with both muscle and those hard, protective plates. I kiss lower, where a happy trail should be, and then move even lower, making a beeline for one of my favorite parts of his body.

My mate groans, his hand tightening in my hair. "Georgie—"

"Shhh. I'm having myself some honeymoon fun." I flick my tongue against his spur and then move even lower, gripping his cock in my hand. He's so big and thick around that my fingers don't quite meet when I circle him, and just giving his girth a squeeze makes me all hot and bothered. "I love how thick you are."

"My cock loves your mouth."

I chuckle, because that's such an absurd thing to say to a girl, but on him it's somehow sweet. I know he doesn't mean it in a creepy way like an Earth guy would. He means it because he loves all of me and how I touch him. I think of the first time I went down on him and blew his mind. Even though he loves to eat pussy—and boy, did I score on that angle—he'd never had a blow job, and every time I give him one, he acts like he's being given the greatest treasure ever.

Which just makes me want to do it more.

I take the head of him into my mouth, lightly running my tongue along the crown. The taste of pre-cum hits my taste buds a moment later, and I moan, lapping at his cockhead. "My handsome alien," I purr, loving the feel of my khui as it starts up, gently rumbling in my chest in time with my mate's arousal. "My mouth loves your cock, too." And I lick him, from root to tip.

He shudders, groaning, and I absolutely love that reaction. God, this man. How is it possible that he's such a damn beast, ferocious and unafraid, and yet so gentle that he holds hands with me and carries me like I'm a princess? How did I get so lucky?

I want to show him how lucky I feel. So I lick him again, letting my tongue glide over those glorious ridges on his cock, and then take the head of him into my mouth again. I suck lightly, and when he's panting and twitching, unable to stay still underneath me, I ease my mouth lower, trying to meet the hand I have gripped around the base of his shaft. It's an impossible task because he's so huge, but I'm going to give it the old college try. I ease down on him, working my mouth and my tongue as I try to go lower and lower, until I hit my gag reflex and come back up for air. I make the most awful sound as I do, but Vektal only groans as if I'm the sexiest thing ever, and I laugh, wiping my lips. "I'll try again," I murmur, already leaning forward. "But you're too big for me."

That elicits another pained groan from my mate, his hand curled tight in my hair. He's not shoving my head down, though I know he really wants to the way his fingers flex against my head. As I lick and suck at his enormous shaft, I take two fingers and tease his spur. He keeps telling me it's not sensitive, but I know when I rub it like it's a mini-cock, he comes unglued. Vektal growls, his hips bucking as I do, pushing him deeper into my throat. I whimper, aroused at his responses and the heady pleasure of going down on him, my senses filled with his scent, his taste, his touch.

"Georgie," he grits out, pumping his hips again and shuttling against the back of my throat. "I need to stop—"

I give the base of his cock another squeeze and rub his spur even as I sink deeper.

His breath erupts in a little grunt, and then he's coming, and I can feel him shooting down my throat without even tasting him, he's so deep. I try to swallow and have to lift my head, my mouth filling with his release.

I drink him down, wiping the corners of my mouth, and when he's done coming, I lean forward and clean his cock with my tongue, loving the little shudders that ripple through him with every touch. When I'm done and there's no more to lick up, I keep tonguing him anyhow, just because I'm aroused and needy and his cock is so amazing. Since meeting Vektal, I've had more sex in the last few weeks than I've had ever, and I'm always hungry for more. There's something about him that just makes me crazy with lust.

Well, I'm sure the khui has something to do with that, but even now, when the khui's sated, I can't get enough of him. Physically, he does it for me. Mentally, he's got a sweetness mixed with his brawn that I find utter catnip. Emotionally? I've never been so loved.

It makes me want to do dirty, filthy things to him all the time.

His cock twitches under my tongue, and then he grabs me and hauls me forward, a breathless laugh escaping him. "Do you mean to lick your mate until he stiffens for your greedy mouth once more?"

"Is that a trick question? I thought it was obvious."

"Your mate has a mouth, too," he murmurs, sliding lower even as he pulls me up. "And he wants to use it. Come and sit on my face."

Now I'm the one that's moaning. I'm wearing only my sleeping tunic, and my legs are thankfully bare of everything, panties included. It takes no convincing for me to move up to where my mate's eager mouth awaits and to slide a thigh over his shoulders. He grips my ass, steadying me over his face, and then leans in and gives me the same long, slow lick I gave him.

I shudder, moaning. With one hand, I clutch at one of his horns, steadying myself as he begins to make love to my pussy. I hold one of my breasts, teasing the nipple through the leather of my tunic and arching against his tongue when it hits me in just the right spot. I'm wet and slick with need, and it doesn't take long before I'm rocking against his mouth, close to my own climax. I want it to last longer, but there's no way I'm going to be able to stand it. It's too much, and I'm too turned on. I love the groans he makes as he licks me, as if I'm the best thing he's ever tasted, and I know he loves it. Hasn't he woken me up dozens of times with his mouth between my legs, just because he wants to?

God, I really am the luckiest woman alive.

He drags a finger along the crease of my backside, one hand stealing closer, and I moan again. He loves to tease me in all the naughtiest of places, and when his finger presses against my butt, I lose it. I come against his sucking, teasing mouth, arching and crying out his name.

I collapse over him, sated, a laugh rising from my throat. He rubs my buttocks, kissing the insides of my thighs and dragging his tongue over my pussy even though I've already come.

"Are you good, my mate?" he asks, breathless.

"Oh yeah," I manage. "I'm amazing." I really am, too.

"Good."

A moment later, Vektal sits up, lifting me into the air. I'm on my back—gently—in the furs a moment later, my knees pushing up to my chest. He moves over me, and I'm giggling even as he presses the hot, thick length of him into my core.

"What is so funny?" he asks, sliding one of my ankles up to his big shoulder. He runs his hand up and down my leg, that possessive, delicious look in his eye.

"I can't believe you're ready to go again, that's all." I smile up at him, and my smile turns into a gasp when he drives deep into me.

"I will always be ready for you, my Georgie," he tells me in a ruthless growl . . . and then he claims the hell out of me once more.

We stay out for a glorious, sex-filled week after that. The little cave in the mountains becomes the honeymoon I promised to Vektal, and there are plenty of days where we don't even leave the furs. It's a vacation, and a great one. We relax lazily, hanging out in the cave, and I share with him my memories of Earth and he tells me stories of growing up in the tribe, which was much bigger once upon a time. There's always more to learn about my mate, and I'm looking forward to a lifetime of discoveries.

Eventually, though, we need to head back. I thought I'd be a little disappointed when we start the long walk back to the home cave, but surprisingly, I'm not. It's been a wonderful, refreshing time alone together, and I feel more connected to my big, burly alien than ever before. Even so, I'm excited for what the future holds for us, and I look forward to rejoining our tribe. I can't wait to see their faces again, and I know Vektal feels the same.

I'm excited to go home.

I'm excited to rejoin our people.

And by the time we round the last bend toward the home caves, I'm practically dancing with excitement.

Vektal laughs with amusement as my steps pick up. "Now you walk fast?"

I laugh, enjoying his teasing. "Uh, yeah. I want to see if anyone resonated while we were gone."

He snorts. "I have told you, my mate, resonances are a rare thing."

"Because you've never had so many hot, single ladies hanging around your cave," I tease back. "Your cooties won't know what to do with all that estrogen in the air."

"Est-roh-what?"

"Girl stuff," I tell him with a wave of my hand. "I admit, I'm a little anxious to get back in general. I want to make sure no one fell apart while we were gone. I worry about some of them." I think specifically of Ariana, who's the tribe's resident weeper, and Kira, who seems sad and distant all the time. And Tiffany, who had plenty to say when we were captive but now that we're free seems to have clammed up entirely. We all have baggage, of course. It's to be expected. But I want to be there for anyone that needs a friend or a shoulder to cry on. I'm going to be chieftess to Vektal's chief, and I want to be the best damn chieftess I can possibly be.

"Ho," a familiar face calls as we approach the cave. It's one of the big blue guys, walking out to greet us, and I recognize Haeden by the scowl on his face. He nods at us.

"Ho," Vektal replies easily. "How fare things?"

Haeden shrugs. "All is quiet."

"Quiet is good," I say, smiling at him. He just stares at me.

Vektal puts a possessive arm around my waist. "Who is out on the trails hunting right now?"

We pause as the two men discuss herd patterns and who's out far from the cave and who's staying close by. Vektal listens to all, nodding, and eventually looks over at me. "It will be my turn to go out on the trail soon. Tomorrow. But tonight, I have one more honey-moons with my pretty mate."

My face gets hot. I'm pretty sure he's using the word "honeymoon" in place of sex, and now he just told Haeden that we're going to go fuck.

"Honey-moons?" Haeden asks, curious.

"Long story," I say before Vektal can speak. I take my mate by the hand and drag him inside. "Let's go, honey, because I'm starving and I smell something good on the fire."

Haeden's frown increases. "Hemalo is dyeing skins over the fire."

Oh. Okay, yeah, that's probably what I smell. No wonder he's looking at me like I'm crazy. If it's the cocktail I remember, the skin dye is made up of pee, brains, and some other unsavory crap, all boiled into a horrific mush.

I tap my nostril, determined to make this lie stick. "Must be my pregnancy nose thinking it smells good."

"Ah." He gives Vektal an odd look but claps him on the shoulder. "Glad you are back, my chief."

"We are glad to be back," Vektal says easily, and puts a hand at the small of my back to lead me inside the cavern that is now my home.

Immediately, the temperature grows warm and slightly humid. I look at the busy cavern, smiling at the sight of familiar sa-khui faces and human faces, too. Over by the fire, Hemalo is stirring something thick and sludgy, all right, and Josie's at his side, helping him. In the center of the cave, Ariana is in the water with her mate, Zolaya, and Nora wrings her hair out and sits on the edge, buck-ass naked while her mate, Dagesh, rubs her shoulders. I see Kira carrying a basket and doing her best to ignore Aehako, who trails behind her. And off in a corner, I see Claire hanging on Bek's arm, blinking big eyes as he tells her a story.

No one's falling apart. No one's a mess. Everyone looks . . . happy.

I'm so relieved.

"Well, well," calls a familiar voice. "Look what the cat dragged in."

Vektal immediately looks around behind us, no doubt searching for a snow cat of some kind. I just laugh and open my arms to hug Liz. "Hey, you!"

She gives me a hug in response, but her expression is a little guarded. Our friendship suffered a bit of a break when Raahosh went into exile and I sided with Vektal. I had to. I can only imagine how dreadful things would have gotten if we'd allowed Raahosh to just cart away Liz with no repercussions. Bek would have stolen Claire away next, and Aehako Kira, and then it would be a nightmare. These people think differently than we do, and even if it's not meant maliciously, it's also not fair to the girls.

I think Liz gets it. Or pretends to get it. Either way, she's firmly on Team Raahosh, which I suppose I get. Sure enough, when I pull back from our hug, he's there nearby, arms crossed and scarred face glowering at me and Vektal.

Liz gives my shoulder a punch. "Where ya been, fearless leaders? Someone said you were on a mooning trip, but I thought that couldn't be right."

"Oh. Did you guys just get in?" I brush my hair back off my face, since the humidity in the cave is making my curls stick to my skin. "We went on a honeymoon to get away, just the two of us. A little bonding time."

She narrows her eyes at me. "Really."

Liz is sharp. I don't know if she's going to believe me or want to know more details. I think of the graves we left up the mountain, and how I left a lot of my own grief and doubt up there with them. I asked Vektal not to mention it, but it's not entirely for the others. I want to leave that part of the past behind myself, and rehashing the fate of our three dead friends and their grave for each person in the tribe will be difficult.

"Honeymoon? Where?" Liz asks.

"The cave we first met," Vektal says, his hand sliding to my waist, and he pulls me close. "It was a good trip. Fine weather. Great company." And he grins at me, fangs flashing.

Liz frowns at me again, and I wait for her to ask. Wait for her to pry into why we needed to get away so quickly after resonating. But then she just sighs. "Well, now I want a romantic honeymoon, too."

"Eh?" Raahosh moves to her side, his grip tight on her arm. For a moment, he looks as if he wants to snatch her away from all of us and hoard her to himself. "You want to travel out into the mountains just to mate? Do we not do that right now, female? It is called exile."

She rolls her eyes. "Where's your sense of romance, Raahosh? This is a trip specifically for sexytimes. We could play 'wampa that discovers a helpless Luke in a cave,' but this time you'd get to eat me." She wiggles her eyebrows at her mate. "Or we could play 'Gollum finds his precious.' Really, the possibilities are endless."

He just frowns at her.

Liz sighs and looks back at me. "Clearly I need to get him on board with such an idea."

Raahosh's mouth flattens and he looks at Vektal accusingly, as if this is somehow my man's fault, and lets Liz lead him away.

I watch them go, biting back a smile. I would say Liz runs roughshod over Raahosh, but I think he's the only one that tolerates her crap and gives her back just as much. It's a surprisingly good pairing, because Liz is definitely a bit acerbic and headstrong.

"You look tired, my mate," Vektal says.

"Do I?" I look over at him in surprise. I don't feel tired. It was a long trip, sure, but I . . . oh. He's giving me a slow, wicked grin that I recognize. "You did say you were leaving me tomorrow, didn't you?"

He nods, pulling me so close that my boobs brush against his chest. "I must go out on the hunt like all the others. It is my duty. But it will make my return twice as sweet to know you and our kit are waiting for me."

It's an aspect of life I'm going to have to get used to. I nod, smiling. "Until then, you did mention you have time for one more honeymoon night?"

"I do," he murmurs, gaze intent on me and a promise in his eyes.

"Maybe we should play Gollum and his precious, then," I say, fluttering my lashes at him as I take him by the hand and lead him back toward the nook of our cave.

"As long as you tell me what it is, I am game."

I chuckle. "It involves lots of rubbing."

"All the best games do."

We end up playing no games at all. I'm too easily distracted. By the time we get to our cave, Vektal's mouth is on me and I lose track of utterly everything in the world but him and his seemingly magic tongue. And his tail. And his big hands. And spur. The spur is always, always a distraction.

It's all wonderful, though. Vektal makes me come so hard that I see stars. Twice. And then we curl around each other and sleep through the night. I put my cold feet on his leg and he doesn't even protest. That's when you know it's love.

I'm asleep when he presses a kiss to my brow and slides out of bed, but even those small movements wake me up. I pretend to keep sleeping, watching him from under my lashes as he puts on his loincloth and his knife-vest and I know he's going hunting. He's going to be leaving me soon for the first time and my throat clenches. I reach up and grab his tail as he tugs on his boots. "You won't leave before I get to kiss you goodbye, will you?"

Vektal groans even as I stroke the furry tip of his tail. I know it's sensitive. I got his attention, though, and that's what I wanted. "I am merely going to get supplies and speak to the other hunters. I will return, my sweet resonance. Never fear. Your mate will not leave without giving his female a proper goodbye."

Ooh, I hope that involves a quickie. I smile up at him from bed. "Okay. I love you. Hurry back soon."

He kneels beside the furs and kisses my brow, then runs his thumb over it. I know he's fascinated by the smoothness there and my lack of horns. "Sleep," he says. "I will wake you before I go."

I nod and snuggle back into the furs as he heads out to the main cave. I can't fall back asleep, though. My mind's already flying through all the things that need to be done. I should visit Maylak and get her to check on my pregnancy, since it's the first human-sa-khui pregnancy in all time and I want to make sure things go well. I need to start sewing. Vektal's got plenty of furs but I don't have much clothing to wear. I need to learn how to do a lot of stuff, actually. I need to check on Claire, who's hooking up with one of the guys without resonance. I need to check on the girls that did resonate and make sure they're doing okay and their relationships are going smoothly. I need to check up on the girls that didn't resonate, because I don't want them to feel as if they're missing out . . .

Really, there's a laundry list of things to do, and staying in bed is a lot less fun when it's just me. With a small sigh, I push the furs back and get up.

Megan's by the fire when I head into the main part of the cave. There are a few of the aliens awake. No, I remind myself. We're the aliens. They're the sa-khui. Megan's the only other human awake, and her face lights up when she sees me so I head in her direction. "Morning," I say brightly. I take one of the cups by the fire and dip it into the hot tea. The sa-khui share cups, and while they're always careful to wash them out, it was strange to me at first, because I imagined all kinds of germs being left behind. But that's why we have cooties, right? To handle those sorts of things. I hold the cup out to Megan. "You want some?"

She hesitates before reaching for it. "Are you sure it's okay?"

"It's for everyone," I tell her. And I know it is. No one would smack Megan's hands for taking a cup of tea. I hand her the cup and scoop one for myself, sitting down next to her. "Sleep well?"

She bites her lip and shrugs. "As well as can be expected on a stone floor?" She rubs her ass as if to demonstrate that not all of her slept well after all.

"Really? I'm surprised you felt the floor. The furs Vektal has are so thick it's ridiculous."

"Oh," is all she says. And the smile she offers me is reluctant and miserable. "He's the chief, though. It's different."

"No, it's not," I tell her firmly. "We live here too, Megan. We are just as valuable as anyone else in this tribe. The food is for everyone. The drink is for everyone." I clink my bone cup to hers in a mock-toast. "If you're thirsty, you get a drink. If you're hungry, you get food. And if you're cold at night, then you get more blankets. We're not interlopers, okay? This is our home now. These are our people."

She gives me a tremulous smile, and there's such worry and uncertainty in her eyes that it makes my heart squeeze. "I just don't want to bother anyone, you know?" Megan bites her lip. "I don't want to be a problem."

I don't know if it's leftover trauma from our horrible time as slaves in the alien ship or if this is Megan's personality, but I wrap a protective arm around her shoulders and give her a squeeze. This is my purpose, I realize. I didn't want to come back from our honeymoon, sure . . . but I'm glad we did. Vektal needs to lead his people and to hunt, and I need to be here for the girls, leading them in my own way. I'm the one that should be setting an example as well as being a shoulder to cry on.

And if Megan needs blankets, I'm going to get her some blankets.

I set my cup down and get to my feet. "Come on."

"Where are we going?" She puts her cup down with a small frown. "Georgie—"

"We are going to get you some extra blankets," I say firmly. "There are plenty of furs in storage so if you're cold, you don't have to suffer. This is your home now, too. You get blankets just like anyone else does."

She gives me such a worried look that it just makes me feel even fiercer in her defense. Poor Megan—someone's done a hell of a number on her self-esteem. "I just don't want to cause problems—"

"Nonsense. If anyone has a problem, they can take it up with me, okay? You don't let anyone give you shit. We're going to learn how to make furs, too, but until then, everyone here is more than willing to share, I promise." I take her hand and squeeze it, then lead her toward the supply cave. I won't let her argue. She'd rather be uncomfortable than "bother" anyone and that's not how it's going to work. We're a tribe and we need to act like one. It's a good reminder for me, too. The honeymoon was nice, but it's even nicer to be home and starting the rest of our lives.

As luck has it, when we approach the supply cave, I can hear the sound of voices. Male voices, deep in discussion. Megan clenches my arm, and I hesitate, not wanting to interrupt anyone's conversation. The supplies are free for everyone to use, but it's also early enough that a conversation in a cave feels like a secret.

"We have questions," I hear one of the hunters say. I mentally flip through my mental list of tribes-folk, trying to match the voice with the face. Hassen? Cashol?

"What is it?"

And that voice makes me flush with pleasure. That's my Vektal. My honey. My sweet resonance. I get a goofy smile on my face.

"One of the females said that Zennek's mate is a man-eater," Cashol says. "Should we warn him to be wary of her? Do you think she truly devours human flesh?"

He sounds so very worried and serious. At my side, Megan buries her face against my arm, stifling her laughter.

I know we should announce our presence, that we're snooping, but really . . . I want to hear the answer. I'm curious how my Vektal will handle it. He doesn't really think Marlene is a cannibal, does he? She's confident and flirty, sure, but . . . eating human flesh?

"Nonsense," my Vektal says. "She is not eating him. Human females like to do that sort of thing to their males. It is very natural for them."

I can feel my eyes go wide. Megan's shoulders shake with silent amusement.

"What . . . are you talking about, my chief? What has Shorshie eaten of yours?" Cashol sounds utterly confused.

Oh jeez. I cringe, waiting to hear the answer.

"Humans have different ways of showing their affection," Vektal says, and he sounds both confident and condescending. "Whatever she puts in her mouth, it is between her and her mate."

I'm dying. I'm really, really dying right about now. Megan makes a crude gesture with a hand and I slap it away, trying not to burst out in a fit of giggles. Are they talking about . . . fellatio? Poor Cashol is just going to get even more confused with the way this conversation is heading.

"I do not know what you are talking about," Cashol admits.

"What do you think I am talking about?" Vektal replies, and it sounds so vague that I think he's realizing they're on two different pages now. My poor mate. I put a hand to my lips to fight back my smile.

"Whatever she is doing to him, Zennek likes it," says a new voice. I know that one—Aehako. "If you are looking to save him from his mate, Cashol, you had best look elsewhere."

"I just worry," Cashol says, and he sounds grumpy. "Do . . . do you think all the females are like Zennek's female? Putting strange things in their mouths that do not belong there?"

"What the hell?" Megan mouths to me.

I just wave a hand, listening in. I should announce our presence soon. Very soon. I'm just enjoying this bizarre conversation far too much.

"We should all be so lucky," Aehako says cheerfully.

"Do you have a female in your sights, Cashol?" Vektal's voice is serious, authoritative.

"The one called Meh-gan is very pleasing to look upon,"

Cashol says. "But she is shy. When I try to smile at her, she looks away. I do not know how to speak to her."

Megan's hand gets tight on my arm and her mouth flattens. It's not a look of dislike, but one of worry and fear. I put my hand over hers calmingly. If she's not ready for a relationship, she doesn't have to have one. I will make that very clear to my Vektal. Megan's had a hard road so far and I'm not going to let anyone make it harder for her.

"Give her time," Vektal says.

"She saw Maylak with her kit and wept," Cashol says, and he sounds concerned. "I think she is frightened of resonance."

"It might be hoar-moans," Vektal says, sounding oh-so-knowledgeable. "My mate told me of such things. They make females cry."

"Hoar-moans?" Aehako echoes. "What is that? Something that dwells inside a female like a khui?"

"Perhaps," Vektal says, and he sounds just as confused as they do.

I clear my throat loudly before Vektal can start telling the others that PMS is a beast that lives inside women or some craziness. I know he doesn't mean it. Humans—and for the most part, women—are pretty mystifying to their men. "Hello in there," I call out, and step forward. Megan shrinks back, letting go of my arm and sinking back. She doesn't follow me in. That's all right, I'll get the blankets for her.

As I enter the supply cave, the three men straighten. I see tails flicking, and Cashol looks uncomfortable even as Aehako grins at me. Vektal just gives me a heated look as if he'd like nothing more than to devour me on the spot.

Now who's the cannibal? I think to myself. "I came to get some extra blankets for, ah, someone." I deliberately avoid Megan's name, remembering how she panicked when Cashol brought her up. "And can I steal you away for a few minutes, Vektal? Before you leave?"

"Of course, my resonance."

We load my arms up with furs while Aehako and Cashol pick through a basket of bones, looking for scraps for some sort of project, or maybe just lurking to overhear anything I say. I gesture that Vektal should follow me out and head back to the main cavern with my armload of furs, but Megan's nowhere to be seen. She's gone off to hide. I'll find her later, then. I head back to the cave I share with Vektal and we set our armloads of furs down on our bed.

"What is it?" he asks the moment I turn to look at him. "Is everything all right? Is the kit well?" His glowing blue eyes are filled with concern, and he moves forward and brushes his knuckles along my jaw, as if he needs to reassure himself that I'm here.

I wanted to bring him back to the cave and tell him not to tell the others about our sex life, or hormones, or any other million things that might come up and be potentially embarrassing. But he puts a hand on my lower belly and tugs me closer to him, and I forget about everything.

There are going to be questions about humans and sa-khui and how we're different. They're going to ask Vektal about our mating. They're going to ask about everything.

And . . . it's not important. Not when I'm looking at my gorgeous, protective mate and he's about to leave me for days on end.

"What did you want to say to me?" Vektal prompts again.

I go up on my tiptoes and pull him down for a quick, hard kiss. "I wanted to say thank you."

His hands are warm on my waist. "For?"

"For my honeymoon." I smile up at him. Let them think I put my mouth all over this gorgeous man. All over. I don't care. We can give them things to talk about. They'll know how much I love him. "And you'll hurry home back to me?"

"No hunter will ever be so fast," he promises, voice raspy as he glides one big hand up and down my back. "My feet will be swift."

I know it's necessary for him to go, just as I know people are going to ask weird questions about our mating, about humans, about everything. It's part of my new life and I'm going to accept it—and my mate—with arms wide open.

Well . . . I'll accept it soon enough. I tug on Vektal's vest and then slide my hand down his stomach. "Think that this swift hunter will have time for a quick round in the furs with his mate before he heads out?"

Vektal's eyes gleam. "For you? I have all the time in the world."

AUTHOR'S NOTE

Hello there!

What a wild ride this has been!

I'm so thrilled to be working with Penguin Random House to make a special edition of *Ice Planet Barbarians*. As the series has taken off and become more popular, one of the things I'm asked about the most is if I'll be doing a special edition. I've been asked to do a fancy one for collectors. I've been asked to do books without all the half-naked men on the covers so they can be read relatively stealthily. I've also (strangely) been asked to do a completely chaste version of the books. And while I don't plan on writing an ice planet book where everyone just holds hands and stares longingly off into the sunset (and that's it!), I hope this fulfills your special edition needs.

Here's a little bit about how *Ice Planet Barbarians* came into being. It was late 2014, and I'd started the Ruby Dixon pen name so I could dip into uncharted ebook territory. No-holds-barred! At that point I'd gone with ménage bikers (because why the fuck not?), and I was burned-out on them. I don't know if you know this, but most motorcycle clubs do not feature nice people. I know! Crazy, right? And I was just tired of writing everything I was writing. I was tired of mean heroes. I was tired of the same old, same old. I was fried. But seeing as how writing is both hobby and obsession for me, I couldn't *not* write.

I decided that I'd write something new and fresh. Something off the rails. Something just for me, and if everyone else in the world hated it, that'd be just fine. It was just to make my brain happy, and then I'd go back to writing . . . all the other stuff. It's not that I don't enjoy writing everything else—I do!—but those of you who have been fans for a while know that I dip in and out of a variety of series. I think of it like hot wings. They're tasty and delicious, right? But if you have hot wings for a month straight, you're going to scream the moment you smell buffalo sauce. That was me. There was nothing wrong with what I was writing, but it was just . . . buffalo sauce.

(If you've followed me for a while, you'll also know I loooove a terrible analogy.)

So I decided to write a science fiction romance. I personally love science fiction. Always have. When I was a kid, my mom would get old science fiction magazines and books from yard sales. Most of them were in such terrible shape that they were given away instead of sold, but as my mom was a voracious reader and I was, too, we'd read them. There were all kinds of stories of men having space adventures. Men exploring the far reaches of space. Men saving the day. Men rescuing the damsel in distress, who appears for all of a chapter and then disappears again.

Loved the concept, hated the execution.

Science fiction romance had been on a bit of a downswing for a while, too. It still existed, but it was mostly a fringe genre.

Everyone knew it didn't sell. There was a bit more of a niche in ebooks, but even then, it wasn't one of those categories you wrote in because you wanted to make truckloads of money. You did it because you genuinely loved this weird, fun little genre. By this point, I think I'd read everything in the science fiction romance category on Amazon that I could find. I knew every author who wrote in the genre, and I searched for covers with Poser-created aliens because they would give me the story-hit I craved. Except . . . not quite. The curse of being an author is that you're constantly wanting a story just so. Most of the science fiction romances I'd read weren't quite what I was looking for. Most of the heroes were cruel and downright brutish to the heroine, and while I am down with enemies-to-lovers, I wanted something a little sweeter, a little more chill for my series. I am also a huge, huge fan of secondary characters (one of my favorite things is to ship a secondary pair in a popular series and wait for them to get their happy ever after), so I made a robust cast. And because I'm an absolute fangirl of all kinds of fated-mates stories, I threw that concept in there, too.

I wanted the planet that Georgie and company were stranded on to be absolutely rotten and inhospitable. I almost didn't make it an ice planet, because that seemed *too* mean, but since this was just for me, I figured . . . fuck it. I had an old story I'd started about a hero who had a symbiont implanted in him that gave him additional powers. I stripped out the powers and gave the khui THE POWER OF LOVE instead. (Again, fangirl.) Now you might be thinking, *Nothing says love quite like a parasite that induces you to mate*, but I swear it made sense in my head, and I figured it was just for me anyhow. I made the hero a rough, Paleolithic sort, but I also made him realize how fucking amazing the heroine was. I gave her agency and let her be a hero in her own story. I put lots of sex and love and made the hero capable but also a bit innocent due to the sheltered nature of his people. I made him fall for the heroine at first sight, and I played with all the fun tropes I could think of. Basically, I put all the things I love in there, and when I was done . . . I kinda liked it.

So I decided to publish it. I figured it would either fail *spectacularly* or I'd find that little niche audience that loved silliness and sexiness together in one weird package. I decided to give it the most on-the-nose title I could imagine—*Ice Planet Barbarians*—and I thought about how it should look. At the time, everything set in space felt very male-reader-centric. There were some science fiction romances lurking here and there in cobwebby corners, but most everything I ran across while shopping seemed written for men. I did everything I could to make the books appeal to the appropriate readers. I put a big blue guy on the cover. I called it SciFi Alien Romance, knowing that using "SciFi" instead of "Science Fiction" would drive off hard-core readers of science fiction (or SF), who consider the abbreviation to be used only by outsiders. I stopped short of writing "There Be Space Cuddles Here" on the cover, but everything else was designed to get the attention of female readers. Serials were also really popular in romance at that time, so I decided to go with a serial format, because I find it a really fun storytelling device.

And I released the first installment of *Ice Planet Barbarians* into the wild.

I don't recall a lot happening at first. I know my motorcycle club readers were like, "Well, this is a bit of a weird detour." But I started to pick up other readers who were excited by it. They loved the concept and wanted to know what would happen with each installment. By the time the sixth (and final) installment of the serial came out, I had a small but growing fan base that couldn't wait for more.

I released the second book in serial format later that year. As of book three, readers had expressed unhappiness about the serial format, so I decided to do a regular novel-sized release instead of the serial chunks. And I just . . . kept on writing. I loved the tribe I'd created, loved the heroines, loved the setting, loved the resonance concept, loved everything about it. It's so much fun to write (still is), and as the series continued on, the story grew and so did my audience. Ice Planet Barbarians became this underground cult hit and just kept chugging along quietly on the sidelines. I wrote full-length novels. I wrote novellas. I wrote a spin-off series about spacefaring corsairs that were the same ancestral race. I wrote another spin-off series called Icehome.

Fast-forward to May 2021, six years after I'd first published *Ice Planet Barbarians*. I was deep into the spin-off series Icehome, and I started to get messages from fans. "Did you know your books were mentioned on TikTok?" "Great," I'd comment, and think nothing of it. I sometimes have people email me to tell me that the books were mentioned on this or that podcast. I don't hunt these sorts of mentions down, because I feel people should be able to talk about my books without me standing over their shoulder, and as a sensitive, precious snowflake of an author, if I saw less-than-glowing reviews of my books, it could throw me off my writing game. So I just avoid that stuff.

But sales started to tick up on Ice Planet Barbarians out of nowhere. I thought that was odd, but pleasing—my popular little niche series kept on finding new readers. Then sales didn't just tick up—they exploded. Uh-oh. Was there some hidden controversy on the Internet that I'd somehow missed that was moving books? Was this a fluke?

I was explaining this fluke to my parents at lunch one day

when my mom shook her head. "Someone on your Instagram said you were trending on TikTok."

TikTok? For books? All I knew about TikTok was that people made videos showing they ate Tide Pods. So I downloaded the app to peek in and was surprised to see how many views I was getting. People were making fan art. People were dressing up as my characters. Bookstores were creating TikTok clips about ordering the books because demand was so high.

(And not a single person was eating a Tide Pod. Go figure!)

From there, things have snowballed. It's been amazing to see the reception the blue barbarians have been getting everywhere. I'm thrilled that new fans pick up the books every day and discover the sa-khui and their mates. Since there's been a demand for a special edition, I wanted to make sure it had exciting content. I've included the novella "Ice Planet Honeymoon: Vektal & Georgie," as it feels like part of their total story. And I've included a new bonus epilogue and a tribal list of who's who.

I've also taken out the initial rape scene in the book. Since it involves a secondary character and many people have found it upsetting, I decided it doesn't belong in the book. Initially I included it to show how high the stakes were for Georgie and company, but that doesn't mean it has to be on-screen. The rest of the book I've left alone. As a writer, we're wanting to constantly tinker with our books but we also have to know when to let go.

I hope you enjoyed your trip to the ice planet!

—Ruby Dixon

THE PEOPLE OF
ICE PLANET BARBARIANS

VEKTAL (Vehk-tall)—Chief of the sa-khui tribe. Son of Hektar, the prior chief, who died in khui-sickness. He is a dedicated hunter and leader, and carries a sword and a bola for weapons. He is the one who finds Georgie, and resonance between them is so strong that he resonates prior to her receiving her khui.

GEORGIE—Unofficial leader of the human women. Originally from Orlando, Florida, she has long, golden-brown curls and a determined attitude. Newly pregnant after resonating to Vektal.

FAMILIES

MAYLAK (May-lack)—One of the few female sa-khui. She is the tribe healer and Vektal's former pleasure mate. She resonated to Kashrem, ending her relationship with Vektal. Sister to Bek.

KASHREM (Cash-rehm)—The gentle tribal tanner. Mated to Maylak.

ESHA (Esh-uh)—Their young female kit.

SEVVAH (Sev-uh)—A tribe elder and one of the few sa-khui fe-males. She is mother to Aehako, Rokan, and Sessah, and acts like a mom to the others in the cave. Her entire family was spared when khui-sickness hit fifteen years ago.

OSHEN (Aw-shen)—A tribe elder and Sevvah's mate. Brewer.

SESSAH (Ses-uh)—Their youngest child, a juvenile male.

KEMLI (Kemm-lee)—An elder female, mother to Salukh, Pashov, Zennek, and Farli. The tribe's expert on plants.

BORRAN (Bore-awn)—Kemli's much younger mate and an elder.

FARLI (Far-lee)—A preteen female sa-khui. Her brothers are Sa-lukh, Pashov, and Zennek.

ASHA (Ah-shuh)—A mated female sa-khui. She is mated to He-malo but has not been seen in his furs for some time. Their kit died shortly after birth.

HEMALO (Hee-mah-lo)—A tanner and a quiet sort. He is mated (unhappily) to Asha.

THE HUMAN FEMALES

ARIANA—One of the women kept in the stasis tubes. Hails from New Jersey and was an anthropology student. She tends to cry a lot. Has a delicate frame and dark brown hair.

CLAIRE—A quiet, slender blonde with a pixie cut. She finds her new world extremely frightening.

HARLOW—One of the women kept in the stasis tubes. She has red hair and freckles, and is mechanically minded and excellent at problem-solving.

JOSIE—One of the original kidnapped women, she broke her leg in the ship crash. Short and adorable, Josie is an excessive talker, a gossip, and a bit of a dreamer. Likes to sing.

KIRA—The first of the human women to be kidnapped, Kira has a large metallic translator attached to her ear by the aliens. She is quiet and serious, with somber eyes.

LIZ—A loudmouth huntress from Oklahoma who loves Star Wars and giving her opinion. Raahosh kidnaps her the moment she receives her lifesaving khui. She was a champion archer as a teenager.

MARLENE (Mar-lenn)—One of the women kept in the stasis tubes. French speaking. Quiet and confident, and exudes sexuality.

MEGAN—Megan was in an early pregnancy when she was captured, but the aliens terminated it. She tends toward a sunny disposition when not abducted by aliens.

NORA—One of the women kept in the stasis tubes. A nurturing sort who seems rather angry she's been dumped on an ice planet.

STACY—One of the women kept in the stasis tubes. She's weepy when she first awakens. Loves to cook and worked in a bakery prior to abduction.

TIFFANY—A "farm girl" back on Earth, she suffered greatly while waiting for Georgie to return. She has been traumatized by her alien abduction. She is a perfectionist and a hard worker.

THE UNMATED HUNTERS

AEHAKO (Eye-ha-koh)—A laughing, flirty hunter. The son of Sevvah and Oshen; brother to Rokan and young Sessah. He seems to be in a permanent good mood. Close friends with Haeden.

BEK (Behk)—A hunter generally thought of as short-tempered and unpleasant. Brother to Maylak.

CASHOL (Cash-awl)—A distractible and slightly goofy-natured hunter. Cousin to Vektal.

DAGESH (Dah-zzhesh; the *g* sound is swallowed)—A calm, hardworking, and responsible hunter.

EREVEN (Air-uh-ven)—A quiet, easygoing hunter.

HAEDEN (Hi-den)—A grim and unsmiling hunter with "dead" eyes, Haeden formerly resonated but his female died of khui-sickness before they could mate. His current khui is new. He is very private.

HARREC (Hair-ek)—A hunter who has no family and finds his place in the tribe by constantly joking and teasing. A bit accident-prone.

HASSEN (Hass-en)—A passionate and brave hunter, Hassen is impulsive and tends to act before he thinks.

PASHOV (Pah-showv)—The son of Kemli and Borran; brother to Farli, Salukh, and Zennek. A hunter described as "quiet."

RAAHOSH (Rah-hosh)—A quiet but surly hunter. One of his horns is broken off and his face scarred. Impatient and rash, he steals Liz the moment she receives her khui.

ROKAN (Row-can)—The son of Sevvah and Oshen; brother to Aehako and young Sessah. A hunter known for his strange predictions that come true all too often.

SALUKH (Sah-luke)—The brawny son of Kemli and Borran; brother to Farli, Pashov, and Zennek. Very strong and intense.

TAUSHEN (Tow—rhymes with "cow"—shen)—A teenage hunter, newly into adulthood. Eager to prove himself.

WARREK (War-eck)—The son of Elder Eklan. He is a very quiet and mild hunter, with long, sleek black hair. Warrek teaches the young kits how to hunt.

ZENNEK (Zehn-eck)—A quiet and shy hunter. Brother to Pashov, Salukh, and Farli. He is the son of Borran and Kemli.

ZOLAYA (Zoh-lay-uh)—A skilled hunter.

ELDERS

ELDER DRAYAN—A smiling elder who uses a cane to help him walk.

ELDER DRENOL—A grumpy, antisocial elder.

ELDER EKLAN—A calm, kind elder. Father to Warrek, he also helped raise Harrec.

ELDER VADREN (Vaw-dren)—An elder.

ELDER VAZA (Vaw-zhuh)—A lonely widower and hunter. He tries to be as helpful as possible. He is very interested in the new females.

THE DEAD

DOMINIQUE—A redheaded human female. Her mind was broken when she was abused by the aliens on the ship. When she arrived on Not-Hoth, she ran out into the snow and deliberately froze.

KRISSY—A human female, dead in the crash.

PEG—A human female, dead in the crash.

BARBARIAN ALIEN

BOOK TWO OF
THE ICE PLANET BARBARIANS SERIES

Twelve humans are left stranded on a wintry alien planet. I'm one of them. Yay, me.

In order to survive, we have to take on a symbiont that wants to rewire our bodies to live in this brutal place. I like to call it a "cootie." And my cootie's a jerk, because it also thinks I'm the mate to the biggest, surliest alien of the group.

Raahosh

My khui is an idiot.

It must be. Why else would it ignore the women of my clan and the moment we enter the den of the dirty, ragged humans, it begins to bleat in my chest like a quilled beast? Or that it chose the frailest of the sick humans to select as my mate?

A mate that glares at me with knowing, angry eyes and refuses to eat the medicinal broth that I bring her? That pushes aside my hands when I try to help her to her feet? Who scowls when I bring her water?

It's clear that my khui is full of foolishness.

"Did you resonate for anyone?" Aehako asks at my side. He stuffs a fur into a traveling bag. We are preparing the humans' cave for travel, since they are too weak to do so. Everything must come with us, Vektal says. It does not matter that it is stained and filthy, or useless. The humans have so little that he is sure they will treasure whatever they have, so it must come. Two of the hunters that resonated for females have been sent off to get furs from the nearest hunter caves, because the humans are poorly equipped to face the harsh snows, and they have no khui to keep them warm.

This will be remedied shortly, however.

A sa-kohtsk is near. The large creatures carry many khui, and we will hunt one for its meat and ensure that the humans will not die of khui-sickness.

I think of the hollow eyes of my new mate and how miserable she looks. Most of the human hides are a pale color, but my human is paler than most. That must mean she is sicker. I will insist she be one of the first to get a khui.

Aehako repeats his question. "Raahosh? Did you resonate?"

I don't like to lie, but I also don't want anyone to know, not when my mate is glaring at me as if she is furious.

Raahosh is scarier than most.

Her words cut. She is smooth and pale and weak, and yet I am the one lacking? I shrug and shoulder the pack. "It matters not. We will see what happens when the khui are in the humans."

"I didn't resonate." Aehako looks glum, his broad features downcast. "Do you think more will resonate when they come into season? Perhaps they're not in season." He gives me a hopeful glance.

"Do I look as if I know human seasons?" I snap. "Finish your bag. We need to hurry if we are to get the humans close enough to the sa-kohtsk to hunt it."

Aehako sighs and returns to work. I tell myself he is young. In fact, he might be the youngest hunter in our clan. He will get over his disappointment, or another human will resonate for him later. Or even a sa-khui woman, perhaps one not yet born.

All I know is that I am resonating for one of the dying humans, and if she dies, she takes all my hopes and dreams with her.

ABOUT THE AUTHOR

RUBY DIXON is an author of all things science fiction romance. She is a Sagittarius and a Reylo shipper, and loves farming sims (but not actual housework). She lives in the South with her husband and a couple of geriatric cats, and can't think of anything else to put in her biography. Truly, she is boring.

CONNECT ONLINE

RubyDixon.com
 RubyDixonBooks
 Author.Ruby.Dixon

Ready to find
your next great read?

Let us help.

Visit prh.com/nextread